DAUNTLESS

Gentlemen of the Order - Book 1

ADELE CLEE

Dauntless
Copyright © 2020 Adele Clee
All rights reserved.
ISBN-13: 978-1-9162774-4-1

Cover by Dar Albert at Wicked Smart Designs

CHAPTER 1

Hart Street, London
Premises of the Gentlemen of the Order

"AND SO I SAID, 'Madam, must you make that god-awful racket? Are you in desperate need of a physician, or do you wish to let the entire street hear of your pleasure?'"

Noah Ashwood almost choked on his coffee. "I thought you preferred them lively in bed." The men's morning banter brought relief from the stringent attitude needed when investigating criminal cases.

D'Angelo laughed as he reclined on the sofa. "Lively, yes, but not wailing like a banshee. It puts a man off his stroke."

"If you have to concentrate on your stroke," Sloane drawled, "you should find another bed partner."

"Choose a woman who stimulates your mind," Finlay Cole said, glancing over the top of his newspaper. "The poets say it makes for an enlightening experience."

"Enlightening?" D'Angelo snorted. "I seek satisfaction, not spiritual instruction."

Noah shook his head. He believed his friend enjoyed acting the rakish rogue. "If you cared for the woman, you would celebrate her howling."

"Blessed saints! Are you suggesting I find a lover who stirs my emotions?" D'Angelo's shocked expression led to fits of laughter until a loud knock on the door disturbed their revelry.

"Enter!"

Mrs Gunning marched into the drawing room. She was a large, steady woman of sixty who prided herself on running an efficient house. She focused her gaze on Noah. "There's a lady arrived, sir. A prospective client. She said she needs to hire an agent."

At twenty-eight, Noah wasn't the oldest of the four men who helped victims of crimes. Nor did his lineage give him a right of entitlement. He was but the nephew of a baron. Still, they had fallen into natural roles, and Noah had no issue accepting responsibility.

"You explained there's no fee? Gave no assurances?" Noah sat forward in the chair. "Explained we take clients on an individual basis?"

Their services could not be bought. The Gentlemen of the Order did not assist wealthy members of the *ton* find solutions to their petty problems. They helped the weak, the needy, those without funds or connections.

Mrs Gunning glanced at the open door before whispering, "I did, sir. The lady seemed confident *you* would hear her case."

"Me?" But he had just finished a lengthy investigation into the blackmail of a bank clerk. One of his colleagues could conduct the interview. D'Angelo needed a distraction, needed to focus on something other than his troublesome lover. "Did the lady present my calling card?"

"No, sir, not exactly." Mrs Gunning toyed with the keys on her chatelaine. "She said she needed a fearless gentleman. Dauntless, she said. I presumed she meant you, sir."

"Dauntless?" How odd. Did the lady know of his moniker? "She used that precise word?"

"Yes, sir."

Curse the saints!

Noah believed in omens and fate, believed one's destiny was written. All one had to do was follow the signs. His friends had called him *Dauntless* since the night he'd stormed into Lady Redford's ballroom, marched onto the dance floor and threw a punch that put his uncle on his arse. The same night he chased two knife-wielding thugs into a dark alley and brought both fiends to their knees.

"The lady practically asked for you by name," Cole agreed, offering an arrogant grin. "That makes it your case."

Noah huffed. "We have yet to determine the nature of her dilemma." He turned to the housekeeper employed to put female clients at ease, to play chaperone and ensure the servants behaved. "Perhaps you should show the lady into the drawing room. Let her choose which one of us is to hear her desperate tale." Yes. Let fate decide.

D'Angelo's brown eyes widened. "Would you care to wager on the outcome? I'll lay odds she'll pick Sloane."

"No wagers," Noah countered. They were professional men, not dissolute rakes looking for ways to banish the boredom. "No. Show her in, Mrs Gunning."

"Right away, sir."

The housekeeper hurried from the room and returned seconds later with their potential client in tow.

Noah had witnessed the grand entrance of many women out to command attention. Most knew the importance of first impressions. Most knew how to alter the energy in the room with a charming smile and a coy tilt of the chin.

Not this one.

The lady ambled behind Mrs Gunning, dragging her feet and mumbling like a bedlamite as she wrote in a small brown note-book. The men all stood, and still, she considered the words she'd just scrawled with her neat little pencil.

"That's it!" she suddenly exclaimed. "Prussic acid."

Noah cleared his throat. "I beg your pardon?"

"Prussic acid. A poison that might kill a man in seconds." The young woman removed her spectacles and pushed them into the reticule dangling at her elbow. "I don't know why I didn't think of it before." She looked up. "Good morning."

A moment of stunned silence ensued before Noah said, "Good morning" and then made the necessary introductions.

Experience led him to expect an older woman—one looking for her runaway husband or light-fingered maid—not a young woman with porcelain skin and eyes of cornflower blue, eyes that sparkled with excitement at the mention of a deadly poison. Interesting. He waited for a faint blush to touch her cheeks, waited to witness a certain bashfulness upon meeting four unconventional men.

But this lady was out to defy all expectations.

"My name is Miss Dunn," she said, slipping her book and pencil into her reticule before studying them through keen, intelligent eyes. "Forgive me for staring. One rarely sees gentlemen with facial hair these days. I thought it was considered unfashionable."

Occasionally they all sported a short, neatly trimmed beard. Today, only Sloane and D'Angelo were clean-shaven.

Noah drew his hand along his bristly jaw. "Fops and dandies care about fashion, Miss Dunn."

"And you're keen to ensure everyone knows you're a virile male." She seemed comfortable making the personal comment. "I mean, masculinity is important to you."

"Indeed." The need to rattle her steely composure forced Noah to add, "A virile male is what you requested, is it not? A man willing to confront thugs in a dark alley?"

Intriguing blue eyes scanned him from head to toe. "I hoped to hire an agent who is not intimidated by a lady of independent means, sir." She raised her dainty chin. "Men are quick to dismiss a woman with ambition."

Yes, men tended to avoid the forthright types. And yet this woman had Noah's undivided attention. His analytical mind scrambled to find the reason why.

Miss Dunn had many feminine attributes to recommend her. Her slender figure and shapely breasts were encased in a plain blue pelisse. He imagined cupping her delicate face, her pink lips parting, those long lashes fluttering with pleasure. The contrast of sensible and sensual seemed to encapsulate her character.

"We could spend all day discussing the failings of a patriarchal society," he said, eager to put this puzzling woman from his mind, "yet I presume you're here on more pressing matters."

That said, she did not seem overly distressed.

"Pressing matters that leave me confounded, sir."

Noah inclined his head and gestured to his friends. "Then you're in luck, Miss Dunn. Any one of us can hear your case."

She frowned in curious enquiry. "Forgive me, Mr Ashwood, are you inviting me to choose an agent?"

"Indeed. We all possess a wealth of experience. We are all fearless men." And for some unfathomable reason, he was beyond desperate to learn of her preference.

"I see." Her gaze drifted to Evan Sloane, the man they called Valiant for his courage and flowing mane of light brown hair.

"Mr Sloane recently solved the case of a child abducted from the street and held captive for ten days," Noah said. "A crime that left Bow Street baffled."

Miss Dunn's hand shot to her breast. "Goodness. I trust you found the child alive."

"Starving and frightened," Sloane said soberly, "but relatively unharmed. I carried his limp body from a filthy fleapit in Southwark."

Sloane was every woman's hero.

The lady's sigh carried the depth of her compassion. "What a tremendous relief."

"And Mr D'Angelo found a runaway husband who faked his death and left his wife and five children destitute," Noah continued. "He was living in luxury with his mistress in Salisbury."

"Oh, the deceitful devil. Some men have no concept of responsibility, Mr D'Angelo." Miss Dunn spoke as if she had experience of wastrels. She considered the lothario, the man they called Dark Angel. "I trust you pointed out the error of his ways. Pray he felt more than the sharp edge of your tongue."

D'Angelo inclined his head and gave a mischievous grin. "The rogue received his comeuppance."

"Excellent."

So, Miss Dunn wasn't opposed to a man using violence when necessary. Fascinating. Most women abhorred such savagery.

Noah cleared his throat. "Mr Cole's case involved the murder of a maid in an alley near Seven Dials." He waited for Miss Dunn's horrified gasp—it didn't come.

The lady raised her gloved hand. "Let me guess. The poor

woman was killed by her employer. She was with child and planned to reveal all, no doubt."

Miss Dunn did not scare easily. She wasn't meek or fragile. So what wickedness forced her to seek their counsel?

"I cannot comment at present." Cole pushed his hand through his black hair, part of the reason for his moniker Raven. "But I believe that an intelligent woman's intuition is rarely wrong."

Sly devil!

For men who were relishing the prospect of a few days' rest and recuperation, they had soon changed their tune.

"And I recently solved a crime at—"

"Forgive me, Mr Ashwood," Miss Dunn implored. "I do not mean to sound rude, but I have already determined your merits and cannot bear to hear another sad tale."

Determined his merits?

What the blazes?

A desire to discover what Miss Dunn had learned of his character during the brief meeting burned in Noah's veins. In the space of a few minutes, he had gone from hoping one of his friends took the case, to praying the lady picked him.

"My investigation involved greed, Miss Dunn. Nothing to tug on the heartstrings." And yet he couldn't help but feel somewhat inadequate. "Now, we're busy men. Perhaps you might make your choice and take a seat in the study across the hall where you may explain your problem in private. Unless you wish to hear an extensive list of our credentials."

"No, Mr Ashwood." Miss Dunn smiled with the self-assurance of a duchess. "That won't be necessary. I made my choice the moment I entered the drawing room."

From the deep inhalations and amused grins of his colleagues, they were as eager as he to learn of her choice.

On first impressions, she might pick D'Angelo, the one with a kind face and a devilish twinkle in his eye. Most women thought they had the skills to tame him. Sloane had the look of a biblical hero who might throw himself into a pit of vipers and leave unscathed. Cole's firm jaw and rugged countenance marked him as a man who got the job done, no matter the cost.

"Then put us out of our misery, Miss Dunn, so we can return to reading our newspapers and drinking our coffee."

"Certainly. I want to explain my story to you, Mr Ashwood."

"Me?" A rush of masculine pride filled Noah's chest. He resisted the urge to punch the air and taunt his friends. "Then allow me to show you to the study."

Noah ignored the men's smirks and escorted the lady from the room. Later would come the barrage of questions and the playful banter bordering on ridicule.

"Please sit, Miss Dunn." He followed her into the study and gestured to the chair opposite his desk. "Shall I have Mrs Gunning arrange tea?"

"Do not put your housekeeper to any trouble." Miss Dunn scanned the walnut bookcases before her gaze came to rest on the trio of crystal decanters on the side table. "May I take something stronger? I've hardly slept a wink, and a little restorative would not go amiss."

He couldn't help but smile as he closed the door.

"Sherry?" he said, though expected her to ask for brandy.

"Sherry is perfect." She sat, removed her gloves, took the book from her reticule and squinted at a page while he poured her a drink. "Will you not join me, sir?" she said, closing her book and accepting the dainty glass.

Their fingers brushed briefly. With any other client, the action might have gone unnoticed. But he was as captivated by the ink stains on her elegant fingers as he was by the sudden spark of awareness.

"I never partake during the day." Noah flicked his coat-tails and dropped into the chair behind the mahogany desk. "Absorbing various elements of a tale requires my complete concentration."

"What must you think of me?" Her light laugh suggested she didn't give a damn what he thought. "Drinking sherry at this hour?"

"It's my job to listen, not judge."

Her inquisitive blue eyes drifted to the sapphire pin in his neckcloth and the monogram buttons on his coat. "Gentlemen of your ilk rarely work for a living."

"I do not work for a living, Miss Dunn." He had inherited his father's wealth and holdings despite his uncle's efforts to prove him illegitimate. "I work for the pleasure that comes from righting injustices."

"A noble pursuit."

"A necessary pursuit."

"I would not disagree." Her shoulders relaxed as she sipped the sherry.

"Miss Dunn, before we begin, may I ask why you chose me?" Devil take it. He sounded like a timid wallflower eager to know why the most eligible man in the room had asked her to dance. "You made your decision rather quickly. If I'm to take your case, I would prefer you were happy with your choice."

The lady studied him with a level of scrutiny he found unnerving. "I chose you for several reasons, sir."

"May I hear them?" Or would she persist in being vague?

"All of them? Even those that might cause mild embarrassment?"

"Madam, there is no shame in having an opinion."

"Oh, I am not speaking of myself, Mr Ashwood. I fear *you* might experience some discomfort."

"Me?" He drew back and laughed. "Nothing you could say or do could make me blush, Miss Dunn." Did she think him a prude? Hell, he had stripped naked to the waist in Green Park and wrestled with Lord Packham. Had pleasured a woman in a theatre box during the second act of *Don Quixote*. "Do not make allowances on my account."

"Very well." She cocked her head and stared at him. "The best way to judge a person's character is to observe how others react around them, is it not?"

"Logic suggests your argument has merit."

"Your housekeeper entered a room occupied by four capable men, yet she addressed you, Mr Ashwood. That tells me you command respect, that she considers you the most responsible."

Oh, this woman was as sharp as a steel trap. "When four men work closely together, someone must act as overseer."

"And the men defer to you. That shows strength of character."

A lesser man might find her comments flattering, but they were delivered as observations, not compliments. "If you mean I have the confidence to speak my mind, am self-assured without being arrogant, that I strive to do what is right, then your assessment is correct."

"I need an agent with unshakable resolve, sir. Not one who is easily distracted."

Noah relaxed back in the chair and steepled his fingers. "And you concluded I was that man before the introductions were made?"

Miss Dunn swallowed what remained of her sherry, shivering visibly as the fortified wine slipped down her throat. "When I entered the drawing room, I gave the impression I was preoccupied. It afforded an opportunity to examine your reactions. Mr D'Angelo's first point of reference was to note my womanly attributes."

"I can assure you, Miss Dunn, we all noted your womanly attributes." He was a man, not a damn saint. "Me included." He decided to test her steely composure. "Pray, is that a faint blush I see?"

She huffed and touched her cheek. "Not at all, merely a mild flush from the sherry." She placed her empty glass on the desk. "I can assure *you*, Mr Ashwood, men usually find my unconventional character unattractive."

"Most men don't think about a woman's character while observing her womanly attributes." And yet he found the entire package rather fascinating. The need to strip back the layers and discover more thrummed in his veins.

"Mr Sloane took one look at my spectacles and lost interest."

"That's because they rouse painful childhood memories of his governess. The woman peered at him through tiny spectacles while whipping him with a birch."

Miss Dunn arched a brow by way of a challenge. "Now you're teasing me. Had that been the case, his expression would have revealed something of his torment." Her playful smile added a certain intimacy to the conversation. "I chose you, Mr Ashwood, because your intelligent eyes flashed with intrigue the moment you saw my notebook."

Noah couldn't help but smile, too. Yet he wanted to see how easy it would be to unnerve her. "Madam, you're rather free with your compliments. A man might get the wrong impression. Perhaps the bare truth of the matter is you picked me purely for my handsome looks."

She pursed her lips, though her eyes danced with amusement. "Well, while on the subject of your manly attributes, your muscular thighs and athletic build played a part in my decision. The scar on your knuckle suggests an injury from a fistfight. I need a man whose physical strength is equal to his mental prowess."

"You need a man?" he said, pressing her further. "Are you certain you've come to the right place, Miss Dunn? But tell me, what if Mr D'Angelo was the only agent available? Your keen observations would have been for nought."

"On the contrary," she challenged.

"Are you suggesting you're capable of dealing with a lothario?" He laughed. Indeed, he could not recall a time when he'd enjoyed bantering with a woman. "Can you manage a man who has contempt for women who wear spectacles?"

"They're hypothetical questions. You will take my case even if stretched to make the time. You see, Mr Ashwood, the truth of the matter is that you're desperate to know what brings me here. You're eager to know what is written in my notebook."

CHAPTER 2

EVA MIGHT HAVE MADE A MISTAKE.

Yes, she had used the principles of reasoning when choosing Mr Ashwood to hear her case. Common sense said he was mentally and physically equipped to deal with the complicated situation. He was a man who took work seriously. A man whose commanding presence radiated from every aspect of his being. Yet she had not expected to find a devilish charm beneath his professional exterior.

"Now I know why there are so many simpering misses in the ballroom, Miss Dunn," the gentleman with exceptional green eyes said. "When distributing honesty and confidence, the Lord gave you the lion's share."

It took immense effort not to laugh. It was easy to feign belief in oneself, easy to speak with certitude. Yet every muscle in her body quivered. The hollow feeling in her chest expanded, bringing the persistent wave of nausea that had plagued her since the violent attack.

"Timidity is a useless pursuit, sir," she said, recalling the strength it took to fight the fiend. "A lady in my position cannot afford to play the meek maid simply because men find submissiveness attractive."

"That's a rather sweeping statement. Some men despise the docile types." His lips curled into a sensual smile that pinned her to the seat. "Some men prefer a challenge, seek a companion with spirit and an intelligent mind."

"I have yet to meet one." Such men were a rare breed.

Mr Ashwood brushed his hand through his golden brown hair. "And yet the slight tension in your voice suggests otherwise."

Good heavens. It was pointless hiding anything from this man. He noted every little movement, every little nuance. He saw beyond the wall she had constructed to hide her pain.

"Then let me rephrase. I have yet to meet one with integrity." For all Mr Hemming's protestations of morality, he was as debased as her brother.

"When it comes to seduction, a scoundrel will use any means necessary to achieve his goal." He scanned her body as if looking for dirty handprints, evidence left by the last devil who backed her into a corner and sought to take advantage. "Tactics you have experienced firsthand. It's why you chose the agent who commanded Mrs Gunning's respect."

"Clearly, I am not the only one with keen observation skills."

"No," he mused. "I learn something new every time you open your mouth, Miss Dunn."

Heavens! His velvet voice made the innocent comment sound highly suggestive.

"Then between us, we should solve this case quickly, sir."

"One would think so." He gave a half shrug. "Though I haven't agreed to help you with your problem."

"Oh, but you will agree." He had to agree. She no longer had the strength to face her mounting problems.

"As your confidence knows no bounds, Miss Dunn, perhaps you should begin your distressing tale." He relaxed back in the chair. His verdant gaze lost its playful sparkle as he stared intently. "All I ask is that you speak plainly. Honestly."

Eva glanced at the quill pen resting on the inkstand. "Will you not take notes, Mr Ashwood?"

"I have an excellent memory, and paper is expensive."

"You will need an exceptional memory if you're to recall the details of my case." Indeed, there were so many elements to the tale she wasn't sure where to start.

"Madam, you have no need to doubt my ability in any regard."

No, he gave the impression he was skilled at most things. And yet she couldn't wait to see a frown appear on his brow, couldn't wait to see the puzzled expression as he tried to make sense of the facts.

Eva smiled to hide the sudden flurry of nerves. The incredulous story was like something from one of her novels. Playing the narrator rather than the victim would make it easier to relay the information.

"Let me begin, sir, by explaining my background. While society considers my father a gentleman, he is a rake and a wastrel and has no concept of moral standards. He has lived in Italy since my mother's death ten years ago and has recently remarried. At four and twenty, I am three years older than my Italian stepmother."

"I see." Mr Ashwood arched a knowing brow. "So, you have lived with a relative since the age of fourteen. You must resent your father."

"As much as any child abandoned by a parent. And yes, I lived with my godfather, Mr Thomas Becker, until he passed away last year."

"Thomas Becker? The poet?" Mr Ashwood's eyes widened. They really were the most magnificent shade of green. "If so, I have his entire collection. *The Wanderer* is a personal favourite."

So, this dangerous-looking gentleman loved poetry. That piqued Eva's interest. "Yes, his love of Norse mythology is evident in many of his works."

"I find the notion of Odin disguising himself as a wounded vagrant to teach humility rather fascinating."

Eva's breath caught in her throat. Mr Ashwood's intelligent comment enhanced his appeal. "A vagrant may be wiser than a king, but without position and power few take notice."

"Indeed." A faint smile played at the corners of his mouth. "Do you pen poems, too, Miss Dunn? The ink stains and the red marks on your fingers suggest you write more than the odd letter. Why else would you have an interest in an acid that can kill a man in seconds?"

She couldn't help but smile. "You're remarkably perceptive, Mr Ashwood." Too perceptive. What else had the gentleman determined during their brief conversation? "Yes, I write, though not poetry. But I shall come to that in a moment."

"Then I await your explanation with anticipation, Miss Dunn."

Eva paused while deciding where to restart her tale. "My brother, Mr Howard Dunn, inherited twenty thousand pounds upon our godfather's death. Though I am sorry to say, he also inherited our father's outlandish behaviour and has frittered away his good fortune at the gaming tables."

Mr Ashwood sat forward. Disappointment marred his fine features. "We help those in dire need, Miss Dunn. We save boys from the hangman's noose. We do not bring wastrel brothers to heel."

No, that was a task beyond a mere mortal's capabilities.

"Even if that were my reason for calling, it would prove an impossible feat considering my brother has been missing for a week." Anticipating Mr Ashwood's next comment, she added, "And no, Howard is not abed with his mistress, nor is he comatose in an opium den. Not this time, at least."

"Perhaps he has eloped with an heiress."

"Howard would never shackle himself to one woman." A fact he had made abundantly clear.

Mr Ashwood smirked. "Most married men keep a mistress, so your point is moot. Have you considered the possibility that he's fled the country to escape his creditors?"

She would have drawn that conclusion, too, had it not been for the other strange happenings. "Having broken the lock on his bedside drawer, I discovered Howard owes three thousand pounds to The Silver Serpent. It's a gaming hell on—"

"Yes, Miss Dunn. I know the proprietor."

Relief burst through her veins. "Oh, then you might discover if Howard's debts have something to do with his disappearance. It's said a man who fails to pay is thrown into the Thames with a sack of bricks strapped to his back."

Mr Ashwood cast a look of reproach. "An intelligent woman should not lend weight to gossip."

"Would you have me believe such things never happen?"

"No," he said with a sigh. "Though you have my assurance Dermot Flannery has not murdered your brother." Mr Ashwood pushed out of the chair. Clearly, he had heard enough. "Forgive me, Miss Dunn, but we haven't the time to search for profligates who should know better. However, I will speak to Dermot Flannery about your brother's debt. If you leave your direction with Mrs—"

"But I've yet to explain my reason for calling."

Mr Ashwood frowned. "You said your brother is missing. I assumed that's why you're here."

"As you say, rogues often go astray." Eva had already enquired at every high-end brothel, every backstreet whorehouse, every gaming hell. She had even sent her footman to the mortuary looking for a fool with a fatal gunshot wound. "Were it not for a catalogue of other worrying events, I would not waste your time, sir."

"Forgive me," he said in the rich drawl that warmed her insides. "I'm used to people so desperate to tell their tale they barely draw breath. Your calm voice belies the distressing nature of your problem."

When one lived with a devil, unsettling situations were commonplace. And crafting frightening tales gave one the courage to converse about matters some ladies found alarming.

"Perhaps that has something to do with my profession."

"You write for a living," he stated, lowering his muscular frame into the chair.

Eva paused. "I presume any discussion remains confidential?"

"Absolutely."

"Then yes, I write fictional stories of murder and mayhem under the pseudonym of Mr Cain Dunnavan."

She waited for the deep sigh, the tut, the derisive snort and roll of the eyes. Howard found the idea ludicrous. Women lacked intellect, lacked the worldly experience necessary to construct a convincing tale. Yet the fickle fool sang a different tune when Eva paid his tailor's bill.

Mr Ashwood shocked her by smiling. "I read *The Blood Pendant* and admire your courage in casting Sister Magdalene as the villain. That's when I suspected Cain Dunnavan was a woman."

Eva didn't hide her surprise. Gentlemen rarely admitted to reading novels. "Why? Do you find the idea of a nun committing a crime unrealistic?"

"Men tend to cast women as foolish victims, or devious vixens who use seduction to corrupt unsuspecting lovers. Sister Magdalene's twisted logic shows that men and women are equally cruel. Only a woman would be brave enough to explore that idea, Miss Dunn."

Eva's pulse raced. Not since her godfather's passing had she engaged in such an interesting conversation, and never with a man whose physical appearance stirred her senses. Heavens. It was all too much. Indeed, she considered informing Mr Ashwood that she had picked the wrong agent. She was far more capable of dealing with Mr D'Angelo's rakish gaze.

"But you didn't come here to discuss literature," he continued. "And we seem to deviate from your purpose with shocking ease."

When one sat opposite a gentleman with such a charismatic character thoughts were bound to stray.

"In summary," he continued, "your brother has not come home, and you write novels for a living. Neither facts seem particularly distressing."

"Then I shall explain my reason for coming in a few sentences."

"I think that's wise. I have another appointment at three."

Eva did not need to glance at the mantel clock to appreciate the man's sarcasm. "Are you sure you do not wish to take notes?"

"You're stalling, Miss Dunn. Give me the facts and let me worry about my memory."

Perhaps she was stalling. It all sounded so ludicrous. The gentleman would blame her wild imagination. Novelists were prone to moments of fancy.

After inhaling deeply, she said, "I am being blackmailed, Mr Ashwood. I received a letter threatening to reveal Cain Dunnavan's true identity. A thousand pounds is the price for the blackmailer's silence else the story shall appear in the broadsheets.

But that is not all. Last night, while walking home from my publisher's office, I was attacked in the street."

"Attacked!" Mr Ashwood sat forward. His panicked green gaze scanned her face and body. "Were you hurt?"

"I have a nasty black bruise on my thigh."

"On your thigh?" Mr Ashwood swallowed deeply.

"Yes. The fiend wrestled me to the ground and stole my boots." The blighter had shoved her skirts up past her knees and practically ripped the boots off her feet. "I had ten pounds in my reticule, a partial advance from Mr Hemming, yet the blackguard was only interested in my footwear."

Mr Hemming had given her the advance to ease his conscience. But she would come to that later.

"Hemming?"

"My publisher."

Mr Ashwood nodded.

"But that is not all. I returned home to find that someone had broken into my house while my servants were taking supper. The thief took every pair of boots and shoes I possess."

"Surely not every pair. You walked here today."

"Every pair." Eva stood. She placed her gloves and notebook near the inkstand before rounding the desk and raising her hem a fraction. "See. These tatty old boots belong to my maid. The poor girl is going about her duties wearing my mother's best dancing slippers."

The gentleman considered the scuffed boots before his gaze climbed slowly over the entire length of her body. "May I ask why the thief failed to take the dancing slippers?"

"They were hidden in a hatbox along with other personal mementoes."

"I see." He gestured to the chair. "You may lower your skirts and sit, Miss Dunn, before I make further study of your trim ankles."

Oh, the man was a terrible tease.

Eva dropped her skirts and brushed the material to hide her mild embarrassment. "But that is not all," she said, returning to her seat.

"No, I don't imagine it is. Though I wonder why you're here

when your profession suggests you have the tools necessary to solve complicated mysteries."

Eva had spent a sleepless night making notes, looking for connections, rummaging through her brother's possessions to find clues. But she had struggled to remain objective and had other reasons for seeking professional help.

"Because emotions cloud one's judgement. I find the situation overwhelming." And due to her brother's wicked ways, she had no friends she could trust. "I need guidance. I need someone to take my hand and steer me through the fog." Eva glanced at Mr Ashwood's strong hands resting on the desk. A woman would never feel afraid when held in his firm grip. "I speak metaphorically, of course."

"Of course."

Silence descended, yet an invisible energy thrummed in the air—a palpable attraction she could not suppress.

"I am also a victim of snowing," she said.

"Snowing? Someone stole garments from your washing line?"

"Indeed. Kathleen, my maid, often hangs out my petticoats first thing in the morning. This morning, someone stole them. But that is not all. My cobbler was found bludgeoned to death, and my publisher is trying to force me into a romantic affair." Eva's shoulders sagged with relief as she caught her breath. She should have kept the last comment to herself but needed to confide in someone. "So you see, Mr Ashwood, why I would be confounded by it all."

The gentleman remained silent for what seemed like an hour.

"Sir, perhaps I should take up your quill and list the events in chronological order. That way, you will have all the information to hand, and nothing will be missed."

"There is no need, Miss Dunn." Mr Ashwood pushed to his feet. He moved to the window and stared at the bustling street. "Your godfather died last year. Your reprobate brother has been missing for a week. Your cobbler was bludgeoned to death five days ago—"

"Five days ago? I don't recall mentioning when—"

"I keep abreast of all serious crimes committed in the city."

"I see."

Perhaps she had made the right choice after all. If she could just get past this inconvenient attraction, together they might solve her problems in a matter of days.

"I suspect you received the blackmail note yesterday, forcing you to visit your publisher at night," he continued in a serious tone. "While you were warding off Mr Hemming's amorous advances, someone broke into your house and stole your shoes. A thief attacked you and stole your boots as you walked home." He turned to face her. "Oh, and someone took your undergarments from the washing line this morning. Have I missed anything?"

"No, sir." Dear Lord. He was so thorough she couldn't help but admire him all the more. "That is exactly as it happened."

If he agreed to take the case, there were many more facts to consider. From the glint of intrigue in his eyes, Eva was convinced he would.

Mr Ashwood folded his muscular arms across his chest and glared. "What the devil possessed you to walk the streets alone at night?" His voice was tight with disapproval, and he sounded more concerned than Howard ever had. "You had ten pounds on your person. For a woman with a logical mind, do you not think it a foolish thing to do, Miss Dunn?"

Eva was torn between telling the man to mind his own business—but she had made it his business—and letting the anxiety of the last few months show.

"I am in dire straits, sir." Eva shot out of the chair. "Writing provides my only source of income. To put food on the table, I must endure my publisher's wandering hands and salacious comments. Yes, I should have visited during the day, or taken a hackney, but desperation makes the most logical behave recklessly."

The gentleman had the decency to incline his head in acknowledgement of her plight. "And I presume those willing to publish the work of a woman are few and far between."

"Indeed," she said, relieved he understood.

Mr Ashwood stroked his short, neatly trimmed beard. "What would you have me do, Miss Dunn? Am I to find your missing brother? Am I to discover who murdered your cobbler? Would you like me to catch a blackmailer or the person who stole your stockings?"

"Stockings?" Embarrassment warmed her cheeks. "I made no mention of stockings."

"No." Amusement danced in his emerald eyes. "But I'm confident they were on the washing line with your other undergarments."

Eva swallowed. "Yes."

"I wonder why you didn't mention it." The devil was teasing her again, flashing the sensual grin that made a simple undergarment seem highly indecent. "Perhaps you think I'm a man whose senses are easily aroused. I can assure you they are not."

So why had his eyes glazed when drifting up past her boots?

"I would like you to find my brother," she began, ignoring his previous comment for she lacked the skills needed when dealing with experienced men. "I want to know who stole my shoes and stockings. Who is blackmailing me? Who killed the cobbler? In short, Mr Ashwood, I need your help in every regard."

"You ask a great deal."

"I am confident you will rise to the challenge."

"I've had no complaints."

"Then I have chosen the right agent. It is my belief, that like the intricate strands of a spider's web, all events are connected."

The man moved to perch on the edge of his desk, the action drawing attention to the breadth of his solid thighs. "If I take this case, I will want to search your house, search your bedchamber. I will ask intimate questions, delve into your private affairs. Can you handle my intrusion, Miss Dunn?"

The smooth timbre of his voice left her a little breathless. "I —I shall tell you anything you need to know."

"I have your assurance you will follow my instruction?"

Eva nodded. There was strength in knowing one's limitations. "Yes. I shall bow to your wealth of experience in all matters. I shall do anything you ask of me."

He arched a sinful brow. "Anything?"

"When it comes to solving the case, of course."

"Of course. And you will be forthcoming with personal information?"

"I have nothing to hide, sir."

That wasn't entirely true.

She would have to tell him about the dreadful thing Howard had done.

Something so awful it shamed her to speak of it.

Something so appalling it gave his enemy a motive to commit murder.

CHAPTER 3

NOAH'S WILLINGNESS TO take Miss Dunn's case had nothing to do with her missing brother. The rogue had either fled the country or was a weighted corpse bobbing on the riverbed. Not that he would speak openly about the latter, not without proof. But he knew with absolute certainty Dermot Flannery was not to blame.

Noah's reason for playing knight errant had nothing to do with blackmail or missing undergarments. Though when Miss Dunn blushed at the mere mention of her stockings, his heart had softened. And while he would do everything in his power to find and punish the villain who attacked her in the street, a different predator prompted his inner fury.

Indeed, he despised men who preyed on women down on their luck. And so his need to free Miss Dunn from the clutches of her lecherous publisher proved his main motivation for accepting the case.

"Did the blackmailer detail when and how you should pay?"

"No, sir. He will inform me where to make the deposit in due course."

"I see." The first demand was a test to see if she alerted the authorities. "And who knows you write as Cain Dunnavan?"

She shrugged. "My brother, my publisher and an old friend."

22

Strange that she listed them in that order as her brother would be top of his list of suspects.

"Would you wait here for a moment, Miss Dunn?"

"Certainly." The lady's affected smile failed to reach her eyes. She was more anxious than she would have him believe.

Noah admired that.

Women used many techniques to incite a man's pity. There was something about Miss Dunn's proud chin he found appealing. There was something about the whole package that held him captive.

Noah left the lady scribbling in her notebook and returned to the drawing room. His friends were still drinking coffee and studying the broadsheets, noting information that might prove pertinent to future cases.

"Cole, may I speak to you privately?"

All three men glanced up from their relaxed positions on the sofas, their expressions brimming with curiosity.

"Of course." Cole folded his newspaper and placed it on the low table next to the coffee pot.

Noah strode to the dining room, and Cole joined him there.

"You're taking the case, I presume," Cole said, closing the door.

"You know I hate to see a woman in distress."

Society had treated Noah's mother like a pariah after his father's untimely death. He had been a boy of ten, but the disastrous event afterwards left a gaping wound in his heart that had never healed.

Cole arched a brow. "Yet Miss Dunn appeared so composed."

"*Appeared* being the operative word."

"And your offer of assistance has nothing to do with the fact you find her interesting? I saw a glimmer of satisfaction in your eyes when she chose you. Women rarely capture your notice."

"You were paying close attention."

"Daventry's stance is firm when it comes to relationships with clients." Cole's dark gaze carried a clear warning.

Lucius Daventry had hired them nine months ago. He was the master of the Order. A man who sought to right injustices, too. Despite Daventry's illegitimacy, he had inherited a vast sum

23

from his father the Duke of Melverley, money he had put to good use. Before that, Daventry had worked tirelessly to help the innocent escape transportation or the hangman's noose. And while the gentleman rarely took cases of his own these days, he was the true overseer.

"I'll admit I find the lady interesting." More interesting than any woman of his acquaintance, Noah thought. "But I have no intention of pursuing a relationship with Miss Dunn. I have a job to do." Every woman he helped eased the pain of regret over his mother's suffering. If only for a short time. "Have I ever broken the rules?"

"Never."

"Then I thank you for your counsel, but you have nothing to fear."

"We need you here," Cole persisted. "D'Angelo needs someone to keep him in line. Perhaps I should take the case."

The sudden flurry of panic in Noah's chest should have served as a warning. Yet the need to discover more about the pretty novelist, the need to soothe her woes, burned in his veins. Working with Miss Dunn would be a real test of his commitment to the Order.

"I'm motivated to help desperate women, not seduce them." Noah clasped Cole's shoulder in a gesture of reassurance. "I give you my word, should lust overcome logic, I will seek your advice."

Cole nodded but seemed unconvinced. "You didn't call me in here to discuss your attraction to Miss Dunn."

"An attraction that will soon pass," Noah reaffirmed. He was confident it would. "The lady's case is complicated. I need you to visit Dermot Flannery and ask about his dealings with a man named Howard Dunn. By all accounts, he gambled away his inheritance at The Silver Serpent."

Though Miss Dunn seemed honest to a fault, Noah never took a client at their word. Facts were often distorted. Tainted by bitter memories. Twisted into a story to support the victim's argument.

"You want to know if Flannery owns this fellow's vowels?"

"Indeed." He decided not to tell Cole that Miss Dunn had

found evidence of her brother's debts. "Ask Flannery if Howard Dunn owes money to another establishment and enquire there, too."

Cole arched a brow. "Daventry will want to know there's more to the case than finding a lady's wayward relative."

"Tell him it involves blackmail and assault. That should appease him. I would visit Flannery myself, but I have a more pressing line of enquiry." Noah didn't mention he would be delving into the matter of the lady's missing stockings.

"I can run your errand after my appointment at Bow Street."

"Excellent." He could trust Cole to do a thorough job.

They returned to the hall and spoke briefly about Cole's meeting with Sir Malcolm Langley. It was important they kept good relations with the magistrate and the constables who worked on the streets.

Cole glanced at the closed study door. "Some women look innocent but know how to get under a man's skin. Hell, she even had me desperate to learn what was written in that damn notebook."

Noah couldn't help but smile. Cole made Miss Dunn sound like a wicked temptress. Like those ladies who circled the ballrooms, flaunting their bulging bosoms, eager to capture every man's eye. They failed to raise Noah's gaze, let alone any other part of his anatomy. So what was it about Miss Dunn that left him eager to learn more?

Cole returned to the drawing room to finish his coffee. Noah returned to the study and found Miss Dunn wearing her spectacles and scrawling frantically in her little brown book. He waited for her to acknowledge his presence—she didn't.

He cleared his throat.

The lady flicked her hand at him as if he were an annoying fly buzzing around her buttered scone. Women were usually eager for his attention. Never had one told him to "hush a moment".

He perched on the edge of the desk like one of the vain vixens he despised, displaying his muscular thighs to advantage in the hope of luring Miss Dunn away from her scribblings. But it seemed nothing could disturb her concentration.

As soon as she'd written the last word, she thrust her book

and pencil into her reticule, removed her spectacles and jumped to her feet.

"Forgive my rudeness, Mr Ashwood. I had an idea for a plot. The slightest distraction and I lose my train of thought."

He glanced around the study. "One wonders what you found to inspire you in here."

"You'd be surprised." Her bright blue gaze turned coy. "Perhaps I might tell you when I have explored the idea further."

"I shall look forward to the prospect."

She stole a glance at his buckskin breeches, and he imagined pulling her between his legs and giving her a far more salacious storyline. A tale of a couple who succumb to their wicked desires while solving a case of mischief and mayhem.

Hellfire!

To rein in his erotic thoughts, he glanced at the painting of the goddess Themis above the mantel. Her weighing scales were a symbol of justice, but a reminder one prospered when life had balance. Perhaps he spent too much time working, not enough time enjoying leisurely pursuits. Perhaps that was why this woman roused a strange craving deep in his chest.

"It is rare for a client to accompany me on an investigation, Miss Dunn. But in this instance, I require your insight."

The lady's countenance brightened. "Oh, how exciting. Are we to visit Mr Flannery's gaming hell? I've longed to see if it's as wild as they say. That would be the most logical way to begin proceedings."

"Indeed. However, my associate will visit Flannery. You can help by answering two questions so I may determine the location of our first appointment."

A frown replaced her look of bitter disappointment. "How do you know you need my assistance if you have no notion where we're going?"

"Just answer the questions, Miss Dunn. I need your address and your given name." He didn't need her given name, just an initial would suffice, but he was curious.

"Yes, of course. I own a house on Brownlow Street, opposite the Lying-In Hospital. It's a short walk from here."

She owned the house?

"You live alone, not with your brother?"

"I inherited the house when my godfather died. Howard got the apartment in the Albany but now lives with me. He lost the apartment to Lord Greymore in a game of hazard."

Howard Dunn was a bloody buffoon. A dissolute wastrel. Everything Noah despised. Yet the information proved useful. It supported his initial theory that Howard Dunn was in hiding. That he sent the blackmail note to his sister hoping to gain funds to pay his debt. Noah would lay odds Miss Dunn had refused to lend her brother money.

"I cannot abide weak men," he said, firming his jaw in irritation. "Be aware, if we find your lousy brother I'm liable to break his nose."

The irony of the situation was not lost on him. All men had weaknesses. Intelligent, interesting women could well be his.

"You're welcome to try anything that might knock sense into his muddled brain." Her tone echoed her frustration. "As to your second question, my given name is Evangeline, but I prefer Eva. Is there a particular reason you asked?"

Evangeline.

It was unusual. Striking. Unique. Much like the lady herself. There was something sensual about the way his tongue wrapped around the syllables as he whispered it almost to himself. Somewhere there had to be the word *Angel*. Just like his need to protect D'Angelo from his tragic past, Noah felt the same compulsion to save Evangeline Dunn.

"I'll explain on the way." Noah stood. "As you live but a ten-minute walk from here, we'll visit a shop in Castle Street first. Mrs Gunning will act as chaperone."

"There is no need to trouble your housekeeper. My brother is a wicked scoundrel. It's too late to consider my reputation."

"Still, I must insist." His uncle's spies were everywhere. Lord Hawkridge sought any opportunity to spread gossip and lies, to blacken Noah's name.

"Very well." The lady pushed her spectacles into her reticule and snatched her dark blue kid gloves from the desk. "I assume there's a reason we're going shopping."

Noah opened the study door and followed Miss Dunn into

the hall. "We're shopping for undergarments. I have three theories regarding the theft this morning." Initially, he'd had two. The fact she lived close to the Lying-In Hospital brought to mind a third.

"Three?"

"An obsessed publisher might want a memento."

Miss Dunn's eyes widened in horror. "Surely not."

"We shall see." He inclined his head. "Excuse me a moment."

He left Miss Dunn waiting in the hall while he informed his friends of his plan to visit Brownlow Street. Investigating scoundrels brought its own dangers, and they always kept abreast of each other's movements. Then he descended the basement stairs.

"Mrs Gunning?" He knocked on the door of the housekeeper's sitting room before entering. He might have tugged the bell to summon her, but he wanted to speak privately. "I need you to accompany me on an outing."

The housekeeper hauled her stout frame out of the chair behind the old oak desk and closed the ledger. "Should I change into my best dress, sir?"

"That won't be necessary. But be prepared. When we reach Miss Dunn's house, I may need you to play a role."

Mrs Gunning failed to hide a grimace. It wouldn't be the first time she had assumed a supposed identity. She crossed the room and snatched her pelisse from the coat stand. "Not the madam of a brothel again."

"No, Mrs Gunning." He laughed. "Not the madam of a brothel."

The housekeeper gave a relieved sigh. "I'll let Cook and Sally know I'll be gone from the house and then meet you upstairs."

He made to leave but paused. "If you discovered someone had stolen washing from the line, what would be your first instinct?"

Noah had a suspect in mind.

The motive would soon reveal itself.

"That depends on how easy it is to access the garden, sir."

"And if the only access was through the house?"

"Suspicion would fall on the servants."

"Indeed." There were many reasons why the maid might have lied about the stolen undergarments, although he was more intrigued as to how Miss Dunn would deal with disloyal staff. "Until we reach Brownlow Street, you will play the part of Miss Dunn's maid."

The thought of beginning a new investigation sent blood surging through Noah's veins. Yet the excitement filling his chest stemmed from more than a need to feel useful. The reason became abundantly clear when he entered the hall and found D'Angelo pressing his lips to Miss Dunn's bare hand.

Jealousy reared like a spitting viper.

D'Angelo straightened upon hearing the clip of Noah's boots on the tiled floor and flashed an arrogant grin. "Ah, the wanderer returns."

Devil!

Noah ground his teeth in annoyance. D'Angelo was lucky he cared for him like a brother.

"Is it not considered the height of rudeness to leave a lady waiting in the hall?" D'Angelo teased.

"It's the height of rudeness to interfere in another man's business," Noah countered. "If you wish to be useful, write a note to Peter Lydford and arrange for me to meet him on the morrow."

From the wicked glint in D'Angelo's eyes, Noah knew to expect a provoking retort. Indeed, the rogue said, "Why? Have you written another book of lewd poems?"

Miss Dunn's delightful mouth fell open. "You write poetry, Mr Ashwood?" Her excitement rang through the hall, the information feeding her innate curiosity.

God's teeth!

"Mr D'Angelo enjoys taunting me." Noah shot his friend an irate glare. "It is merely a hobby. I once wrote a collection of rather salacious poems. Poems unfit for a lady's delicate ears. Mr D'Angelo persuaded me to publish them, anonymously, of course."

"They're remarkably good." D'Angelo grinned. "So exceptional one can almost feel the poet's crippling torment when he denies himself that which he desperately craves."

"How interesting." Miss Dunn's animated smile reached her

cornflower eyes. "I wonder, might the book be entitled *Every Man's Desire?*"

Good Lord! Surely she had not read the volume.

Noah swallowed deeply. "Men are driven by a multitude of passions. They strive to be great landowners, doctors, tailors. Yet their base desires are the same. In that regard, rich or poor, we share an affinity." He cleared his throat. "That is but one topic explored."

The lady continued to study him intently. "Fascinating. Perhaps we might discuss your work in more detail."

"You wish to discuss erotic literature?" Noah spoke past the hard lump in his throat. He tried to ignore the tightening in his groin, tried to ignore D'Angelo's satisfied grin.

"That would be inappropriate, sir. But I am most interested in your creative process."

"Trust me, Miss Dunn. You do not want to explore the mind of a man who commits his desires to paper." It wasn't just his deepest desires laid bare. His fears and anxieties were evident, too. "Now, I hear Mrs Gunning stomping up the stairs, and so we shall be on our way."

Noah reminded D'Angelo that he was to send a note to Mr Lydford, then he took his hat and gloves from the console table and escorted Miss Dunn out onto Hart Street.

They walked towards Long Acre in companionable silence, Mrs Gunning ambling behind playing chaperone. A list of unanswered questions bombarded his thoughts, and so he took the opportunity to gather answers.

"May I ask why you came to Hart Street without your maid?" he said, keen to delve deeper into the workings of the lady's mind.

It took her a few seconds to reply. "I no longer know who to trust, Mr Ashwood. Indeed, I find myself growing more suspicious by the day."

"You're right to be cautious." Now was a good time to prepare her for the inevitable outcome of their morning visit. "I imagine we will solve the problem of your missing undergarments within the hour. Once your maid has confessed, we will have a better understanding of whether she's involved in the theft of your boots."

"My maid!" Miss Dunn sucked in a sharp breath although her gait did not falter. "You're convinced she is to blame?"

"It seems likely."

"Kathleen is not a bad person, I can assure you."

He admired her sense of loyalty. "Good people commit crimes. More often than not, the motive is money. What's the price of silk stockings? Eight shillings?"

"Twelve, sir, though I suspect three shillings is the going rate for second-hand hosiery."

He thought it best not to mention that wealthy men with strange obsessions paid more than five pounds for a soiled pair.

"Might a friend not have acted as your companion today? Or do your misgivings stretch to all those of your acquaintance?"

This time, her brief silence was fraught with tension.

"To be blunt, sir, I have no friends. My brother is a lying scoundrel. Decent ladies avoid me like the plague. The only person foolish enough to value our friendship is now paying a hefty price. Indeed, she was sent to live in Northumberland and is not permitted to write."

The dissolute usually amassed enemies. There would be plenty of people who wished Howard Dunn dead. The innocent were always caught in the crossfire. Indeed, Noah's father had not thought of his poor wife and child when fighting a duel over his mistress.

"I know what it's like to suffer because of a selfish man's deeds," he said, his body stiffening in anger. It took effort to keep his rage at bay as he told her briefly how his father had died. It might help her to know she was not the only person tainted by the behaviour of another. "I'm sorry life dealt you a similar hand."

She came to an abrupt halt and turned to face him. Mrs Gunning almost bumped into them, for she was busy looking at the summer bonnets in Farthings' window.

"Thank you, Mr Ashwood." Miss Dunn's blue eyes brimmed with appreciation. "Few people would reveal something so distressing, so personal, merely to put another at ease."

Heat filled his chest for the umpteenth time this morning. Perhaps he was coming down with an ague. "The actions of family members do not define us, Miss Dunn. I thought it important to remind you of that fact."

The lady moved to touch his arm but snatched her hand back. "I appreciate your wisdom, sir. More than you know."

Devil be damned. The tender words penetrated his rapidly failing reserve. Did she have to look upon him with doe-eyed admiration? Could she not say something distasteful to dampen his ardour?

"Let us be on our way before people accuse us of blocking the pavement," he said lest he spout fanciful sentiments, too.

They arrived in Castle Street moments later, at the clothes shop owned by Bernard Peters. At Noah's request, Miss Dunn entered first while Mrs Gunning remained outside. The tinkling of the bell brought the beaming proprietor hurrying to the door until he caught sight of her companion and came to a crashing halt.

"Mr Ashwood, sir." Peters gulped a breath and fiddled with his fat fingers. He shuffled back and reluctantly bid them welcome.

"You know why I'm here, Peters."

Noah glanced at the array of garments hanging from hooks on the walls—men's coats and shirts in all shapes and sizes, some new, some carrying the stale, musty stench of old clothes. Gloves and reticules, cravats and stockings, filled the drawers in the glass-fronted counter. An array of dusty hats and bonnets, scuffed shoes and boots, littered the space.

Peters shook his head repeatedly before blurting, "I've not bought a thing off Jack Higgins, sir. I swear it on my dear mother's grave. God rest her soul."

"Your mother is alive, Peters."

"Yes, sir, but I'd swear it all the same."

Noah glanced at Miss Dunn. "Although Peters sells new clothes, he also pays people for their old linens."

Miss Dunn pressed her fingers to her nostrils. "Yes, I soon discerned that most of his stock is second-hand."

"Second-hand but all above board, miss. Those thieving

rascals won't get a penny for their booty here." Peters gestured to the oak barrel full of walking canes and swordsticks. One did not need a vivid imagination to picture how he might use them. "And I check the pockets of any coat what comes in, for soil and the like."

"Soil?" Miss Dunn's curiosity was piqued.

"I caught Peters selling a dead man's clothes. A man last seen wearing them in an open coffin."

Miss Dunn frowned and glared at Peters. "You bought clothes from a grave robber? Had you no thought for the deceased man's family?"

Peters pressed his chubby hands together in prayer. "If I'd have known that canny devil and his crew were digging up the dead, I'd have told him to sling his hook."

Once again, they were straying from the point.

"We're not here to discuss your previous misdeeds," Noah said curtly, "but rather to determine if you purchased a petticoat and stockings early this morning." Miss Dunn's house was a two-minute walk from the shop and an ideal place for a maid to dispose of stolen goods quickly. "The petticoat will bear the embroidered initials E. D."

Miss Dunn touched his arm and whispered, "How do you know the garment bears my initials? I am, after all, the only lady in the house."

Noah stole any opportunity to explain his logical deductions. And he needed something to distract his mind from the dainty fingers resting on his coat sleeve.

"Because you were keen to inform me that Kathleen is a good person. One might assume that she stole an old garment, one that would not be missed as much as a recent purchase."

"Yes."

"And because I believe your godfather's last poem, *Castle of Corpses*, relates to the time he took you to stay at Briden Castle two summers ago."

It was a poem about an angel made to suffer the company of the undead. A battle to remain pure and uncorrupted. Becker had mentioned his charge in the acknowledgements but not named her.

"When attending a large house party," he continued, "a maid would want to ensure no personal items went astray."

Miss Dunn's eyes remained wide. "While some would argue that you make sweeping assumptions, I find your insight rather remarkable." She continued to stare. "And yes, a month spent with pretentious prigs takes its toll."

Peters cleared his throat. "Begging your pardon, sir, but I opened late this morning. You're the first people to walk through that door."

Noah dragged his gaze away from Miss Dunn. "Then you won't mind if I inspect your stock."

"No, Mr Ashwood, sir. Do as you please." Peters gestured for Noah to come behind the crude counter. "The lady is welcome to rummage through the drawers while you search the cupboards out the back."

"Wait here, Miss Dunn. Scan the rows of shoes. See if any seem at all familiar."

To keep Peters on his toes, Noah strode into the storeroom and searched through the petticoats. Based on Peters' sudden burst of confidence, he knew the maid had not hurried to the shop to sell her ill-gotten gains.

Upon his return, he found Miss Dunn examining a rack of old boots, her pretty lace handkerchief pressed to her nose to mask the foul stench that resembled rotten cabbage.

"Anything of interest?"

"No. Nothing." She straightened and tucked her handkerchief into her reticule.

Peters' smile filled his chubby face. "As I said, sir, you're the first people I've seen this morning."

"Then let's hope you speak the truth. I shall be in a devil of a mood if forced to return." Noah captured Miss Dunn's elbow and guided her towards the door.

Touching her only deepened his attraction.

"Where to now?" She looked up at him and held his gaze. The tightness around her eyes revealed a sense of unease.

"Now we question your maid."

CHAPTER 4

THEY COVERED the brief walk to Brownlow Street in silence, though Eva's mind was far from quiet. Her chaotic thoughts had nothing to do with her worrying situation. On the contrary, the confident gentleman striding beside her commanded her attention.

Eva studied his handsome profile.

Mr Ashwood embodied a wealth of contradictions. His neat beard and devilish grin gave him a rugged appeal. That of a man capable of beating a villain to death with his bare hands. Yet his powerful jaw and proud bearing spoke of his upstanding moral character. He was serious in his approach to work. Determined. A man to admire. Yet it was the teasing way his golden brown hair curled at the nape, and the playful glint in those alluring green eyes, that fed her curiosity.

"You'll have a crick in your neck if you keep staring, Miss Dunn." Mr Ashwood did not look at her but continued to survey their surroundings as they approached the Lying-In Hospital.

"I find you somewhat of an enigma, sir." And she did so love a puzzle.

"Then we have something else in common, madam, other than our feckless fathers and a love of books."

He came to an abrupt halt opposite the hospital. The building might have been mistaken for a row of townhouses were it not for the grand entrance supported by Doric pilasters and a vast Greek pediment.

"Something else in common?"

"With shocking frequency, I'm surprised by elements of your character, too." He studied the sash windows covering the hospital's facade. "I've never met a woman like you."

Thank goodness he wasn't gazing into her eyes when conveying what sounded like a compliment. "Being considered an *original* comes with its problems."

"I fail to see how," he said before his attention drifted. "Excuse me a moment."

Without another word, Mr Ashwood dashed across the road and came to the aid of a heavily pregnant woman struggling to carry her valise. He took hold of her bag and let the woman grip his arm as he helped her hobble towards the entrance.

A matron appeared, and a lengthy discussion ensued. Mr Ashwood motioned to Eva, no doubt explaining that he was not the father of the unborn babe but a mere bystander offering assistance.

"The men call him Dauntless," Mrs Gunning said, admiration for her employer evident. "Dauntless because of his strength and courage they say. It doesn't do him justice in my humble opinion."

"No," Eva mused as she watched the gentleman approach. She imagined any woman witnessing the act of kindness might fall a little in love with Mr Ashwood. "I suspect there isn't a word to sum up the complex nature of his character."

"Forgive me," the gentleman said, joining Eva on the pavement. "What husband lets his wife make the journey to hospital alone?"

"A negligent one." Eva glanced at the hospital, the place paid for by wealthy subscribers to care for impoverished pregnant women of reasonable social standing. "Although some ladies who arrive are unmarried and have forged the paperwork."

She had heard many sad stories, seen many desperate women attempt to gain entrance without having first submitted an affidavit of marriage and the necessary letter of recommendation.

Guilt flared as her thoughts turned to Miss Swales.

Eva knew she shouldn't blame herself for what happened. Had she known of the secret assignations, of the lies and deceit, she would have intervened. Yet every time she stepped out onto the street to see another woman heavy with child, she was reminded of her brother's wickedness.

Perhaps Howard had journeyed to Northumberland to reunite with the woman he had used so callously. The need to know the truth was yet another reason she had sought professional help. And yet she hadn't found the strength to speak to Mr Ashwood of her family's shame.

"Marital status shouldn't matter when a woman is in dire straits," he said, sounding cross. "Not when some men are slow to keep their promises."

Something in his tone suggested he spoke from experience. It was the sort of bitter comment made by an illegitimate son. Yet while waiting in the hall at Hart Street, Mr D'Angelo mentioned that Mr Ashwood was Lord Hawkridge's nephew.

"Some men have no concept of responsibility," she said. Indeed, Mr Ashwood's disdain for rogues was the reason she decided to hold on to her secret a little longer. "My father being a prime example."

"A fate we share, Miss Dunn. Now, let us continue with our business. You said you live opposite the hospital."

"Yes, here." She motioned to the black door behind her.

"You live at Number 11?"

"Indeed. Why? Is something wrong?"

"I live at Number 11 Wigmore Street, off Cavendish Square."

"How remarkable," she said, slightly surprised by the growing number of coincidences. "I don't know why, but I presumed you had rooms in Hart Street." The house belonging to the Gentlemen of the Order seemed more like a family home than a business premises.

"I have a room there should I wish to stay, but every agent has his own house in town." He spent a few seconds surveying the road. "Am I right in saying there is no way to access your garden from the street?"

"No obvious way, no. But if you enter the alley leading to

Castle Street, you might scale the wall into the garden of Number 12."

If a man could clear the first wall, there was no reason why he couldn't climb into her garden. Although she doubted a thief would think it worth the effort. Not when it increased the likelihood of getting caught.

Mr Ashwood nodded. "I would like to examine the garden and then speak to your staff, if I may. Before I leave, I shall inspect your bedchamber."

Though his tone was as measured as a sergeant from Bow Street, a coil of heat swirled in her stomach at the thought of him invading her privacy.

"Then you must come inside," she said, feeling suddenly nervous about welcoming him into her home.

Eva escorted Mr Ashwood and Mrs Gunning into the house. She employed four servants, all of whom had worked for her godfather Mr Becker. Bardsley, the middle-aged butler, relieved them of their outdoor apparel.

"Bardsley, show Mrs—"

"Mrs Sawyer," Mr Ashwood interjected.

Eva forced a smile. "Show Mrs Sawyer into the drawing room while I take Mr Ashwood out into the garden."

"Yes, ma'am."

Mr Ashwood spent a few minutes surveying the brick wall. He crouched by the flowerbeds, his muscular thighs almost bursting from his breeches as he examined the borders. Then he brushed soil from his hands and asked to speak to the servants but not the maid.

The staff gathered around the kitchen table while the gentleman asked if they'd heard anything unusual the previous evening.

"We were taking supper, sir," Bardsley explained, "and never heard a sound. The devil was as quiet as a mouse."

Henry, the footman, and Cook supported the butler's claim.

"All four of you ate supper?" Mr Ashwood asked. "Including Kathleen?"

"Yes, sir."

"And how long did you remain here?"

"About an hour, sir," Bardsley replied.

"And no one has seen or heard from Mr Dunn since his sudden departure?"

"No, sir," they all said in unison.

"Is anything missing from his room?"

They all turned to Henry, who shook his head.

Mr Ashwood studied them before saying, "That will be all for now."

Next, having instructed Bardsley to summon her maid, Eva led Mr Ashwood to the drawing room where Mrs Gunning sat waiting.

"Do you recall your promise, Miss Dunn?" Mr Ashwood said after declining the offer of a seat. His voice was so utterly compelling he might tempt her to say anything. "You agreed I might intrude into your affairs."

Eva swallowed past another rush of nerves. "Yes."

"Then no matter what lies fall from my lips, I ask that you do not contradict me in front of your maid."

Eva nodded. "As long as you're not unkind."

"Do you suppose I'm a man who treats servants with disrespect?" He cast Mrs Gunning a sidelong glance. The woman seemed aghast at the suggestion.

"Not at all. I merely wish to remind you I have a duty to protect my staff."

"Noted."

A light tap on the door brought Kathleen. The young woman bobbed a quick curtsy. She stood rigid, yet her gaze flicked nervously from side to side.

"Kathleen, this is Mr Ashwood. He is investigating the theft that occurred here last night and again this morning. He wants to ask you a few questions."

"Yes, ma'am." Kathleen's bottom lip quivered as she examined Mr Ashwood's broad, athletic frame. The man radiated a power that would make the innocent drop to their knees and beg for clemency.

"Fear not," he said and offered a smile to soften the hardest woman's heart. "This will take but a moment, and then you may return to your duties."

ADELE CLEE

Kathleen clasped her hands and pursed her lips.

"Tell me exactly what was stolen this morning," he continued.

The maid swallowed. "A petticoat and a pair of stockings, sir."

"Was there anything else on the washing line?"

"No, sir."

"And yet the stolen stockings were not the ones your mistress wore yesterday," he stated. "They were ripped during the attack in the street."

How the devil did he know that?

"Yes, sir. I mean, no, sir. They were the stockings from the previous day."

"Do you not keep to a strict washday?"

"No, sir, not when I've just the mistress' clothes to launder."

"What about Miss Dunn's chemise?" Mr Ashwood's verdant gaze journeyed the length of Eva's body as if she stood in nothing but the flimsy garment in question. "Why would you wash her petticoat and not the linen worn closest to the skin? You did wash her chemise?"

Kathleen's blonde lashes fluttered in a panic. "Y-yes, sir."

"So why was it not on the line?"

The maid stared blankly.

"This is Mrs Sawyer," he continued in an impersonal tone. "She's the matron who attended those entering the hospital this morning. She dealt with the distraught woman seen crying in the street."

Eva studied the gentleman, in awe of his calm, controlled manner. Was there ever a time when he lost the firm grasp of his faculties? Was he ever unsettled, ever fearful?

"Is there something you wish to confess?" he said, taking a few slow steps towards the maid, swamping her petite frame. "Or shall I have Mrs Sawyer tell your mistress what happened this morning?"

Kathleen's eyes widened. She sucked in a sharp breath and swung around to face Eva. "Forgive me, ma'am. I didn't know what else to do. I shouldn't have lied. I should have explained what happened, but with Mr Dunn missing and the issue with the money, I thought you'd be angry."

Heavens above. Did she have to mention the money? When

hunting for information, Mr Ashwood was like a hawk and could spot a mouse in a sprawling wheat field.

"You gave my petticoat and stockings to someone from the hospital?" Eva asked, hoping to steer the conversation away from Howard.

"A woman must provide clothing for herself and her babe before she can enter the hospital," Mr Ashwood said. "Am I correct, Mrs Sawyer?"

"Yes, sir," the housekeeper replied, perfectly at ease in her acting role. "That's correct."

Kathleen whimpered. "I was out scrubbing the step this morning, and I saw a woman sobbing further down the street. She had given her papers two weeks ago and secured a place at the hospital. But her husband said she must have the babe at home and refused to let her take all her belongings."

Eva frowned. She felt foolish for troubling Mr Ashwood over a mere household affair. "But if you'd come to me, I would have given the woman the clothes she needed. You know I make regular donations to the hospital."

"But that was before Mr Dunn disappeared taking the—"

"The less said about Mr Dunn, the better," Eva interposed far too abruptly. She tried to steal a covert glance at Mr Ashwood only to find the gentleman staring at her intently.

"You were still upset about what Mr Dunn did, ma'am, I didn't want to add to the burden," Kathleen said, much to Eva's chagrin.

Eva pasted a smile and faced Mr Ashwood. "Forgive me for wasting your time this morning. It seems the undergarments were not stolen after all."

"No," he mused. The word carried a wealth of suspicion. "But the last few minutes have proved insightful." Presumably, he had a host of questions for her, but he turned to Kathleen. "I trust you didn't encounter a woman in the street who needed boots and shoes."

"No, sir." Kathleen rubbed her chapped fingers. "And I was taking supper when the thief entered the house."

"And the intruder took nothing but Miss Dunn's footwear?"

He glanced at the maid's feet. It was evident she wore boots, not dainty dancing slippers.

"Not that I noticed, sir."

"Are those your boots?"

Kathleen shook her head. "They belong to Cook. They're too small, sir, but I didn't want to ruin my mistress' beloved slippers."

Mr Ashwood nodded. "And do you have any idea how the villain entered the house?"

Kathleen shrugged. "Bardsley must have left the front door unlocked when Miss Dunn went out last night."

"That would have been rather fortuitous for a passing thief." Mr Ashwood's voice dripped with sarcasm. He shot Eva a curious glance. "There was no sign of forced entry?"

"No." She knew what he was thinking without him uttering a word. He believed Howard had returned and stolen her shoes and boots.

Her theory proved correct when Mr Ashwood said, "Presumably Mr Dunn has a door key."

"He does, sir, but no one has seen the master for a week."

The master!

Had Kathleen forgotten who paid her wages?

"That does not mean he wasn't here." Mr Ashwood's expression remained unreadable, though there was a devilish glint of amusement in his eyes when he said, "Would you escort me to your bedchamber, Miss Dunn? I'm sure Kathleen will fetch tea for Mrs Sawyer while the matron awaits our return."

"Of course." Eva's heartbeat pounded in her chest. "Come with me, Mr Ashwood."

Climbing the stairs proved an arduous task with a handsome gentleman in tow. Her legs were as heavy as lead weights. She had to grip the handrail to propel herself forward. Mr Ashwood's gaze bored into her back as he trailed too closely behind.

"Might I examine your brother's room first?" he said when they reached the landing.

"Certainly." The distraction would give her time to gather her composure, and so she gestured to the door at the far end of the corridor.

He pushed open the door to Howard's chamber and entered. "Do you recall the last conversation you had with your brother?"

Eva followed Mr Ashwood into the room. "Yes."

They had fought. Howard had said terrible things. Called her every cruel name. Cursed her to the devil. Hurt her for the last time.

Mr Ashwood opened the top drawer of the gentleman's dressing chest, removed a gold cravat pin and twirled it between long, elegant fingers. "Are you determined to keep me in the dark, Miss Dunn, or will you explain the reason for your argument?"

"How do you know we argued?"

Mr Ashwood closed the top drawer. He opened the one beneath and rummaged through the silk cravats. "Your brother is a wastrel. You cut your maid short when you feared she would reveal something of his scandalous ways."

It was time to make a small confession. "Howard wanted money. I refused, and so he stole the paltry sum I kept hidden in a box under my bed."

"I see. Then it's possible your brother sent the blackmail note." He moved to the armoire and studied the array of well-tailored coats and embroidered silk waistcoats. "If I press you further—and I intend to press you much further, Miss Dunn—you will tell me he asked for a thousand pounds. The exact sum requested in the demand."

Silence ensued.

Was there anything Mr Ashwood didn't know?

The man was so perceptive he could tell fortunes at the fair.

Her reasons for secrecy had nothing to do with protecting Howard. The cad was capable of the worst kind of atrocities. No. The last thing she wanted was for Mr Ashwood to think her a naive fool.

But pride be damned.

"Howard's initial request was for two thousand pounds," she admitted. "I was shrewd enough to invest the small sum left to me by Mr Becker. Howard pleaded poverty and insisted I visit the bank." There was no reasoning with a man whose evil addictions had taken possession of his character. "He demanded my footman serve as his valet. Indeed, he seemed to think he had the run of the house."

Mr Ashwood turned to face her, his jaw firm, his expression severe. "When we find your wayward brother, I shall blacken his eyes and break his nose."

"And I shall applaud you for it, sir."

"Excellent. I'm glad we understand one another." He motioned to the assortment of polished boots and shoes in the armoire. "It's evident your brother had every intention of returning." He paused. "What strikes me as odd is that the intruder stole your shoes and left your brother's expensive Hessians."

"Odd indeed," she agreed.

He released a weary sigh as he scanned every inch of the room with unblinking focus. "Take me to your bedchamber, Miss Dunn."

The demand sent her pulse soaring. Heavens, she had no control over her emotions when in this man's presence.

"Certainly. Follow me."

Eva led him into her chamber, a sumptuous space decorated entirely in gold and pale blue. It was where she came to read and relax, came to get away from her brother's annoying diatribe.

A faint smile played on Mr Ashwood's lips as he stroked the rich hangings on the large canopy bed. "You like to sleep in luxury, Miss Dunn."

"One spends almost a third of one's time in bed, sir." Heat rose to her cheeks despite her logical reply. "It pays to be comfortable."

"Comfort should always be a consideration when spending any length of time in bed."

"Indeed."

"And your bathtub is a permanent feature?" he asked, moving to examine the tub positioned on the wooden plinth in the corner. With an amused hum, he studied the lavish dressing screen bearing a naked image of Venus surrounded by a host of cherubs.

"I read when I bathe, and I do both often."

He removed the delicate glass bottle from the side table next to the tub, pulled out the stopper and inhaled deeply. The pleasurable sigh breezing from his lips played havoc with her insides.

"There is nothing like the sweet smell of rosewater on a woman's skin," he drawled.

Good Lord! Her heart thumped hard in her throat. "I'm glad you approve, though what that has to do with my stolen boots is beyond me."

There, a sharp snipe worked wonders to cool the blood.

He threw a wicked smile in her direction. "One can learn a great deal about a person from their habits and surroundings."

Eva snorted. "And what have you learned about me, sir, other than I prefer the smell of roses to lavender?"

"You're pragmatic, efficient." He sauntered towards her, clutching the bottle. "Yet a practical woman would have the bath removed for it clutters the space."

"A practical woman might decide it saves the servants time if the bath is a permanent fixture," she countered. "It bodes for better use of limited resources."

"But that is not the reason it's here." The gentleman brought the bottle to his nose and inhaled again. "A practical woman rarely indulges her senses. Rarely yields to her inclinations. And yet you strike me as one who refuses to suppress her passions." He withdrew the glass stopper and dabbed rosewater on the pad of his finger. "May I?"

Eva knew what he meant to do, but found she could not refuse.

"I work hard, sir," she said almost choking on the words as he leaned closer and pressed the scent to the pulse point below her ear. "But ... but I am still a woman."

"Of that, I am acutely aware, Miss Dunn."

The delicate fragrance drifted to her nostrils. "Perhaps you might like to examine the armoire if you have finished analysing my character." A nervous energy made her voice sound an octave higher.

Mr Ashwood studied her for a moment before dabbing the scent on his wrist and removing the rosewater to the small table. He crossed the room and pulled open the double doors of the large wardrobe.

"As you can see, sir, someone cleared the bottom shelf."

"Indeed." He studied the dresses hanging on the hooks, but one in particular captured his attention. "Is a red silk gown not a rather extravagant item for a practical woman's wardrobe?"

"Well, as you so rightly pointed out, I often indulge my whims."

Mr Ashwood glanced at her and smiled. "But you've never worn it, have you?"

"No. Never." And the likelihood of her ever wearing it was slim to none.

Seconds ticked before he said, "Two questions. Might I ask if the room was in disarray when you returned home? And where do you keep your jewels?"

The first question was easy to answer.

The second roused bitter memories.

"The room was exactly as you see it now." There had been no reason to suspect a thing. It wasn't until she opened the armoire that she learned of the theft. "And I do not possess jewels, sir. I'm afraid my brother took the few items that belonged to my mother and sold them."

"Took?"

"Stole."

Mr Ashwood muttered a curse. "Then we shall add three broken fingers to the list of his impending injuries." He took one last look around the room before removing his pocket watch and checking the time. "I think that is all for today."

Eva was grateful for his intervention but hadn't taken a full breath since meeting him this morning. "Now we've solved the mystery of my missing undergarments, what shall we tackle next?"

"Next, we visit your publisher."

"Mr Hemming?" A boulder of a lump formed in her throat. The man had a wicked streak. He manipulated events to suit his purpose. "Must we involve him?"

"Arrange an appointment and send word to me in Hart Street. I shall have my carriage collect you in ample time."

There was to be no discussion on the matter.

"I can see myself out, Miss Dunn. Spend the next few days preparing yourself for our next meeting."

"Preparing myself?" Eva snorted. "For what exactly?"

Mr Ashwood arched a brow. "For divulging those elements of the tale you've neglected to mention." He brought his wrist to his nostrils, his lips curling into a sinful grin as he inhaled. "I'll have the complete story, or Mr D'Angelo will take your case. The decision is yours. Good day, Miss Dunn."

Eva watched him stride from the room, though his powerful presence lingered in every conceivable space long after he'd descended the stairs.

Perhaps it would be better if she changed agents.

And yet she had grown surprisingly attached to Mr Ashwood. Indeed, his intense green eyes and intelligent mind held her spellbound. His sensual smile sent pulses of pleasure to all the wrong places. One thing was certain. When she lounged in her tub tonight, when she dabbed rosewater onto her bare skin and slipped into her luxurious bed, she would think of nothing but the enigmatic man who wrote erotic poetry.

CHAPTER 5

"Howard Dunn's situation is worse than you thought." Cole crossed the drawing room and dropped onto the sofa. His grave expression confirmed Noah's worst fears.

Noah returned his coffee cup to the silver tray on the low table. They were the first men to arrive at Hart Street this morning, and so he probed his friend further.

"You mean the devil's debts far outweigh his ability to pay?"

Cole reached for the coffeepot and 'poured himself a cup. "Howard Dunn's debts amount to twelve thousand pounds. For affluent men, that's an average month's losses at the tables. But I'm told Mr Dunn's creditors are tired of hearing his excuses."

"So he owes Flannery twelve thousand pounds?" Much more than the paltry sum Miss Dunn mentioned.

"Five thousand," Cole corrected. "Flannery extended Dunn credit as he'd had no issue settling his account before."

"Presumably he owes another gaming hell the remaining seven."

Cole's tight lips and deep frown roused a wave of trepidation. "You won't like the answer." He paused. "Dunn owes the Turners four thousand."

"The Turners!" Hellfire! Noah almost shot out of his seat. "Has the man lost his mind? Howard Dunn is a bloody imbecile."

The Turner brothers—no one knew their given names—were

48

violent men who worked out of The Compass Inn in Rosemary Lane. Fixing boxing bouts was their speciality. No doubt Howard Dunn had been fool enough to gamble on a prizefighter with bow legs and a weak left hook.

"Then there's every chance Howard Dunn is dead," Noah said, dreading the thought of explaining the seriousness of the problem to Miss Dunn. "It's said their bull terrier can sink its teeth into a man's jugular and rip his throat clean out."

Cole snorted, yet the sound held no amusement. "Ordinarily, I would taunt you for lending weight to gossip, but that dog is reputed to be as vicious as its owners."

Noah cursed.

The news complicated matters. Logic said Howard Dunn hadn't fled to France for the summer, looking to charm a wealthy widow into covering his debts. The fact his clothes still hung in the armoire did not bode well. An unpaid debt to the Turners was like a signature on a death warrant.

"And what of the other three thousand?" Noah asked, foolishly thinking that nothing could be worse than owing a debt to the Turners.

Cole drained his cup as if it contained something far more potent than coffee. The temporary distraction failed to conceal his look of dread. "The idiot borrowed money from a lender in Gower Street."

"Gower Street?" Noah's blood ran cold. "Tell me you're not referring to Mr Manning."

Or Mortuary Manning as he was known on the streets. Anyone who crossed the moneylender ended up stiff on a mortuary slab. He was the sort to bludgeon a cobbler to death for information.

Cole nodded. "Most men would rather do a stint in the Marshalsea than borrow from Manning."

"Bloody fool," Noah muttered.

"And what relation is this fool to Miss Dunn?"

"Her brother."

"Then you should prepare her for the worst." Cole's dark eyes conveyed the gravity of the situation. "I don't need to remind you that Manning harasses the family of those who cannot pay their debts."

"No, you don't need to remind me. With luck, we'll find the blighter before it comes to that."

Noah scrubbed his face to ease the tension. Manning didn't care who he hurt as long as he got his money. Though if Miss Dunn's attacker had been working for the brute, she would have a broken leg, not a bruised thigh.

A vision of the woman's marred thigh filled his mind. Vengeance simmered. The thug would pay for attacking a help-less woman in the street. A frisson of desire rippled through him, too. What was it about Miss Dunn he found so alluring?

"I have no appointments today," Cole said, disturbing Noah's reverie. "Perhaps I might assist you in your investigation."

Only a fool would attempt to deal with Mortuary Manning and the Turners without support. "I'm to accompany Miss Dunn to an appointment in Tavistock Street at eleven. I'll explain more when I return." He couldn't mention the publisher, couldn't break Miss Dunn's confidence without gaining her permission. "Howard Dunn lost his apartment at the Albany to Lord Greymere in a game of hazard. I need to know if there's truth to the story. And see if you can compile a list of Dunn's friends and associates."

Cole nodded. "We should inform D'Angelo and Sloane that we're investigating Manning and the Turners."

"Agreed."

It paid to be cautious.

And yet Noah couldn't shake the feeling that the case was about to become even more complicated. Indeed, Miss Dunn had a secret. A terrible secret. Something far worse than admit-ting her brother was a wasteful degenerate.

Noah hoped to spend a few minutes alone in the carriage, composing himself and settling into the role of investigator, yet punctuality was another trait of Miss Dunn's he admired.

"Good morning, Mr Ashwood." She fixed her gaze upon him and smiled. "I see you've shaved."

"Good morning, Miss Dunn." He stroked his smooth jaw. "We don't want your publisher thinking you've formed a friendship with a vagrant."

"I rather liked your beard."

"I'm certain you'll see it again."

She accepted his proffered hand and climbed into the carriage. Today, she wore a dark grey pelisse, the matching bonnet adorned with delicate red rosebuds. Grey, because it was practical. The silk flowers added a hint of sensuality.

He inwardly sighed.

Even a damn fashion accessory managed to raise his pulse.

He wasted no time getting to the point. "I trust you've had time to consider what I said the other day. I cannot work on a case without knowing all the facts."

The lady settled into the seat opposite, her gloved hands clasped in her lap. "I spent hours lounging in the bathtub thinking of nothing else."

He doubted Miss Dunn meant to tease him with thoughts of her naked body rising Venus-like from the water. And yet he wondered if she'd thought of him when tending to her ablutions.

"And while indulging your whims, did you come to a decision?" Having witnessed her opulent bedchamber, it wasn't difficult to picture her satisfying her desires—or satisfying his desires for that matter. "There is little point moving off unless I'm certain of your willingness to comply."

She had the decency to look sheepish. "I had planned to tell you soon, once I mustered the courage." A stain of shame tainted her cheeks. "But I am so hurt and humiliated I cannot bear to speak of my brother's betrayal."

Her choice of words tied Noah's stomach in knots. By all accounts, his mother had made the same claim upon learning of his father's duplicity. Noah inhaled a calming breath. Had fate sent Miss Dunn to torment him, torment him in every conceivable way?

Her strength and intelligence roused his admiration. Her underlying sense of vulnerability spoke to the virile male determined to prove his worth. The veil of mystery that shrouded the real woman behind the calm facade left him desperate to learn more.

But she was his client.

"You need my help, and I'm the last person to judge," he said, hoping that working on the case would command his full attention. "You may be assured of my discretion. You may be assured that every member of the Order will keep your secrets."

She considered him through curious eyes. "Tell me something about yourself, Mr Ashwood. Something that brings you shame."

"Me?" Harrowing images flashed into his mind. Images that threatened to steer a man off course. But he was used to battening down the hatches and riding out the storm. "We are not here to delve into my past traumas, Miss Dunn."

"I have yet to meet a man who proved trustworthy, sir. Confide in me. Give me a reason to trust you."

Noah snorted. The woman had come to Hart Street of her own volition. He'd not kidnapped her off the street. Did she want his damn help or not?

He was about to refuse when she said, "Please. I must learn to trust someone. Let it be you."

Hell!

Cole was right. Miss Dunn had a way of getting under a man's skin. The need to protect her and please her outweighed all rationale.

"Very well." He sighed to make his frustration known. She wanted to hear of a past trauma. She could bloody well hear them all. "My father was as reckless as yours. He married my mother over an anvil in Gretna Green two days before I was born. My uncle has spent years trying to prove the marriage took place after the birth in order to lay claim to my inheritance. My father died in a duel fought because of an argument over his mistress. My mother died of a broken heart two months later, under tragic circumstances I refuse to discuss." Too tragic for a son to witness. "Would you care to hear more?"

"Forgive me." Pity filled the lady's eyes. "It must have been dreadful. I assume you were a boy when your parents died."

"A boy of ten." The painful ache in his throat returned.

"Childhood memories are often the most traumatic."

"Yes."

They both fell silent. Yet he was still navigating through the turmoil, the nightmare.

"I cannot help but notice the similarities between us, sir," she eventually said, and he was grateful for the distraction.

"Similarities?"

"Both our fathers are undeserving wastrels. We strive to shake the ugly stain on our names left by their deplorable actions. We have a family member who serves to test our resolve and remind us of our tainted history."

"Indeed." And they both used confidence as a shield. "Thankfully we were saved from a terrible fate by respectable men," he added, his equilibrium restored. "My paternal grandfather took me in when my parents died. You were fortunate to have Mr Becker."

He expected her to nod in agreement, to be full of praise for the kind poet, but her expression turned pensive. It took a few seconds for her to recover.

"When one admires a man's work it is easy to place him on a pedestal," she said, gazing thoughtfully out of the window, though the carriage was still parked on Brownlow Street. "Being a creative genius does not mean one is principled."

The comment shouldn't have shocked him. And yet he was as guilty as the rest for presuming intelligence conveyed a person's worth.

"Creative frustration is a kind of mental torture," he said, drawing from experience. It sounded as if he were defending Thomas Becker without the merest notion of his crime. "But that is no excuse to behave badly."

There was a stiffness about her features when she said, "My godfather cared for us, of that there is no doubt. But work was his greatest passion. He worked best when indulging his cravings."

"His cravings?"

"Wine and women."

"I see."

"The house was his *pleasure dome*, Mr Ashwood. I lost count of the many lovers he entertained."

A mental picture formed. A young woman woken at night by the rampant activities of her guardian. Now he knew why her bedchamber was her sanctuary, why she had no desire to play the coquette in a room of men.

"So," she began in the confident tone she used as a crutch, "now we understand one another a little better, I shall explain the true depth of my brother's depravity."

"Let's start with the fact he's a delinquent. A debt-ridden scoundrel who's stolen from the one person who cares for him."

"Cared. I have cut all emotional ties."

"Cared," he corrected just as icily. "He's a liar and has chased away every friend you've had."

"Yes. Minds get muddled when a handsome gentleman pays a lady attention." She gave a derisive snort. "I have yet to meet an attractive man who isn't a scoundrel." She sucked in a breath upon noting her misstep. "Present company excepted, of course."

"Of course."

"My closest friend, Miss Swales, fell for my brother's charms and—" Miss Dunn stopped abruptly. She closed her eyes tight for a moment.

Noah feared she might cry. "I do not wish to cause you distress, Miss Dunn. But I must know of this terrible deed. It may prove important to the case." In a move that was wholly inappropriate for a gentleman of the Order, he reached across the carriage and gripped her gloved hand. "The shame is not yours to bear." They were familiar words, words spoken by his grandfather many times.

The lady's eyes shot open. She looked to her lap but did not pull her hand from his grasp. "Thank you, Mr Ashwood. Miss Swales was a dear, dear friend. A dear friend whose loss I have mourned deeply."

"I understand," he said, releasing her dainty fingers and relaxing back in the seat. "When you have blood ties with a scoundrel, people treat you like a leper."

Ladies did. Men often held a secret admiration for those able to shake themselves free from the shackles of responsibility.

Miss Dunn gathered herself. "You wish to know my shameful secret. I shall speak quickly and plainly. Telling a long, emotional tale is like rubbing salt into a weeping wound."

"You may speak freely to me, Miss Dunn."

She forced a smile before inhaling deeply. "Howard gave Miss Swales the impression he would offer for her. It was a ridiculous notion. Her brother, Lord Benham, sought a more lucrative match for his only sister. Clara's naivety was part of her charm. She foolishly believed Howard was her missing half. Foolishly believed in love."

Did Miss Dunn know that the way a person told a tale revealed much about the storyteller?

"You do not believe in love, Miss Dunn?"

The question took her by surprise. "Me?" She shrugged but pursed her pretty lips as she considered her response. "I'm afraid I am rather cynical when it comes to affairs of the heart."

"And why is that?" He knew the answer but wanted to hear her explanation. Besides, it served as a distraction from the pain of her brother's antics.

The lady arched a brow. "You know very well. I have seen how Howard, my father and Mr Becker treat women. They all have one thing in common when it comes to romantic relationships."

"They're disloyal?"

"Despicably so. Perhaps I am the naive one. Perhaps I might easily fall under the wrong man's spell."

"Then, you must strive to fall in love with the right man." He should have been questioning her about Miss Swales yet couldn't help but say, "May I give you some advice?"

Miss Dunn blinked rapidly. It was evident she didn't welcome a man's opinion, yet she said, "You may speak freely to me, Mr Ashwood."

He inclined his head respectfully while wondering how this woman managed to be so readable and so mysteriously seductive at the same time.

"If you can trust a man with your life. If he puts your needs before his own." Noah cleared his throat, determined to continue. "If his eyes make love to you with a passion that transcends the physical realm, then he is worthy of your esteem."

She remained silent, yet her penetrating gaze never left him.

Noah took the opportunity to rap on the roof and alert McGuffey of their wish to proceed to Mr Hemming's establishment on Tavistock Street.

Miss Dunn clutched the seat as the carriage lurched forward. "Your last comment brings to mind your poem, *The Journey*. The parched nomad drops to his knees before a glistening oasis. He describes the coolness of the water as he imagines it slipping down his throat, the moistness on his lips, yet he is reluctant to thrust his dirty hands into the pool and so doesn't drink."

Good God!

Every muscle in his abdomen tightened. Never had anyone spoken intimately about his work. "You mean, why would a man make love to you with his eyes and not his body? Assuming both parties were willing, of course."

"Of course."

"Like the nomad, perhaps he fears the reality will fall short of the dream. Ruin the illusion."

"Yes," she mused. "The nomad draws on past disappointment. It's the reason he would rather die in blissful ignorance." It was evident she wished to delve into the depths of his soul. "You've been hurt. Not just by the selfish actions of your father and uncle, but by a woman."

Hellfire! How had the conversation turned from him offering advice to tearing open his chest and baring his bruised heart?

"It was a long time ago. A young man's disappointment."

It was not the bitter pain of a lover's rejection, as she might suppose. But a woman had hurt him, had cut deep with her sharp blade, left him to live like a nomad, forever wandering, scared to settle, scared to take the plunge. Perhaps it was another reason he strived to help the weak, fought against injustice.

"It's not something I wish to discuss," he continued. "Yet the pain served as inspiration for my creative efforts."

Not all desires were sexual.

Not all desires were obtainable.

Her blue eyes softened. "Again, we both have reasons to

distrust people's motives," she said as if hearing his thoughts. "We will be at my publisher's office soon, and so I should finish telling you what happened to Miss Swales."

Noah welcomed the change of topic as a miner welcomed fresh air. "I presume Miss Swales succumbed to your brother's desire to express their love in the physical act."

"Unfortunately, yes. The lady is with child and has removed to Northumberland to continue her confinement. Though you must not breathe a word of this to anyone outside the Order."

"You can trust me." His tone echoed his assurance. "Are you certain your brother hasn't ventured to Northumberland?"

"Most certain." She bit down on her bottom lip to stop the sudden tremble. "Howard cares for no one but himself."

Noah removed his handkerchief from his pocket and handed it to Miss Dunn just as the silent tears trickled down her cheek.

"I do not weep for myself, you understand, but for the infant." She took the silk square and dabbed her cheeks. "My brother added to our family's humiliation by refusing to marry Clara. I can assure you, there is not a respectable bone in Howard's body."

Silence ensued while the lady dried her tears. She offered to return Noah's handkerchief, but he insisted she keep it.

"If I had a sister and a rogue abused her in such a cruel fashion, I would kill him with my bare hands." He paused. "Are you certain you want me to find your brother?"

Was Howard Dunn not best left to conduct his nefarious business elsewhere? Assuming he was still alive. A fact that was becoming increasingly doubtful.

"I am not certain of anything, sir, not anymore."

Noah glanced out of the window. It was a mere five-minute journey to Tavistock Street, and so he would have to return to the subject of Lord Benham being a suspect once he'd dealt with Hemming.

He pulled his gold watch from his pocket and checked the time. "We can continue this conversation later. Unless there is another secret you wish to divulge."

"No, no more secrets." She hesitated. "There is something you should know about Lord Benham, but we can discuss it after the appointment. I hope you understand why I was reluctant to speak of this matter. I hope you understand why this was a hard tale to tell."

"Indeed."

Noah wondered how she fared living across the road from the hospital. Did witnessing the women's struggles firsthand remind her of Miss Swales' ruination? Did seeing proud mothers cradling their babes rouse painful regrets?

He cleared his throat. "As we're fast approaching our meeting with your publisher, I must ask a few personal questions, if I may."

Miss Dunn nodded confidently, though he sensed an underlying tension at the mere mention of Mr Hemming.

"What do you want to know?" She gripped the seat.

"Have you given Mr Hemming any indication you would be open to his romantic overtures?"

She straightened abruptly. "Certainly not."

"And have you ever embraced, ever kissed?"

"No!"

"Has he mentioned marriage?"

"On occasion."

"And has he touched you intimately without your permission?"

Miss Dunn's cheeks flamed. She closed her eyes briefly and nodded. "He said he misread the signs. That I gave the impression I was open to his advances, particularly after accepting his gift."

"Gift?" Noah muttered a curse. It was a common ploy used by a seducer to shift blame.

"A pretty silver bookmark in a velvet case. I returned it the moment I realised it gave him an excuse to manhandle me in a rakish fashion."

Noah's hands throbbed to manhandle the blackguard, too.

"Are you loyal to Mr Hemming? What if I found you another publisher?"

Hope sprang to life in Miss Dunn's eyes. Indeed, her whole countenance brightened. "You know a publisher who is willing to consider a woman's work?"

"I do," he said, his heart feeling suddenly full at the prospect of helping her. "Mr Lydford is a forward-thinking man, and a friend. He published my poetry when most thought it unsuitable reading material."

She smiled. "And yet I'm told every man in London owns a copy."

"Mr Lydford did not regret his decision."

"I would be eternally grateful if you could arrange a meeting with the gentleman. The sooner I untangle myself from Mr Hemming's web, the better."

"Excellent."

Miss Dunn's contented sigh became a groan when the carriage rattled to a halt outside the goldsmith shop in Tavistock Street.

"How will this work?" she said, the sudden onset of nerves evident. "I do not want Mr Hemming to know I sought the help of a professional investigator."

Noah had no intention of revealing the real reason they were meeting with the publisher. "How are your acting skills?"

She blinked in surprise. "Poor at best. Why, what would you have me do?"

"All I ask is that you agree to everything I say. That you support whatever claims I make regardless how ludicrous. You must be convincing if we're to establish if Mr Hemming is guilty of a crime against you."

"A crime?" She fell silent, though he could almost hear the cogs turning in her mind. "You think he might have sent the blackmail note?"

"He is one of the few people who know you write as Cain Dunnavan. When frightened, women tend to seek help from men they know."

"You think he wrote the note to lure me to his office?"

"I think it's worth testing the theory, worth laying a trap. Don't you?"

CHAPTER 6

TELLING Mr Ashwood of her family's shame brought a surprising sense of relief. For the last month, ever since Clara had been spirited away to Northumberland in the dead of night, Eva had lived with the guilt. She should have done something to protect her friend. She should have spoken to Lord Benham the moment Howard's behaviour roused her suspicions.

It was too much to hope her brother had fled the country never to be seen again. The coward had created a scandal and left Eva to suffer the shame.

How could one's sibling be so callous, so cruel?

"Remember, we must dangle the bait if we're to lure vermin into our trap," Mr Ashwood said as he opened the wrought-iron gate leading to the alley between the goldsmith shop and the apothecary.

Eva nodded, a sudden rush of confidence filling her chest.

Mr Ashwood was the most capable, most sincere man she had ever met. She had been waiting for the moment he proved a disappointment, and yet the more time she spent in his company, the more she admired him. Every kind and competent action restored her faith. And despite being a sensible woman, she struggled to fight her growing attraction.

Foolish gal!

"And if Mr Hemming is not the rodent we seek?" she asked.

Her publisher had wandering hands but lacked the backbone necessary to commit a crime.

"We dangle our bait elsewhere. Namely, Lord Benham's door."

Lord Benham!

Heavens above. Now she knew why Mr Ashwood's colleagues called him Dauntless. Lord Benham had money, connections, rights that came with his position. The viscount could afford to prosecute her for defamation. Could ruin her for good. Had she not suffered enough in her brother's name?

"I doubt a gentleman of Lord Benham's standing would hire someone to steal my boots." And what would he have to gain from the murder of her cobbler?

"It's highly likely he's responsible for your brother's disappearance," Mr Ashwood countered.

She could not argue. It was only a matter of time before the lord sought vengeance. "Still, you cannot pry into a peer's affairs."

Mr Ashwood came to an abrupt halt beside the shiny brass plate bearing Mr Hemming's name. He faced her and arched a reprimanding brow.

"Miss Dunn, I will give you another piece of advice. Learn to use your weaknesses to your advantage. As I have done."

Eva snorted. "If you have weaknesses, sir, I've yet to see them."

"When your father is a shameless devil, you have two choices. You can hide in the corner, afraid to meet anyone's gaze, or you can let people believe you possess the same dangerous streak."

She considered this tall, broad-shouldered man, with his determined eyes and firm jaw. Beneath his devastatingly handsome face lingered a deadly force. Yes, she could imagine people fearing what he might do.

"No one respects a coward," he added.

"What should I do, sir? March into Lord Benham's house and demand to see his sister?"

She knew the answer before he spoke.

"If Miss Swales is important to you, then yes. Climb onto

your plinth of shame, shout and scream and incite the crowd to riot. Do what you must until you have Lord Benham's attention. Be clever about it. Use your brother's recklessness to your advantage."

Eva stared at him, a little in awe of his strength and resolve. He proved a conundrum. Never had she met anyone so fascinating.

"You're right," she said, aware she was gaping like a besotted fool. She could not recall ever wanting to kiss a man. But she had an urge to kiss Mr Ashwood. "I should not have given up so easily."

"No."

Their gazes remained locked.

The nervous tension in the air grew palpable.

"Well, Mr Hemming will be waiting," she eventually said before she took his advice and did something unbelievably reck-less. "And how will we bait my publisher?"

"We will improvise." He opened the door leading to the tiled hall and narrow flight of stairs. "I prefer to let the suspect's actions determine how I proceed."

Mr Ashwood sneered at the brass plate on the wall before gesturing for her to enter the premises. As she mounted the stairs, it took every effort not to trip for she could feel the heat of his gaze scorching her back. A glance behind confirmed Mr Ashwood was watching the sway of her hips, not minding his step.

Mr Hemming's clerk sat at a cluttered desk in the room opposite the stairs. He pushed to his feet, straightened his spec-tacles and wiped his hands on his trousers before hurrying forward to greet them.

"Good m-morning, Miss Dunn." The young clerk bowed and then fussed with his mop of blonde locks to hide his receding hairline.

"Good morning, Mr Smith." Eva motioned to the commanding gentleman beside her. "This is Mr Ashwood. He will join me when I meet with Mr Hemming today."

The clerk's eyes widened as he scanned the breadth of Mr Ashwood's chest. His nervous tic made him wink incessantly. "Is

Mr Hemming aware you've b-brought company?" Mr Smith's voice trembled the way it always did when speaking of his employer.

"Not to my knowledge." Eva offered a reassuring smile.

Mr Smith glanced at the door at the end of the hall as if it were the entrance to Hades. "Then I had best inform him of—"

"There's no need," Mr Ashwood interjected. "Miss Dunn has an appointment, and I am here at her behest."

"Yes, sir, but—"

"Rams butt, Smith. We haven't time to waste lingering in the corridor."

"N-no, sir," the clerk stuttered.

Mr Ashwood placed his hand at the small of Eva's back. "Lead the way, my love."

The clerk frowned with confusion upon hearing the endearment, while Eva shivered with delight. Oh, her reaction bordered on ridiculous. Clearly, Mr Ashwood wished to make it known he had a vested interest in her welfare.

It was a warning.

A claim of ownership.

Bait.

"Follow my lead," Mr Ashwood whispered in her ear as they neared Mr Hemming's office, though it must have looked highly inappropriate to the poor clerk watching while shuffling his papers. "Play the role."

Eva swallowed deeply before knocking on the publisher's door.

"Enter," came the usual lofty reply.

"You enter," Mr Ashwood muttered. "I'll wait in the shadows."

Eva pasted a smile and burst into the room. She looked to the desk only to find the wingback chair empty. Then she spotted the devil, who thought his handsome countenance gave him a right of entitlement, relaxing on the sofa near the hearth.

"Good morning, Mr Hemming," she said, succeeding in banishing her nerves. "Thank you for seeing me."

Mr Ashwood did not follow her into the room.

"Everett. Call me Everett. How many times must I tell you,

Evangeline?" Mr Hemming stood. His wicked grin matched the suggestive look in his eyes as his gaze caressed her body. "After our last little interlude, I think we've moved beyond the use of formalities. Obviously, you're just as keen to continue our stimulating conversation."

The man made her skin crawl.

"You speak of our misunderstanding."

"Was it a misunderstanding, my dear? I think not."

The lying toad. "You cannot think I welcomed your advances."

Mr Hemming moistened his lips. "You came here alone at night. Invented a tale of blackmail to gain my attention. What else is a man supposed to think?"

"It wasn't a tale."

"Well, let's continue our discussion away from Smith's pricked ears." Mr Hemming moved to close the door, but Mr Ashwood blocked it with his booted foot.

"Miss Dunn is here in a professional capacity." Mr Ashwood's stern voice echoed through the musty space as he pushed open the door and strode into the room. "She has no desire to hear more of your pretentious claptrap."

Mr Hemming reeled from the insult and shuffled back. "Who the devil are you?"

"Someone keen to protect Miss Dunn from lecherous leeches."

Mr Hemming stared. Open-mouthed shock turned to seething arrogance. "Miss Dunn and I have been friends for three years. If the lady needs protection, the responsibility falls to me."

"You're only her publisher."

Bristling, Mr Hemming puffed out his chest. "I'm a damn sight more than that. What gives you the right—"

"The lady has agreed to be my wife. I believe that gives me a greater claim."

His wife!

Mother of all saints!

This wasn't dangling bait in the hope of trapping vermin. This was a pistol shot between the eyes.

Shock didn't even begin to define the look on Mr Hemming's face. His cheeks turned deathly pale. He shook his head repeatedly as if attempting to dismiss the last words spoken from Mr Ashwood's lips.

Guilt and pity fought to conquer Eva's resolve. But that was her problem. Mr Hemming had a way of making her feel responsible for their frequent misunderstandings. He often accused her of being too familiar—reminded her of promises never made.

No one spoke.

The heavy sound of Mr Hemming's ragged breathing disturbed the deafening silence. His gruff gasps became snorts and then loud, hearty laughter.

Eva glanced sideways and met Mr Ashwood's calm, reassuring gaze.

Play the role, came his silent plea.

Indeed, she could not let her soft heart rule her head. She had given Mr Hemming too many chances, and the devil knew how to play to her weaknesses.

Mr Hemming clutched his abdomen as he continued to find Mr Ashwood's declaration amusing.

"Oh, I have to admit you had me fooled for a moment," the publisher said before letting out another loud guffaw. "My dear, if this is a ploy to make me jealous, I must say you succeeded." He exhaled to gather his composure. Then, mimicking Mr Ashwood's deep voice, he said, "The lady has agreed to be my wife." He laughed again. "Oh, for a second, I was floundering."

"What is it about our betrothal you find hard to believe?" Mr Ashwood said in a manner so cool, so composed.

"Anyone who knows Evangeline would find the suggestion of marriage highly improbable." Mr Hemming dabbed the corners of his eyes. "Marriage! Ha!"

Mr Ashwood cleared his throat. "Why is that? And before you answer, I must warn you that I will not tolerate your blatant use of her given name."

Mr Hemming's smile fell, but then he laughed again. "Very well," he said, taking time to get his emotions under control. "No doubt Evangeline wishes to bring me up to the mark, so I'll play this game."

"Trust me. This is by no means a game." Mr Ashwood's voice held a sinister edge, though her publisher was too full of mirth to notice.

"Then tell me how and where you met. Evangeline rarely leaves the house these days and has made no mention of you before."

"I shall let Miss Dunn explain." Mr Ashwood gestured to her, and with remarkable poise added, "The next time you use her given name, I shall grab you by the throat and knock that arrogant smirk off your face."

Mr Hemming's eyes narrowed as he struggled to know whether to take the threat seriously.

"I met Mr Ashwood three months ago," Eva lied. Still, it felt like she had known him a lifetime. "In Vincent and Teale's book shop in Bedford Street."

"We share a love of poetry," Mr Ashwood said, his tone soft and warm as if recalling a treasured memory. "She is, without doubt, the only woman ever to hold my interest. I found myself desperate to deepen our acquaintance."

Oh, he was so convincing.

So good at this.

"We meet in the park every Wednesday, take a picnic and discuss a particular poem." Creating a romantic fantasy proved easy when Mr Ashwood was the object of one's desire. It occurred to her that she would like to stretch out on a blanket in the sunshine and have him read poetry.

Mr Hemming seemed unconvinced. "What was the last poem you discussed?"

Eva smiled, grateful for the recent conversation in the carriage as it would add authenticity to their tale. "We spoke about how the metaphor of a nomad failing to drink from an oasis relates to a man's fear of commitment."

Mr Hemming focused his attention on Mr Ashwood. "What's the poem called?"

"*The Journey*. Last week we discussed her godfather's poem, *The Wanderer*. We share an interest in Norse mythology, too."

Mr Hemming's gaze hardened. "And what if I told you Miss

Dunn promised to marry me? That we agreed to announce our betrothal."

"Then I would call you a liar. You're her publisher, nothing more. She has no interest in pursuing a relationship with you when she is in love with me. Indeed, I have come today to return your advance and to inform you that she has found another publisher."

Mr Ashwood reached into his pocket and removed a folded note. With a contemptuous glare, he threw it onto Mr Hemming's disorderly desk.

A muscle in Mr Hemming's cheek twitched. "You think ten pounds will free Miss Dunn from her contract? She owes me a damn sight more than that."

"The note is for a hundred pounds. I'm certain that should suffice. I expect your clerk to issue a receipt."

"A hundred pounds!" Eva gasped. She turned to Mr Ashwood in a state of blind panic. Matters were spiralling out of control. Lord, she could not repay such a huge debt. "I cannot let you part with such an extortionate sum."

In a move that rocked her to her core—and one she suspected was done to rouse the publisher's ire—Mr Ashwood cupped her cheek gently and said in his velvet voice, "I would pay a king's ransom in the hope of making you happy."

Eva swallowed past the lump in her throat as she gazed into his eyes. He sounded so sincere she struggled to distinguish between fantasy and reality. Heat flooded her body. Three times her stomach flipped as a nervous excitement raced through her veins.

"I cannot accept your charity," she whispered. "It's too much."

It was all too much.

"Nothing is too much where you're concerned." He stared at her mouth. "Your publisher needs proof of our commitment. Let us show him the depth of our affection."

Eva's heart raced so fast she could barely breathe. Heaven help her. Did Mr Ashwood mean to kiss her? In the office? With her publisher as a witness?

"Give your permission, Eva," he said, clearly serious in his intention, "for I am not a man who takes liberties at a lady's expense."

Eva's mind whirled. Somehow she managed a weak nod while scrambling to know how to make the kiss look convincing when she lacked experience in that department. But she liked Mr Ashwood, found him appealing on every level. Indeed, she was rather desperate to feel those muscular arms holding her in a warm embrace.

Mr Ashwood took hold of her face between his hot hands. He ran the pad of his thumb over her quivering bottom lip. It wasn't raging lust she saw in his eyes as he bent his head, it was a tender look that spoke of genuine affection.

Despite fearing she would not appear credible, Eva came up on trembling toes, and their mouths met.

Oh, Lord!

Mr Ashwood kissed her in a slow, sensual way, melding himself to her as if he wished to savour every second. She could taste nothing definable, nothing but a potent masculine essence that swirled through her body to tease her sex. With every skilled caress, the ache intensified. And the heat, oh, the heat from his lips journeyed southwards to warm her lonely soul.

Using nothing more than the satisfying movements of his mouth, he drew her closer. The space between them evaporated. She seemed to melt into him, into the powerful aura that made her feel so safe, so secure. Men had shown an interest in her before, but not like this. Never with such depth of feeling. Never with the promise of unbridled passion.

The highly pleasurable moment was brought to an abrupt end by a loud thud and Mr Hemming's vile curse.

"You bloody bastard."

Mr Ashwood dragged his mouth from hers, yet the desperate ache remained. They were both a bit breathless, both a little dazed by the arousing experience. It took a few seconds to break the spell that held them only a few inches apart.

But this was acting, she reminded herself.

This was playing a role.

Eventually, Mr Ashwood cleared his throat and straightened.

He turned to face Mr Hemming, who in a wild fit of temper had swiped the pile of books off his desk onto the floor.

"I think it's obvious to anyone watching, we are desperate to wed," Mr Ashwood said, his voice echoing the intense longing still thrumming through her veins.

Mr Hemming stood rigid, his fists balled at his sides. His face was so red with rage he looked ready to explode. A feral growl rumbled in the back of his throat.

"Are you saying our little interludes meant nothing to you?" Mr Hemming snarled.

How could a man be so misguided?

"Sir, ours was—and always has been—a business arrangement. Any breach of propriety stemmed from false belief." It was the first time she had spoken so openly. Having Mr Ashwood at her side gave her the confidence to speak her mind. "I am in love with Mr Ashwood and plan to marry him."

Mr Ashwood captured her hand and brought it to his lips.

Oh, the sooner this meeting was over, the better. Whenever he touched her intimately, her knees practically buckled.

Mr Hemming's face contorted into an ugly grimace. "It will be nigh on impossible to find someone willing to publish your work. And certainly not for the generous sum we agreed."

It was Mr Ashwood's turn to laugh. "*The Blood Pendant* outsold all other works of fiction published last year. Besides, Miss Dunn has secured another publisher, though she certainly won't need the money when she marries me."

"Ah! So that's it!" The publisher wagged his finger. "Don't you see? He will want to control you once you're wed. This gentleman is only pretending to show an interest in your work, whereas I have the utmost respect for your creative talents."

Eva had feared Mr Hemming's manner bordered on obsessive.

Now she knew it was true.

"Mr Ashwood has nothing but my best interests at heart," Eva replied. "And our last *misunderstanding* was a step too far."

In a fit of frustration, Mr Hemming thrust his hands through his generous mop of brown hair. "Madam, a man cannot help but follow the signs. Do you not admit to being too free with your compliments?"

Anger surfaced. She was about to fire a retort, but Mr Ashwood dropped her hand and stepped forward.

With wide, uncertain eyes, Mr Hemming shuffled back until his legs hit the sofa. "Stay back, sir, else I shall call my clerk." He lost his footing and collapsed onto the padded seat.

Mr Ashwood towered over the quivering milksop. "If you don't like it, Hemming, if you feel you've suffered some slight, then call me out."

The coward's face turned ashen.

"No?" Mr Ashwood continued. "A wise decision because you would be dead before you pulled the trigger. Indeed, speak ill of Miss Dunn to anyone, harass her in the despicable manner you have of late, then honour be damned. I shall drag you from this office and force a pistol into your clammy hand."

Mr Ashwood straightened.

The urge to add a threat of her own bubbled in Eva's chest. She charged forward. "And if I discover you sent the blackmail note to intimidate me, I shall pass the evidence to the magistrate at Bow Street. Do you hear?"

Mr Ashwood slipped his arm around her waist and said, "Come, we have wasted enough time here. Let us away."

As always, Eva could not get out of the office quick enough.

They moved towards the door, but Mr Ashwood turned on his heel. "Perhaps you should have your clerk write your obituary, Hemming. I have a strange suspicion you're going to need it."

CHAPTER 7

WHAT THE DEVIL was wrong with him?

Noah was a logical man, a sensible man, not a boy with uncontrollable urges. A violent threat would have been enough to silence Hemming. And yet the need to taste Miss Dunn's lips, the need to stake his claim, had burned fiercely in his chest.

Damnation!

Even as they rattled along in the carriage—when he should have been planning which problem to tackle next—he thought about pulling her into his lap and ravaging her senseless.

And why in blazes had he spoken of marriage?

Dangle the bait, he'd said, not offer himself up as the sacrificial lamb.

Noah relaxed back in the seat and considered the lady sitting opposite. Her lips were pulled as tight as a miser's purse strings. She had barely spoken since leaving her publisher's office. Numerous times he had caught her studying him intently. Now, sitting with her hands clasped in her lap, she struggled to meet his gaze.

He should say something, something to banish the tension.

"You played the role well," he said, frustration giving way to a sinful smile. Indeed, she had played the role too damn well. Miss Dunn tasted divine. Sweet like nectar. "Forgive me for overstepping the bounds of propriety, but your publisher is a little more than misguided."

There. Did that not sound like a reasonable explanation?

Miss Dunn looked at him. "You might have warned me that acting amounted to more than telling a few lies."

He could not argue. He had taken a shocking liberty. Made it impossible for her to say no and still maintain their story. Did that not make him as wicked as Hemming?

"Please accept my sincere apology. I never meant to cause you distress. You have my word it won't happen again."

Disappointment sank like a brick to the pit of his stomach. Cole was right. Miss Dunn had worked her way under his skin. Putting distance between them was the only solution to this inexplicable attraction.

Her gaze softened. "Thank you, but I must apologise, too. I —I doubt you've had to kiss a woman so lacking in experience." Obvious embarrassment had her nibbling her lip. "Though I suppose Mr Hemming was convinced."

It was her lack of experience, her purity of mind and soul, that made it a kiss to remember. How could he explain that one small sip of her sweetness had fired a passion in him that had barely reached a simmer in recent years? Oh, he could have had her panting and writhing, had her stripping off his clothes in a mad frenzy. Had her begging for his touch.

"Freeing you from that pompous letch is all that matters. It took effort not to force my fist down his arrogant throat."

Miss Dunn smiled. "I would have offered no objection. Though I'd rather you didn't exert yourself on my account. Besides, your threats seemed to do the trick."

Had they? Time would tell.

A slight sense of trepidation surfaced. "Hemming thinks he's in love with you, but he's mistaken. If he truly loved you, he would not have abused you in such a cruel fashion."

Perhaps he should wait for the publisher to leave his office tonight and remind him how to treat a lady. All in the name of reform, of course.

"No," she mused. "I suspect love requires an element of sacrifice." Her expression changed abruptly from contentment to shock. "You don't think Mr Hemming will retaliate? Cause problems to prevent us from marrying?"

Marrying? She made the ruse sound plausible.

"It's a possibility." Noah could not lie, and she should be prepared for any eventuality. "If Hemming sent the blackmail note, he might seek to manipulate you. We've set the trap. Now we must wait and see if he nibbles the bait. I shall have a man keep track of his movements. Have another watch your house in case Hemming should call."

The flash of fear in her eyes made his heart lurch.

"I have no issue if he makes a house call," she said despite swallowing numerous times. "I just don't want to be alone with him in his office."

"I would avoid all contact for the foreseeable future."

The carriage rattled to a halt outside her home in Brownlow Street. Again, the comings and goings at the hospital drew his attention. A woman pushing a perambulator had stopped at the entrance while a matron cooed over the infant.

"Living across from the hospital must remind you of your poor friend's plight," he said. "It must take its toll."

Her strained smile and watery eyes revealed an inner torment.

"Perhaps your brother grew tired of the reminder and has sought refuge elsewhere for a time," Noah added. He didn't necessarily believe that. Indeed, he would visit the mortuary before returning to Hart Street and examine those bodies dragged from the river.

"Howard constantly complains about the noise from the hospital. But then he complains about everything, money mostly."

She was best rid of the rogue, in Noah's opinion.

The thought of Howard Dunn's demise prompted him to say, "On the subject of your brother's recklessness with money, I must convey the full extent of his debts." But how did he tell her about Manning without scaring her half to death? "He's in the mire. Deeper than you suspect."

"How deep?" Mild panic pervaded her tone.

"He owes twelve thousand pounds to various creditors."

"Twelve thousand?" Her mouth fell open. "The fool."

"He borrowed from a notorious moneylender." Noah paused, overcome with the sudden suspicion the cad was already buried in a shallow grave. "And from men who will most likely beat him to death if he fails to pay."

"He deserves nothing less," she said, though her face grew pale, and she covered her mouth with her hand.

"Know that I will ... that the Order will do everything in their power to see this matter right."

She nodded. "I have a lot to thank you for, Mr Ashwood. And while we're discussing money, I hope you understand why I must repay my debt in instalments."

"Your debt?"

Her shoulders sagged. "The hundred pounds you gave to Mr Hemming."

"It was not a loan, Miss Dunn. We are permitted to claim expenses when dealing with a case." Noah briefly explained Lucius Daventry's role as master of the Order. He could hardly say that he'd paid the publisher from his personal funds.

She seemed disappointed that he was not solely responsible for the generous gesture. Hell, Daventry would never have parted with such an extortionate sum. Not when Hemming was guilty of nothing but having wandering hands and amorous intentions.

"I cannot accept Mr Daventry's charity." She shook her head numerous times to make her point. "I assume some people who seek your help are penniless. My circumstances are far better than most. No. Please explain to Mr Daventry that I will repay the debt as soon as reasonably possible."

Noah nodded and smiled while fighting the urge to kiss the sadness from her downturned lips.

"My publisher is out of town for a few days though he has agreed to see you upon his return. Based on previous sales, I'm sure your current work in progress will be of interest to him."

Her pained smile said something was amiss. "Thank you, Mr Ashwood. You have been most helpful. Inspiration is a little slow at the moment, but I'm confident things will improve. And I can always take work at the hospital in the interim."

The structured speech hid a wealth of torment. He would lay odds she had not written a word since the shameful situation with Miss Swales. And yet to survive, she would place herself in a hospital full of tragic stories and crying infants—a constant reminder of her brother's failings.

Damn the devil.

Noah rubbed his jaw and unleashed another silent curse. He should be solving the mystery of her missing brother, not worrying about healing Miss Dunn's wounded heart.

"I wonder, might I have the blackmail note to examine?" he said, attempting to focus. "Do you have a sample of Mr Hemming's writing and that of your brother's?"

"Yes, I have both. But if you're trying to identify the sender, I have already concluded neither man wrote the note. Of course, that doesn't mean someone else didn't write it on their behalf."

Based on his last case, he believed the villain would rather work to disguise his penmanship than take a partner in crime. "Still, I would like to be sure before moving to other lines of enquiry."

"Then I shall find anything pertinent to the case and have my footman deliver it to you in Hart Street."

It occurred to him there was another suspect not yet named. "And who is the friend who knows you write under a pseudonym?"

A veil of sadness fell over her features, and he knew the person's identity before she said, "Clara Swales."

"Of course. Lord Benham's sister."

"Though Clara is not a suspect."

"No." Not unless she was looking for funds to escape her Northumberland prison. Not unless Howard Dunn had put her up to the task.

"Either way, we should add another name to the list—Lord Benham's. He may have inadvertently stumbled upon your secret." Perhaps the viscount sent the note to prevent Miss Dunn from visiting Northumberland. Perhaps he sent it to frighten her as a means of revenge.

A heavy silence descended.

It was time to depart, though he found it impossible to leave.

He recalled the fantasy she had created to appease the publisher. An afternoon spent stretched on a blanket in the park while he read poems. An afternoon relaxing in the sunshine, picnicking, drinking wine, more passionate kissing.

The image spoke to him deeply.

So deeply, he feared he was losing his grasp on reality.

"Now you have dealt with the matter of my stolen undergarments and released me from Mr Hemming's clutches," Miss Dunn said, her sweet voice drawing him from his reverie, "what do you propose we do now?"

Oh, he had plenty of ideas as to how they might fill their time.

"I suggest you think carefully about the night of the attack. Did the thug say anything? Is there a reason your boots might hold some particular value to him?"

One reason sprang to mind, and he would give the matter his consideration upon his return to Hart Street.

Miss Dunn swallowed deeply. "So, you don't need me to accompany you on another outing?"

"Not at present." Though he wished he could invent another appointment, wished to banish the loneliness from her voice. "But while I wait for your publisher to pounce, I intend to question Lord Benham. After all, the man has a motive for murder."

She clutched her throat as if she were Benham's next target. "Howard deserves to pay for his crimes, but I pray Lord Benham has not gone too far. Vengeance will not heal the heartache. And how can a man reform if he's dead?"

Reform?

"Men like your brother are beyond redemption," he said, attempting to keep his contempt for Howard Dunn from his voice.

"Of course they are, but one must not give up hope."

"No. Hope is all we have."

After another brief silence, Miss Dunn straightened her bonnet. "Well, I am sure you will keep me informed of your progress, and I shall arrange to have the information you require sent to Hart Street."

"Excellent."

They sat there ... waiting ... stalling. Noah reached for the door handle a second after Miss Dunn leant forward and wrapped her fingers around the metal.

Damnation! It looked like he was trying to prevent her from leaving, as if he had something important to say.

The lady gave a light laugh. "Good day, Mr Ashwood. And thank you for your help. I'm rather ashamed I lacked the strength to deal with Mr Hemming."

"Don't be." Noah squeezed her hand in a gesture of reassurance. "Like a true predator, Hemming knew to play to your weaknesses. As soon as Mr Lydford returns, I shall arrange a meeting."

Her blue eyes brightened. "That would be wonderful." She glanced at the ungloved hand clasped around hers. "Good day, sir."

Noah released his grip.

She opened the carriage door, and her footman hurried out of the house. The young, golden-haired servant offered his hand. A lonely woman might take advantage, suggest a way the servant might supplement his income. And yet he knew Miss Dunn would never abuse her position.

"Miss Dunn!" he called, leaning forward in his seat.

"Yes." She swung around, excitement flashing in her eyes.

"Please inform me when you receive the next blackmail note. Equally, send word to Hart Street should your brother return."

She nodded. "I will."

"And it would be wise to err on the side of caution when venturing about town."

"You mean don't walk the streets alone at night." Her amused smile tugged at his insides.

"Exactly." Hell, why couldn't he simply say goodbye and shut the damn door? "If you must go out, take your maid and hire a hackney."

"Have no fear, sir. I rarely attend functions and have no need to revisit Mr Hemming. Goodbye, Mr Ashwood."

"Goodbye, Miss Dunn."

Noah slammed the door and rapped on the roof. He fell back into the seat as the carriage lurched forward and rattled along the cobbled street. Later this afternoon he would meet Lucius Daventry. It would afford an opportunity to address his priorities. To forget about this little infatuation and focus on what mattered—working to right a catalogue of injustices.

"Cole tells me you have a new client, a new case." Lucius Daventry splashed brandy into a glass and swallowed the contents. Despite his tall, athletic frame he looked tired, a little weary. "When I asked him about it, he told but half a tale. You know it's important to keep the men informed of your whereabouts."

Noah sat behind the desk in the study, elbows resting on the polished surface, his hands clasped. "It's a complicated case." Made more complicated by the fact the client was an original with a mouth as sweet as honey.

Daventry left the glass on the side table and came to sit in the chair once occupied by Miss Dunn. "I'm all ears."

"Are you certain you wish to hear about it now? You look as exhausted as Sloane when he carried the boy from the slums. And he'd not slept for three days."

Daventry rubbed his eyes. "It's what comes from having two infants cutting teeth at the same time. Perhaps I should have listened to my bull terrier of a nursemaid and set up the nursery in the east wing."

"You could sleep in the east wing. Though I imagine you let Sybil get a good night's rest."

While Lucius Daventry was as determined and as dangerous as all the members of the Order, he did not hide the fact he was deeply in love with his wife. Noah couldn't help but be slightly envious of his situation.

Daventry grinned. "She's extremely grateful, and that's all I wish to say on the matter. Now, for some reason, you're reluctant to reveal certain aspects of the case."

"Not at all," he lied.

Daventry would see through his facade. He would remove Noah from the case and have Cole assist Miss Dunn. Perhaps it was for the best. But what if Hemming refused to accept he had lost his lady love? What if they had to play the betrothed couple a while longer?

"Miss Dunn, isn't it?" Daventry replied. "Cole said that before giving her name, the lady was preoccupied with remembering an acid that can kill a man in seconds. What a novel introduction."

"The lady is unique."

"Annoyingly unique, or temptingly unique?"

There was little point postponing the inevitable. It was better to use reason with Lucius Daventry than to get caught in a web of lies.

"A man who admires courage and intelligence might lose his head."

"I see." Daventry studied Noah through narrow eyes, or maybe he was so tired his lids were too heavy. "Perhaps you should tell me her story."

Noah wasted no time. "Her reprobate brother has been missing for a week. He is in debt to Flannery, the Turners and Mortuary Manning for a total of twelve thousand pounds."

"Hell!" Daventry cursed. "Then the man is as good as dead unless he can find the funds." He paused. "Still, we're not in the game of helping—"

"Her cobbler was bludgeoned to death over a week ago. She received a blackmail note threatening to reveal a secret identity, forcing her to visit her publisher at night. While warding off the publisher's amorous advances, someone broke into her house and stole every pair of shoes she owns. A thief attacked her and stole her boots as she walked home. Oh, and someone stole her undergarments from the washing line."

Daventry relaxed back in the chair while absorbing the catalogue of information. "Publisher, you say? The lady writes?"

"Novels."

"No wonder she captured your interest."

"You know I hate to see a woman without family or means struggling to defend herself against threats from all quarters."

Daventry's penetrating stare softened. "Indeed."

ADELE CLEE

The man had once found himself in similar circumstances and was now married to the woman he had saved.

"We help those without funds, without connections," Daventry continued.

"Miss Dunn has no friends and rarely ventures into society."

Noah explained about her brother's dastardly deeds. How he ruined his sister's closest friend and stole his mother's jewels.

"He ruined Benham's sister?" Daventry's features twisted in disdain. "And you agreed to find this devil? Is he not best left to rot in whatever sewer he's crawled into?"

"I don't care if the fool is a bloated corpse bobbing about the Thames. Manning will want his money and will go to any lengths to get it. The lady needs our protection. Manning is not averse to kidnapping."

It wouldn't come to that, but Noah's current task was to get Daventry onside. Sir Malcolm Langley, a magistrate at Bow Street, had made it his mission to see Manning hang. He was busy gathering evidence and witnesses to crimes. Hopefully, Manning was too occupied to worry about punishing Miss Dunn.

"No." Daventry sighed. "Manning is not averse to anything."

"And you know what will happen to Miss Dunn should Manning take her in payment for the debt."

"She'll be sold to an evil bastard abroad who enjoys beating women." Daventry rubbed his jaw as he considered the dilemma. "If the brother is dead and Miss Dunn is short of funds, we will pay the debt to Manning."

If only that were possible.

"We cannot intervene. Sir Malcolm is getting closer to securing evidence to arrest Manning. There'll be a trial. The Order must be seen to follow the law. If we're to continue to offer support to the needy, we cannot be held to ransom by murdering scoundrels."

That didn't mean Noah couldn't personally assist Miss Dunn.

"Agreed." Daventry pursed his lips. "What about the Turners?"

"They'll kill Howard Dunn if he fails to pay. But I've never known them take revenge on an innocent woman."

Silence ensued.

80

"One thing is clear," Daventry said. "You cannot work this case alone. There are too many loose ends. Good God, you have the mystery surrounding the blackmail note, the stolen boots and the murder of her cobbler to solve."

Noah explained all that had occurred so far, omitting to mention he had kissed Miss Dunn for the hell of it—because he couldn't resist. He made no mention of their fake betrothal, either. Daventry would be sure to warn him over his foolish lapse in judgement.

"I've arranged for someone to guard her door and another to keep watch on Mr Hemming." They had a group of capable men to call upon, ex-sailors and soldiers, good men who had fallen on hard times but who sought to make an honest living.

"That's fine for the publisher. But if Manning is involved, I'll send Bower to guard the lady's house."

Despite his military background, Bower worked as Lucius Daventry's butler and played coachman on occasion. He had assisted his master during many late-night skirmishes at the docks and in the rookeries. He was loyal to a fault and would report directly to Daventry.

"Sloane and D'Angelo will work with Sir Malcolm to secure Manning's arrest," Daventry added. "Cole will assist you until the brother is found, and the debts satisfied. Perhaps let him deal directly with Miss Dunn. There's not a woman alive who can rouse affection in his chest."

Noah fought the urge to jump to his feet and protest. But the master of the Order cared about his members. Daventry had seen men die while working to save innocent victims. He was on a mission to ensure no one else died while in pursuit of the truth.

"What of Lord Benham?" Noah said. "He has a motive for murder."

Daventry despised men who used their positions in society to escape their crimes. Not that Howard Dunn didn't deserve punishment.

"It's not as though I can call at his residence and question him about the disappearance of Howard Dunn," Noah added. "I imagine the peer will go to great lengths to protect his sister."

"And we would do the same in his position. Finding the

brother is paramount." Daventry spent a moment in quiet contemplation. "Lord Newberry is having a ball at his home in Cavendish Square. Benham will surely be there. I shall arrange for invitations. A few questions exchanged while sipping champagne will allow an opportunity to gauge Benham's reaction."

Noah inwardly groaned.

No doubt his uncle would be in attendance.

"It will take more than a glass of champagne to loosen Benham's tongue."

Lucius Daventry cast a wry smile. "Then use Miss Dunn as bait."

CHAPTER 8

"MA'AM, YOU MUST MAKE A CHOICE SOON." Kathleen held up the bright blue gown Eva had worn the last time someone forced her to parade amongst quality. "You're to leave for the ball in two hours, and I might need to make alterations."

Eva didn't want to make a choice. She wanted to slip beneath the coverlet and hide until dawn. While logic said Lord Benham was a prime suspect in her brother's disappearance, the thought of being within a few feet of the viscount filled her with dismay.

"Ma'am?"

Eva's gaze drifted to the exquisite red gown draped over the chair. She had purchased the material on a whim. Had taken it to a seamstress in Spitalfields who made the most remarkable creations for a reasonable price. The fantasy of being the most confident woman in the room—not the need to attract a gentleman's eye—had been her motivation.

And yet all thoughts turned to Mr Ashwood.

One kiss—one pleasurable kiss—one kiss that had curled her toes and roasted her insides, had turned her mind to mush.

"The blue reflects the colour of your eyes, ma'am," Kathleen continued, dragging Eva from her reverie.

"The blue is best worn with jewels. And the only slippers I possess have red bows." She was making excuses. Trying to delay the inevitable. The only saving grace was that she didn't have to face Lord Benham alone.

Kathleen winced before daring to say, "Ma'am, I can change the bows."

The suggestion brought a lump to Eva's throat. "They were my mother's favourite slippers. I haven't the heart to change a thing."

Thoughts turned to the diamond earrings, the ruby brooch and the pretty topaz and cannetille necklace, stolen by the rogue whose desire to cherish the jewels should have taken precedence over saving his own scrawny neck.

"No, I shall wear red," Eva said with renewed determination.

But how would she maintain an air of confidence with Mr Ashwood at her side? A mere glance from the man turned her into a quivering wreck.

And how was she to hold her head high knowing of the dreadful things her brother had done? Equally, her father was famous for being one of the greatest profligates of his time. And she still hadn't explained to Mr Ashwood how she knew Clara Swales, let alone inform him of Lord Benham's role in this dreadful business.

"The red is so daring I won't need jewels."

"You'll need rouge, ma'am," Kathleen said, returning the blue dress to the armoire. "Just a touch on your cheeks. A light pass of carmine blush will do the trick."

Eva groaned as an internal war raged.

The thought of a night spent mingling in society brought on a bout of nausea. The thought of a night spent laughing and dancing with Mr Ashwood filled her with a different feeling entirely.

Disappointment hit like a savage blow to the stomach. A hard wallop to wake her from her pathetic fantasy.

It was Mr Cole, not Mr Ashwood, who stood in the hall, dressed in black. While he looked the epitome of elegance and sophistication, there was no mistaking the dangerous undertone hidden beneath.

"Good evening, Miss Dunn," came Mr Cole's gruff greeting. He scanned the red gown but appeared totally indifferent.

The gentleman lacked Mr Ashwood's charm, lacked the teasing gleam in his eyes that made a lady's heart flutter. He seemed so cold, so detached from all personal thoughts and feelings. Oh, this would be a long, insufferable night.

"Good evening, Mr Cole." If she could rouse a glimmer of a smile on his solemn face, it would be an achievement.

"No doubt you were expecting my colleague," he said dryly.

"I presumed Mr Ashwood was dealing with my case, yes."

It was Mr Ashwood who sent the note sealed with his monogram. The note—informing her of the need to attend Lord Newberry's ball—carried the gentleman's teasing tone and unique scent. The man's alluring persona oozed from the page. Excitement had squeezed the breath from her lungs. And her thoughts had turned to dancing, to touching him, to a romantic stroll in the garden, to another toe-curling kiss.

"Your brother's debts make this a complicated case," Mr Cole said, scanning his environment through dark, critical eyes. "Mr Daventry wishes me to assist Mr Ashwood."

"Mr Daventry? Ah, yes. The gentleman who hired you to help right the imbalance of justice." Eva was intrigued to know what prompted wealthy men to chase criminals and put their lives in danger.

Mr Cole motioned to the rectangular mark on the wall. "What happened to the painting that used to hang there?"

She glanced at the dirty smudges. "I had to part with it, sir."

"It wasn't stolen?" Suspicion coated every word.

"No. I sold the painting this morning. Has Mr Ashwood informed you I have parted ways with my publisher?"

Had Mr Ashwood mentioned they'd shared a long and lingering kiss while standing in the middle of Mr Hemming's office? Was that the real reason Mr Cole stood in her hall looking like the devil come to claim another soul?

"Out of concern for your safety, Miss Dunn, my colleague had no choice but to convey details of the case."

"I see. I trust I can speak in confidence."

"Absolute confidence."

"Then with regard to the painting, not only do I need funds for household expenses and the purchase of new boots, but after Mr Ashwood's kind gesture, I am now in debt to Mr Daventry to the sum of one hundred pounds."

Mr Cole's expression remained stone-like, but the slight widening of his eyes said he knew nothing of Mr Ashwood's generosity. Surely he had recorded the expense.

"To whom did Mr Ashwood pay a hundred pounds?"

"My publisher."

"For what purpose?"

"To release me from a contract."

"Hmm," he mused, yet two frown lines appeared between brows almost swamped by a mop of sable hair.

Kathleen's sudden appearance brought light relief. "I have your cloak, ma'am. There's a mighty chill in the air tonight."

There was a frosty atmosphere in the hall, too. Mr Cole was so difficult to read. So reserved. So stern.

"Allow me." He snatched the gold cloak she had not worn for two years and draped it around her shoulders.

His fingers brushed absently against her nape, though she felt nothing. Not the delightful shiver that shot to her toes as a result of Mr Ashwood's touch. Not the need to turn on her heel and meld her body to his. Not the desperate hope that he felt the same way, too.

"Will Mr Ashwood be attending tonight?" she asked as Mr Cole led her to his carriage. If she were to face Lord Benham, she would rather have a man named Dauntless as her companion.

Mr Cole ignored her question and gestured to the hulking figure sitting atop the box of an unmarked carriage parked at the end of Brownlow Street. "Bower will watch your house until we bring an end to these troubling matters. He's a strong, capable man, one used to dealing with villains."

"I see."

Witnessing the burly individual should have settled her

nerves. But Mr Ashwood would not have appointed such a sturdy watchman if there was nothing to fear. Indeed, the sudden thought of sleeping alone tonight chilled her to the bone. Filled her with dread.

Dread held her rigid in the carriage seat as they rattled through town on their way to Lord Newberry's ball in Cavendish Square. In Mr Ashwood's company she felt safe, protected. Mr Cole made her want to run for the hills, not race into his embrace.

To pass the time, she studied Mr Cole's conveyance. The black leather seats were so opposed to the inviting red ones in Mr Ashwood's carriage. The potent smell of Mr Ashwood's cologne—bergamot, exotic spice and some woody essence—roused primal urges when in the confined space. In Mr Cole's carriage, she was too scared to breathe.

Oh, this was ridiculous.

"Will Mr Ashwood be attending tonight?" she repeated.

Mr Cole glanced in her direction. "Does it matter?"

It did matter.

It mattered more than it should.

Perhaps an estrangement was for the best. Nothing would come of this bedevilling attraction. The addiction had kept her awake last night, imagining all sorts of lewd fantasies.

"What if word gets out I am betrothed to Mr Ashwood? Will it not look highly irregular if I attend a ball with you, sir?"

Mr Cole shot forward in the seat. "Betrothed? To Ashwood?" The atmosphere grew heavy, charged with tension, like the prelude to a violent storm. "Madam, if this is a game to rile my temper—"

"I never play games, Mr Cole." She gave an outline of the meeting in Mr Hemming's office. If Mr Ashwood failed to mention their fake betrothal, he most definitely hadn't mentioned the kiss. "And so you see, Mr Ashwood wished to send the rogue a clear message."

Mr Cole's eyes flashed as black as his mood. "Oh, I understand the message. I understand the message all too well."

"Whatever you're implying, sir, you have me at a loss."

"Then it seems neither of you has control of your wits."

It occurred to her that Mr Cole's annoyance stemmed from a need to protect his friend and colleague. But from what? Did he think she'd invented her problems merely to seduce an unsuspecting agent into marriage?

"It was merely a ploy. Bait to lure a rodent into a trap."

"What sort of trap?" Mr Cole snapped.

"Mr Ashwood is trying to determine whether my brother sent the blackmail note to gain funds, or if my publisher sent it to entice me to his office in the dead of night." She offered a confident smile. "It is not a trap to lure an eligible gentleman into marriage if that is your fear."

"Fear?" He snorted. "I'm not afraid of anything, Miss Dunn."

"No. Nothing except for experiencing the pain that has made you so hard and unforgiving."

Well, that took the wind out of his sails.

The gentleman stared open-mouthed for a few seconds until he mastered his senses. "Then I shall follow your lead, madam, and be blunt. I intend to help my friend overcome his fleeting infatuation."

Infatuation!

Eva's heart lurched.

So, she had not imagined the vibrant energy that charged the air when in Mr Ashwood's company. The taste of passion on his lips had not been part of the ruse. They had many things in common, too many to ignore. One might be forgiven for believing fate had brought them together.

"Then let us be clear, sir. I have the utmost respect for Mr Ashwood." Indeed, he had restored her faith, given her the belief there were honest men in the world. "I have no intention of making the case more difficult than it is already. So, for the third and final time, will your colleague be joining us this evening?"

After a moment of reflection, Mr Cole said, "The official answer is no. Another matter requires his attention. As his friend, I would not be surprised if he made an appearance."

Her stomach grew hot upon hearing the news.

Perhaps Mr Cole had every reason to express his concern.

This fleeting infatuation had taken command of her faculties, too.

A heavy silence ensued.

Nerves took hold as they neared Cavendish Square and the home of Lord Newberry. The fop had been a guest at Briden Castle two summers ago, along with his friend Lord Benham. Both men had lavished her with attention. It was Clara who first made Eva aware of the bet. A kindness that was a catalyst for the wealth of suffering that followed.

"It might help if you explain our objective for attending the ball this evening," Eva said. She needed to prepare mentally for the clash with the viscount. "I presume we have invitations. That said, Lord Benham will probably have me thrown out." And yet it wasn't the viscount's anger she feared, more his cunning and his need for vengeance.

"No one will ask us to leave. Daventry knows too much about Newberry's nefarious dealings."

"And will Lord Newberry provide a chaperone? Surely you know what people will say should they see us alone together."

Eva didn't care what people said. Most expected the worst. Like those poor souls during the revolution, her name was proof of her guilt. Besides, those who professed to be holier than thou and the epitome of high standards, were drunken debauchers who would murder their own mothers to move up the social ladder. Although seeing her in the company of another man was certain to rouse the viscount's ire.

Mr Cole exhaled a weary sigh. "Mr Ashwood insisted I arrange for a companion. Someone respectable, trustworthy. Someone of his choosing. Someone with whom I share a history."

Whoever this *someone* was, Mr Cole's tone turned irritable the moment he spoke about the mystery lady. But there was no time to press him further. The carriage slowed, joining the queue stretching as far as Henrietta Street.

For fifteen minutes, they sat in morbid silence. Every jolt and jerk forward added to the crippling sense of trepidation. Music and the faint hum of laughter drifted through the cool night air, but it did nothing to ease the tension.

Mr Cole was every bit the respectable gentleman as he escorted Eva into the mansion house. From her brief encounter with Lord Newberry, she knew him to be a man who liked to flaunt his wealth. Tonight was no exception.

Magnificent ice sculptures, lavish champagne fountains and an alarming number of standing candelabra made for an extravagant affair.

Mr Cole's mouth curled in disdain as he led Eva to their position near a grand marble fireplace, above which hung a huge portrait of their host.

Despite Mr Cole's stony appearance, many men inclined their heads respectfully as they passed. Indeed, they seemed a little in awe of the brusque gentleman who had barely spoken two words to Eva since their arrival.

"At last," he muttered beneath his breath as a graceful woman approached. Mr Cole scanned the lady's figure-hugging emerald dress with a little more than indifference. He gave the silver-blonde curls teasing her elegant neck the same scrutiny.

"Finlay," the lady said, her blue eyes as bright as her smile. "Or am I supposed to call you Raven?"

Mr Cole ignored the question and introduced Lady Adair, a widow approaching thirty whose porcelain skin would rival that of any young debutante.

"I must say, I was a little surprised to receive your note." A slight tension lingered behind the lady's friendly manner.

"Miss Dunn is without family or connections," he replied soberly, "but it was imperative she attend tonight."

"Is there a gentleman here you wish to impress, Miss Dunn?" Lady Adair scanned Eva's red gown with a look of admiration, and yet a sliver of jealousy invaded her tone.

"I dress to please myself, my lady." It wasn't a complete lie. Tonight was the first time she had ever wanted to look beautiful as opposed to confident. She had thought of Mr Ashwood when dabbing rosewater to her throat. She had thought of Mr Ashwood when insisting Kathleen pull her stays tighter.

Lady Adair laughed. "Then you're either a woman of great fortune or one of strong moral character."

"I am neither." She could not profess to be moral after the

sinful way Mr Ashwood had devoured her mouth. Indeed, her traitorous body was in danger of permitting more shocking liberties. "But I have yet to meet a man worthy of my effort. Most are debauched degenerates filled with self-importance."

That was not entirely true, either.

Mr Ashwood was the exception.

"On that point, I must agree." The lady laughed as she stole a glance at Mr Cole. "And yet in my experience, good men rarely commit."

Mr Cole cleared his throat. "A good man wants a woman who can warm his heart with the same fervent passion she warms his bed."

One did not need to be skilled in reading subtext to know this couple shared a tumultuous history.

"And what would a lady need to do to melt the frost around your heart, Mr Cole?" Lady Adair said, adding emphasis to the point that she had not used his given name.

Mr Cole was about to answer, but the arrival of Lord Benham seized his attention.

Eva recoiled as panic rose like a tidal wave ready to engulf her.

Lord Benham was not a handsome man. Not by any stretch of the imagination. Looking into his eyes was like looking into the bottomless pit of a well. Cold and dark and dank. He bore the nose of a tyrant, hooked, long and dreadfully ugly. His mouth would be his redeeming feature were it not drawn tight into a cynical line.

Mr Cole turned to Lady Adair, who had undoubtedly hurt him at some point in his life. "Can I trust you to stay with Miss Dunn for a moment?"

"Of course. That is why you summoned me."

"Do not let her out of your sight."

Eva watched Lord Benham bull his way through the crowd. She hoped to shrink back into the fireplace, to get lost amongst the soot and coals. But Lady Adair had an inherent beauty that captured every man's eye. Indeed, Benham glanced in their direction, his lifeless eyes widening as their gazes locked.

That vicious mouth twitched.

If only Mr Ashwood were here. In his company, she felt invincible. Had she explained the whole story, he would not have left her to face this devil alone. But she could not hide from the wicked creature forever. She had sought professional help to bring an end to her nightmares. And yet she couldn't help but think her nightmares had only just begun.

CHAPTER 9

Despite Mr Cole's cunning effort to extract information from Lord Benham, he returned to the ballroom disappointed and in a devil of a mood. Lady Adair had removed to speak to Lady Cartwright, and so Mr Cole aired his frustration.

"Benham said he saw your brother at the tables in Cockburns a few days ago." Mr Cole sneered. "Your sibling fled with his coat-tails flapping. Benham is lying through his teeth and knows a damn sight more than he claims."

"That would not surprise me." Was Howard playing a game? A game to force her hand? Would he continue to cause her distress until she loosened the purse strings and parted with the full two thousand pounds? "I refer to my brother gambling. Lord Benham is undoubtedly a liar."

Mr Cole eyed her suspiciously. "Benham asked about the nature of our relationship and seemed annoyed you're here with me. Jealousy formed the basis of his enquiry." He paused. "Would you care to elaborate?"

Elaborate!

Eva had banished the memories to the far reaches of her mind. Still, she had made a commitment to deal with her problems, not hide from them.

Elaborate?

93

There was no easy way to say it. Perhaps a short explanation would suffice.

"Lord Benham tried to bed me during a month's stay at Briden Castle. He had to bed me to win a bet." She paused for breath, and to banish the terrible images from her mind. "For three tiring weeks, he did everything in his power to dupe me, to capture me in his snare. It was his sister Clara who confessed to his devious plan."

"They say Benham always gets what he wants." Disgust imbued Mr Cole's tone. "They say he can be extremely persuasive."

"Deviously so." Eva shivered at the memory. A lady needed her wits to stay one step ahead. She lowered her voice. "But please, tell me you didn't speak about Clara's predicament. The viscount will do anything to keep his sister's shame a secret."

"I'm not a fool, Miss Dunn."

"No."

"Has it occurred to you that your brother acted out of revenge? That he treated Benham's sister the way Benham treated you?"

A choked laugh burst from Eva's lips. She had never heard anything so absurd. "Sir, I can assure you, my brother wouldn't care if I were carried away by a horde of rampaging Vikings."

Mr Cole did not share in her amusement.

Nor did anyone else in the room.

All laughter and conversation died.

Eva craned her neck to see what had captured the crowd's attention. What had made them nudge their friends, press their heads together and whisper?

"Ashwood is here." Mr Cole's comment almost knocked Eva off her feet.

"Is he?" Her lungs contracted, squeezing out her last breath. Her head spun as her heart plunged to the depths of her stomach. She caught sight of him then—the enigmatic gentleman who sent her giddy.

Heaven help her!

She patted her simple coiffure and brushed her skirts. Would he look upon the sumptuous red gown with admiring eyes?

Would that wickedly sinful gaze linger in daring places? Would she see the fleeting infatuation Mr Cole mentioned?

Lady Adair returned. "Mr Ashwood has come to cause a stir, I see. If he's searching for his uncle, he'll find Hawkridge in the card room."

"He's not here for Hawkridge," came Mr Cole's disgruntled mutter. "No doubt the crowd will be disappointed. They enjoy a good show."

"Well, he seems determined in his cause." Lady Adair arched a brow, seemingly intrigued. "So determined he forgot to dress in evening attire. As heir presumptive, perhaps he wishes to frighten Hawkridge into an early grave."

Mr Ashwood was Lord Hawkridge's heir?

Mr Cole scoffed. "Ashwood hopes his uncle will sire a son before meeting his maker. The last thing my friend wants is a title."

"I fear his hopes may be dashed," Lady Adair replied. "Everyone knows Lady Hawkridge is barren."

Mr Ashwood continued to push through the crowd. All Eva could do was drink in the splendid sight. He was as fearless as his moniker implied. While all the men wore black coats, breeches and buckled shoes, he was dressed in buckskins and Hessians. Eva imagined he would look devastatingly handsome in black. Yet there was something about his defiant air that made him utterly irresistible.

He turned his head in her direction and their gazes locked. A sinful smile formed on his lips as his attention journeyed over her gown. The power of it hit her hard. Heat flooded her cheeks. Blessed saints. Every person in the room must know of her desire for this man. Mr Cole must surely see that she was more than obsessed with the agent who wrote lewd poetry.

But then a pretty woman with vibrant red hair stopped Mr Ashwood in his tracks. The temptress placed her hand on his arm in a way that seemed far too familiar. Jealousy slithered like a serpent in Eva's chest, its poisonous venom adding to her delirium.

"Please excuse me." Her words escaped her on a breathless pant. "I—I must visit the retiring room."

If she could not take control of her heightened emotions, Mr Cole would assume responsibility for her case. The thought of not working closely with Mr Ashwood, of not seeing him again, made her feel sick to her stomach.

"You should not go alone," Mr Cole said, gesturing for his friend to join them. "Sophia, would you accompany Miss Dunn to the retiring room?"

The lady's coy smile spoke of mischief. "Certainly. Come, Miss Dunn." She threaded her arm through Eva's. "Let us discuss Mr Cole's bad temper in private."

As Lady Adair steered her away through the ballroom, Eva didn't dare steal a glance at Mr Ashwood. There were many excuses she could make for her sudden departure. Based on his appearance, she could say that she presumed he wished to discuss something urgently with Mr Cole. That was if she ever found herself alone with Mr Ashwood again.

The queue to the retiring room stretched the length of the corridor. Lady Adair spent the time probing Eva about Mr Cole. Had he mentioned their fathers were close friends? Had he spoken about his wife, about the woman who died three years ago? Had he expressed a desire to remarry?

Eva explained that she barely knew him and that it was Mr Ashwood with whom she shared an acquaintance. The mere mention of the gentleman's name caused desire to unfurl like the first petals of spring. The memory of him dabbing rosewater to her neck, of his mouth moving over hers with complete mastery, roused a physical ache.

Oh, this was absurd.

Never had a man taken command of her senses.

In the retiring room, she joined the queue to use a booth. Not because she wished to attend to her ablutions, but she needed a moment alone to catch her breath.

By now, Mr Cole would have spoken of Lord Benham's deplorable antics at Briden Castle. Mr Ashwood made no secret of his disdain for men who took advantage. Would he go in search of Lord Benham? Would he seek answers? Would he make more shocking claims to prove a point?

A loud knock on the dressing screen made Eva jump.

"Are you all right, Miss Dunn?" Lady Adair's concerned voice was barely audible amongst the bird-like chatter in the room.

"Yes. Just a moment." Eva inhaled deeply before straightening her skirts and parting the screen.

Lady Adair entered the booth. "Wait for me on the sofa." She gestured to the adjoining salon occupied by a host of young women and their dithering mothers. "Before we return to the ballroom, there is something I want to ask you about Mr Cole."

Eva groaned inwardly but forced a smile. "Certainly."

She had no intention of waiting, and every intention of seeking Lord Benham. It was time she stopped hiding. Time she spoke honestly. Time the viscount understood that his licentious actions were partly to blame for the whole dreadful affair.

After scanning the corridor to ensure Mr Cole wasn't lingering in the shadows, Eva left the retiring salon and quickly hurried to the refreshment room. Lord Benham stood a head taller than most men, and she soon discerned he was not amongst the crowd enjoying claret and conversation. The card room was her next port of call, but he was not seated at the tables where men sought refuge from interfering mamas, either.

There were but a few places left to look.

The young buck leaving the billiard room informed her the viscount wasn't playing and to his knowledge loathed the game.

Eva stood for a moment and considered her options. Lord Benham would never speak openly about his sister's predicament. Certainly not to Mr Ashwood. Certainly not where cunning gossips hovered like vultures waiting to scavenge morsels of meat.

And then she spotted the devil glaring at her from an alcove, his arms folded in defiance.

The icy grip of fear chilled her to the bone.

It wasn't his unpleasant appearance that made her mouth dry and hands shake. It was the callous look in his eyes, the brutal curl of his lips.

He pushed away from the wall—his curt nod a command to follow—and entered the room opposite.

Only a fool would do his bidding. Only a fool would place herself at risk. But she cared about Clara. Guilt's blade was still embedded in Eva's chest. Firmly rooted. Deeply painful. Something had to be done about this man who was, without doubt, the cause of her problems.

And so, after waiting a moment until the corridor was clear, she entered Lucifer's lair.

"Lock the door, Miss Dunn." Lord Benham's strict instruction echoed from the dark depths of the room. "I'll not have anyone stumble upon our tryst."

Eva swallowed to temper her nerves. She pressed her foot against the door, turned the handle and fiddled with the key, tricking him into believing it was locked.

"This is not a tryst," she said, whirling round to look for his monstrous silhouette amid the shadows of Lord Newberry's library. "It's an attempt at a treaty, an opportunity to form an alliance. After all, we share a common interest."

"I gave you an opportunity to form an alliance, Miss Dunn. An opportunity you've refused at every turn." His derisive snort turned her stomach. "We have no other common interest."

Gathering her courage, Eva took a few tentative steps forward. "That's not true. We both care about Clara."

Lord Benham ground his teeth. "You permitted your brother to take advantage of a naive girl. Is that how you treat those you care for, Miss Dunn? No doubt you saw it as a means of revenge."

Eva ignored his cruel taunts. "What have you done with Howard? Is he ... is he dead?"

The devil prowled towards her, closing the gap between them. The shadows made his disproportioned features seem more grotesque. "As I told Finlay Cole when he probed me earlier, I've not seen the pathetic fop for days. With luck, his creditors have strung him up from Bloody Bridge and spilt his innards."

"I don't believe you."

He shrugged. "Do I look like I care?"

No, those black eyes were soulless pits. Pits of nothingness.

"Did you arrange for someone to attack me in the street? Was it revenge for the callous way my brother treated Clara?"

An inscrutable smile formed on the viscount's lips. He

stepped closer, forcing her to shuffle back until her bottom came to rest against Lord Newberry's imposing desk.

"I can protect you from mindless thugs. I can save you from those who might seek to take advantage of a woman living alone. I shall permit you to see Clara and the child. I'll give you one last chance to surrender. Surrender yourself to me, and you may make amends."

Make amends?

Lord Benham was a man of threats and ultimatums. Winning was his only motivation. His power made most women overlook his mean spirit and repulsive countenance. There wasn't an incentive in the world that could make Eva overlook his callous manner.

"I don't blame you for hating my brother. I despise him, too."

"*Hate* is too mild a word."

"And yet this all started because of a bet *you* made." Eva raised her chin, determined to continue, though her defensive walls were shaking, close to crumbling. "This began because you were intent on ruining an innocent for sport. You've insulted me at every turn. Even now, you offer a place in your bed but not as your wife." Not that she would ever accept an offer from this beast. "You're no different from Howard. You're both scheming, lying cheats who frighten women to get your own way."

Eva was so keen to tell this blackguard what she thought, she failed to note the hardening of his jaw or the sparks of rage in his eyes. Indeed, it wasn't until he grabbed her chin and pressed his overbearing body to hers that she feared she had gone too far.

"Damn beguiling witch." His empty eyes fell to her heaving bosom. "You tease men with your smart little mouth. Taunt them with rare glimpses of flesh. You profess independence, but it's a guise for you to behave like a wanton."

Eva gulped. "Howard verbally defiles me when he cannot get his way." Fear forced her to push the viscount's chest. "You're the same. Both equally delusional."

This time he grabbed her cheeks in a bruising grip and squeezed hard. "Give yourself to me, else you shall suffer the consequences."

A sudden sliver of light sliced through the darkness as the

door creaked open. Eva sought to cry out, to beg for help, but there wasn't a man alive who would challenge Lord Benham.

Well—perhaps there was one.

"Release the lady, Benham. Take your complaint up with me." Mr Ashwood closed the door and stepped into the room. The way he tugged the cuffs on his coat said he meant business. "Though I should warn you, this is a battle you won't win."

The viscount shot Mr Ashwood a scowl. "This has nothing to do with you, Ashwood. If you're looking for a fight, your uncle is in the card room."

"My fight is with you, Benham. Release the lady, else I shall break every one of those fingers marring her skin." Mr Ashwood's menacing tone would have Satan seeking sanctuary. Dark shadows danced across his fine features. His green eyes were serpent-like. Focused. Deadly.

"We're done here," Lord Benham said so as not to look cowardly when he released his grip and stepped back. "Miss Dunn clings to her chastity with the lofty arrogance of an abbess. Your threat leads me to conclude the abbess has already strayed from the righteous path."

"Some men have a deep-rooted need to protect women, not abuse them," Mr Ashwood countered.

Did the need to play protector stem from the tragic loss of his mother? As a child, he must have felt helpless. As a man, he took command of every situation.

The viscount sneered. "Some might believe your admirable protestations, but you want to bed her as much as I do."

To her shock, Mr Ashwood did not discount the lord's claim. "Every man has his torments. Miss Dunn is kind and intelligent, courageous, beautiful. Why wouldn't I want to bed her?"

Eva struggled to breathe.

It wasn't the list of compliments that sent her head spinning, but the knowledge of his intimate thoughts.

She imagined him naked. Pert buttocks and rippling muscles. Hard and male. She imagined him scooping her up into his powerful arms and lowering her down onto her plush mattress— entering her, pleasuring her, loving her.

"But I am assisting Miss Dunn in a professional capacity," he continued, dousing her inner flames. "The lady wishes to find her brother, wishes to punish the coward who attacked her in the street. I seek justice on her behalf. That is all."

That was not all.

There was something more between them. More than duty. More than lust. Something intangible. Something that spanned centuries if one believed in destiny and fate. The need to fuse herself to him, to meld together body and soul was so great she could think of little else.

"I'm not surprised Hawkridge is ashamed of your familial connection," the viscount scoffed, attempting to gain ground. "Perhaps he's right. Perhaps there is doubt over your lineage. Your father spent his days too drunk to notice your mother's indiscretion. Why else would you soil your hands when you're wealthier than your uncle?"

Eva froze.

The atmosphere turned volatile seconds before Mr Ashwood flew across the room and grabbed Lord Benham by the throat. For all the viscount's arrogance, he was nowhere near as strong as his opponent. Despite a violent struggle, he could not break free.

"You do not want to make an enemy of me." Mr Ashwood's vicious growl practically shook the chandelier. No doubt hell's sinners were diving into the inferno to escape the terrifying tremors. "My father's blood flows through my veins—wild and reckless—though I'm an expert shot and fight for honourable causes." He tightened his grip, choking the lord. "I don't care who you are. Insult my mother, issue one more threat to Miss Dunn, and I'll put a lead ball between your brows."

Good Lord. Eva had never seen him so angry, so out of control. She couldn't help but feel responsible. In questioning Lord Benham, she had been trying to prevent an argument, not start one.

Lord Benham managed a curt nod, but still, Mr Ashwood maintained his firm hold. The viscount's cheeks flamed red. His eyes bulged in their sockets.

Eva gripped Mr Ashwood's arm. "I think Lord Benham understands the gravity of the situation, sir. Let him go. Let him go before you throttle him to death."

The library door creaked open again, but—thank the Lord— it was Mr Cole who entered. He took one look at the situation and cursed beneath his breath. "Listen to Miss Dunn. Let Benham go."

Mr Ashwood released his grip.

The viscount sagged forward and clutched his throat as he gasped for air.

"If you wish to take this further," Mr Ashwood said, the fire in his eyes still burning, "I shall await your dawn invitation. I name Finlay Cole as my second."

Lord Benham was a cruel individual, but he was not a fool. Still, Mr Ashwood's anger radiated, and the viscount might easily provoke him.

"I'm sure Lord Benham understands that he said something wholly inappropriate," Eva said with some desperation. "That he deserved your retaliation. Let us leave him to catch his breath and reflect on who was to blame." She flashed a pleading gaze at Mr Cole.

"I'm sure Benham knows that an enemy of Ashwood's is an enemy of mine," Mr Cole said, his tone razor sharp. "A wise man chooses his battles."

"Come." Eva tugged Mr Ashwood's coat sleeve. "We should leave."

Mr Ashwood shot her an irate stare. "Damn right, we should." Without warning, he captured her elbow and propelled her towards the door.

Lord Benham remained silent, though Eva felt the whip of his disdain lashing her back, sharp enough to draw blood.

Mr Cole peered around the jamb and surveyed the corridor before ushering them out of the room. "I presume you walked here. We can take my carriage."

But Mr Ashwood had other plans.

"Stay here, Cole. Entertain Lady Adair. I shall see Miss Dunn home."

"I'm not sure that's wise. Daventry will have something to say about—"

"Sod Daventry."

Mr Ashwood didn't care for his friend's opinion. He didn't care who saw him steering her possessively through the corridor.

A gentleman with a patrician nose and an arrogant mouth pushed away from the wall as they approached. "Ah, Ashwood," he said, attempting to block their path. "I heard you were here. Causing trouble again, I see. And who is this delightful—"

"Bugger off!" Mr Ashwood barged shoulders with the fellow and continued towards the front door.

"Who was that?"

"Hawkridge."

"Your uncle?"

His reply was but a muttered curse.

"Where are we going?" she whispered as numerous people turned their heads and gaped as he led her out into Cavendish Square. "I thought you were concerned about my reputation."

"Your brother is a scoundrel. Your recklessness this evening will be a talking point for months. The damage is done."

She could not argue with his logic.

"When I said you should get Lord Benham's attention," he said, navigating her around the row of parked carriages in the square, "I advised you to use your wits, not place yourself in a perilous situation."

"But he refuses to acknowledge me in public. How else was I to gain an audience?"

"You wait until you have something with which to bargain."

"Then what was the purpose of attending the ball?" She would have preferred to stay at home.

Mr Ashwood sighed. "To gauge his reaction when Cole mentioned your brother. To see how he would behave knowing you were here. To find an excuse to call at his home and question him further."

Eva swallowed hard as she marched beside him, trying to keep pace. Lord Benham had behaved as expected—like the vile hypocrite of old.

"Slow down. These slippers will be threadbare when we reach our destination." She shivered against the chilly night air. "What about my cloak?"

"You don't need it," he said, keeping his hand at her elbow. "I shall have my maid collect it tomorrow."

"I am capable of walking without assistance." And yet she rather liked the protective way he held her arm. "Where are you taking me?"

"To Wigmore Street."

"Wigmore Street?" His home! "Is that wise?"

"We need privacy, Miss Dunn. And I intend to make damn sure we get it."

CHAPTER 10

NOAH COULDN'T FOCUS. His mind was a muddled mess. Anger had woken from its slumber, disturbed by Miss Dunn's desire to place herself in precarious situations.

It began the moment she sought to avoid him, when she fled Newberry's ballroom as if her gown were ablaze. Then Cole told him of her confession. Spoke of Benham's desire to bed the woman. But that's not what fed the beast's fury. No. The fact Miss Dunn neglected to mention a crucial piece of information had him hopping on hot coals.

"Sir, you're walking too quickly." The lady—this mystical temptress who had possessed his mind and body—stopped and gasped a breath. "Just give me a moment."

"Madam, you may catch your breath once we're safely inside." Indeed, they were but twelve feet from his front door.

"I'm not sure I should come inside." A slight frisson of fear darkened her tone. "Not when you're in the devil's mood."

Frightening her was not part of his plan.

"Eva, I want to talk to you." He faced her and softened his tone. He needed a drink, needed her to soothe the devil back to bed. "Trust me. I shall behave in the way you've grown accustomed, not like the reckless rogue you saw tonight."

"I found the reckless rogue rather charming." She gave a coy shrug that drew his gaze to the delightful swell of her breasts.

"You defended your mother's memory. That was the reason for your violent outburst."

"One reason," he said, capturing her elbow again. "Come, you're cold. Let's continue this conversation inside. A large glass of brandy awaits."

"Are you trying to tempt me with liquor, Mr Ashwood?"

"Come because you want to, not because I offer an inducement or force your hand." It occurred to him that, after her recent experiences, she would seek to avoid being alone with unbalanced men. "Your virtue is safe with me. I seek your company, nothing more. But I can have McGuffey take you home if you prefer."

She studied him for a moment. "Lord Benham gave me a fright. A glass of brandy and an hour of interesting conversation would be most welcome."

The mere mention of Benham had his inner devil leaping up, ready to bring eternal damnation down on anyone who hurt her. To calm his temper, he did not speak again until they were ensconced in his drawing room.

"You should have told me what happened at Briden Castle," he said, prodding the fire with a poker while she poured two glasses of brandy. She should have told him because he felt a duty to protect her that went beyond all reason. "It is important to the case."

"I tried." She crossed the candlelit room and offered him the crystal goblet half full of amber nectar. "I mentioned it before we entered Mr Hemming's office if you remember."

"Of course I remember." He had an exceptional memory. And yet he struggled to focus on anything other than the kiss that left him famished, ravenous, hungry for more.

"But you're right. Lord Benham hopes Howard is dead. It all started with the bet at Briden." Sadness swam in her eyes. "I should have told you about that when we spoke about Clara."

Her obvious regret soothed the beast inside.

Noah gestured to the sofa. "Please, sit."

He watched her smooth her silk skirts and settle into the seat. She looked breathtaking in red. Exquisite. Indeed, it wasn't just anger flowing through the beast's veins. Lust—and something infinitely more alarming—flared whenever he was in her company.

"Ask me anything about Lord Benham," she said, cradling the brandy glass between her palms, "and I shall speak honestly."

Noah dropped into the seat opposite. "For a woman who believes her character is wholly unattractive, there are at least two men eager to gain entrance to your bedchamber."

Three if he counted himself.

A flush crept across her cheeks. "Mr Hemming speaks of marriage because he wants to take control of my work. Lord Benham wants me for a mistress, not a wife. Winning the bet is his only motivation."

Noah didn't want to control her, nor did he want her for his mistress. So what the hell did he want?

"You ran away from me tonight. You seemed pleased to see me but then fled from the ballroom without so much as a greeting. Why?"

The lady sipped her brandy, gasping as the fiery spirit burned her throat. It was a ploy to distract him while she gathered her wits. Was she keeping another secret? If so, he would walk away, never look back.

"After the debacle with Lord Benham, have we not established that honesty is the only way forward, Miss Dunn?"

"Miss Dunn?" she teased. "I like it when you call me Eva."

That had been a slip of the tongue, a moment of weakness. "You're stalling."

"Am I?"

"What is it you're not telling me?"

Her light laugh was forced. "I had to use the retiring room."

"If that's the truth, why can you not look me in the eye? Why do you squirm in your seat? And your ears are as red as your gown."

"Must you examine every nuance?" she countered, gazing at the amber liquid sloshing about in the glass. "Why does your need to study mannerisms border on obsessive?"

"Because I was once duped into believing a lie." The words tumbled carelessly from his mouth. He gave a weary sigh. Aware of the tension he'd held inside for nigh on two decades.

Miss Dunn gave him her full attention. "You were hurt, betrayed by someone you loved."

Noah's throat constricted. "Yes."

His inner torment must surely be evident. But it was wrong to insist she reveal her secrets and demand the right to keep his own.

Miss Dunn's pretty blue eyes softened. "Then she was a fool to reject you, sir. Your qualities are superior to any man of my acquaintance. A woman would be proud to have you for a husband."

Though the lady had drawn the wrong conclusion, her faith in him stole his breath. "I—I was not duped by a lover." No. Were that the case, he might have fallen in love again, been happy. "My mother convinced me all was well hours before she swallowed a fatal dose of laudanum."

In the crippling silence that followed, Miss Dunn's breathing grew as ragged as his own. The distress in her eyes mirrored the pain in his heart. Confusion and disbelief hung in the air, as heavy as they had on that dreadful day.

Noah drained his glass, then stood and placed the goblet on the mantel. Staring into the fire's flames turned his mood reflective. Perhaps he might have prevented the tragedy. Perhaps he could have said something to alter the turn of events.

He felt a gentle hand on his shoulder. The lady placed her glass next to his—hers full, his empty.

"Forgive me," she whispered. "I would not have pressed you had I known."

"Now you understand why I despise secrets, Miss Dunn."

"Please, call me Eva," she said in the gentle voice that touched him like a deeply moving melody. "Yes. And I understand your need to help women in distress."

Despite her comment, he could feel the dark cloud of grief descending. The guilt. The frustration. The never-ending questions. "The irony is I can barely remember her, yet that one incident is like a black stain on my conscience."

He'd never spoken those words to another soul, not even to his grandfather.

"You were a boy. Innocent. Naive to the ways of the world."

"And yet I blame myself for that, too."

Silence ensued.

Her comforting hand never left his shoulder.

"Then never again shall I keep anything from you, regardless of my embarrassment." She inhaled. "An independent woman should not admit such a thing, but I dressed for you tonight. I wore the red gown because I wanted to show you the woman whose heart is bursting with passion."

He turned to face her, his grief dissipating. "You show me that woman every time we're together."

"But you believe I'm practical and efficient." She looked up at him through wide, sensual eyes, her full lips parted, just waiting to be kissed.

Noah couldn't help but smile. "You're a delightful package of contradictions." And he wanted her in every conceivable way.

She screwed her petite nose. "A package?"

"A box of wonders." He drank in her radiant beauty. "Indeed, a man might marvel for hours while examining every gift. You must have been disheartened when Cole arrived to play escort."

"I doubt I have ever suffered a greater disappointment."

He couldn't help but reach out and tuck a stray tendril behind her ear. "And yet in the ballroom, you ran away the moment our gazes locked. Why? Was it my failure to dress appropriately?"

She squared her shoulders as if affronted he should think so. "I prefer a man with a strong mind."

"Strong mind?" He laughed. "I had no intention of attending, yet could not stay away."

"Why, because you refuse to relinquish control of the case to Mr Cole?"

"No. You know why I came." His need to see her had taken command of his senses. The urge to touch her now saw him capture her gloved hand. "Why did you run?"

She swallowed hard. "Because I did not want Mr Cole to witness the change in me, the change brought about by your arrival."

"Change?" He slipped her white glove past her elbow, sliding it down to her wrist. "Must you insist on being vague, Eva?"

"Y-you leave me breathless, sir." She watched as he stripped the glove from her hand. "I find my legs struggle to support me when I'm in your presence. Mr Cole is determined to save you from your fleeting infatuation."

Noah stroked his finger across her palm, following each fascinating line. "Is that what he said?"

"Indeed."

"We're like brothers. He knows me better than anyone, fears the bonds may be broken, snatched from his grasp like every good thing in his life."

"He wishes to protect you, to protect himself."

"Yes. Our work for the Order has given us a purpose. Cole doesn't want me to throw it away for a woman."

"Then you won't mind if I remind you of your own advice." She visibly shivered as he trailed his finger to her wrist and drew circles. "The wrong woman might insist you stop these dangerous pursuits. The right woman won't want to change a thing. The right woman will want you exactly as you are."

Was Eva Dunn the right woman?

Instinct said so.

"There were so many beautiful ladies at the ball tonight," she said, flutters of desire evident in every breath. The nervous energy radiating from her was perhaps the reason she kept talking. "You stole their attention the moment you entered the room."

"I wouldn't know." He took her hand and placed it on his chest. "I saw no one but you, Eva."

They fell silent, but the roaring of their suppressed passions seemed to vibrate through the room. The air was suddenly charged with the need to ease this insistent ache. To satisfy the base desire that kept him awake last night.

"I swore I wouldn't kiss you again." And yet he had thought of little else.

She shuffled closer. "Some promises are made to be broken."

"Things may progress beyond a kiss."

"I fear I might die if you don't touch me, Mr Ashwood."

"Noah," he corrected as he slipped his arm around her waist

and drew her close. "I'm of a mind to satisfy your cravings. To pander to your whims."

"I'm of a mind to let you."

He drew the backs of his fingers gently across her cheek, across skin pale as porcelain, soft as silk. "Then I'm going to kiss you, Eva."

Her nod was the only signal he needed to lower his head and claim her mouth. He intended to take his time, to teach her to express her desire, to awaken her passions, tease a deeper reaction, a slow and gentle caressing of tongues.

God help him.

It took every effort not to devour her senseless. It might have been easier had she not clutched the lapels of his coat, ready to rip it off his back. Easier, had her need not been evident in the rocking of her hips, had she not released a throaty hum.

Indeed, as their mouths moved together in a sensual dance, it became evident neither had control over their desires. What should have been a chaste, experimental kiss turned into something so damn hot he burned to shove her skirts to her waist and thrust home.

Hell!

The temperature in the room soared when she slipped her tongue into his mouth. Damn, it was so warm and sweet, so bloody seductive. He could taste a hint of brandy. The contradiction of innocence and the independent streak he loved sent blood rushing to his cock.

He was so damn hard.

So damn desperate.

The need to consummate their union threatened to consume him. Him! A master of control and level-headedness! Except when he was with her. With her, he could be himself, could let down the barriers. He might have laughed had he not been obsessed with making love to her mouth.

Eva tore her lips from his to catch her breath. "Oh, it is so hot in here. Perhaps we should move away from the fire."

He might have suggested they remove their clothes, but he didn't want to frighten her, didn't want to press her too hard.

Indeed, he had to temper his inner flames before they over-whelmed him.

He knew lust, but not this all-consuming passion.

"Perhaps I should escort you home," he said, his erection jerking in protest, though he knew where their amorous inclinations would lead. "Before I end up throwing you over my shoulder and taking you to bed."

She laughed as she looked at him through inviting blue pools that made a man want to strip naked and plunge deep. "Things tend to get a little heated with us, do they not?"

"A little? Madam, the brigade would refuse to tackle the blaze."

"Some say lust is the devil's curse." Her eyes turned all soft and dreamy, her smile wistful. "I say lust is heavenly."

"So, you crave my body, Miss Dunn."

She hit him playfully on the arm and giggled. Hell. She was so damn irresistible when happy. "You know I find your mind just as stimulating."

Did she mean to use such a provocative word?

Did she mean to tease him to distraction?

"The feeling is mutual, hence the reason we're likely to lose our heads."

Lord, how he longed to see her lose control, longed to see her writhing in his lap, panting, shuddering as her climax ripped through her. He longed to see her hair wild and untamed, her lips moist and swollen, longed to have her clinging to him, urging him to thrust harder.

Blast. He had to cease with this mental torture.

"Let me escort you home," he said. Bower would be keeping watch in Brownlow Street, would report directly to Lucius Daventry. "Your problems are far from over. It's imperative we remain focused. There's plenty of time to explore our growing attraction."

And yet he couldn't help but slide his hand into her hair, draw her closer, steal one last kiss.

A sweet hum left her lips when they parted. "Lust is like an addiction."

"More a delightful obsession," he said, though he suspected

their feelings were more complicated than a hunger for physical release.

He collected her glove from the floor and watched her slip her fingers inside. The fact he found the action erotic came as no surprise. Indeed, the fact he didn't give a damn what Lucius Daventry thought was telling, too.

Once inside the dark confines of his carriage, his thoughts turned to seduction, to easing desire's deep ache. Anyone would think he was a boy of fifteen, not a mature man who should have a handle on his passions.

"I know you've been preoccupied of late," he said, attempting to focus on something other than the alluring smell of roses, "but if you could arrange for your footman to deliver the documents you mentioned, that would be helpful." Besides, he had to get his mind back on the case.

The lady sat forward and frowned. "But Henry brought them to you this morning. I gave him samples of Howard's and Mr Hemming's writing along with the blackmail note. He assured me he handed them to you in person. Indeed, I meant to mention it before our ... our interlude."

Such alarming news forced him to push memories of their kiss aside. "If Henry came to Hart Street this morning, he did not hand the documents to me." And Mrs Gunning would have mentioned taking receipt of important information.

"Oh." She sat back. "That is odd. Henry was adamant."

It seemed the lady was surrounded by deceitful scamps.

"Is this where you tell me Henry is a good person?"

She shrugged. "I've had no cause to doubt his word before."

No, because when her brother was too busy gambling away his inheritance, he had no reason to corrupt her staff.

"Perhaps your brother had other reasons for wanting Henry as his valet. Perhaps they had an arrangement, colluded together to extort money. Why else would the servant tell such a blatant lie?"

That said, they had worked for Mr Becker. When one's master indulged his cravings for wine and women, the servants were prone to lapses of morality, too.

A weary sigh escaped her. "The staff have been acting

strangely. They're more attentive. I assumed it had something to do with Howard taking the money, and their guilt over the intruder entering the house while they enjoyed supper."

Guilt undoubtedly formed the basis of their actions. "Then let us deal with the matter now. Tonight." He didn't like leaving her alone with servants who caused mischief. "Let me challenge Henry's account."

Miss Dunn fell silent before saying with some determination, "You may join me inside, Mr Ashwood, but I will be the one to challenge Henry's account."

Noah was unused to letting someone else take control. But he sensed her frustration, knew she had a point to prove.

"If that is what you want," he said, his tone conveying confidence in her ability.

"And I must ask that you do not intervene or overrule me."

"Madam, I shall be as quiet as a mouse." He didn't need to speak to be intimidating.

The carriage turned into Brownlow Street and rumbled to a halt outside Number 11. Noah became aware of Bower's presence long before he opened the carriage door and vaulted to the pavement.

Indeed, he glanced at the hulking figure sitting atop the box of a carriage parked further down from the hospital. Bower recognised him and tipped his hat, as did his companion. Daventry would hear about the late-night visit and make obvious assumptions.

But Lucius Daventry could go to hell.

Noah would help Miss Dunn with her problems and woe betide anyone who tried to stop him.

CHAPTER 11

THERE WAS a fundamental difference between men and women, Eva noted as she escorted Noah Ashwood into the drawing room and told him to help himself to a drink, though she only had port.

Indeed, having asked Bardsley to summon Henry from his room, she returned to find Mr Ashwood relaxing on the sofa like he hadn't a care in the world. One wondered if the man might close his eyes and take a nap. He offered a smile and gestured to the glass of port on the side table, the drink he had poured for her.

Was his mind not consumed with thoughts of their passionate kiss? Was his body not burning to strip away their clothes and indulge their desires? No? Was he not alarmed, disturbed by Henry's blatant lie? Apparently not.

"I didn't know you were a connoisseur of port wine," he said, raising his glass in salute.

"I'm not. Howard insists on the best. I cannot tell you how many times I've wanted to pull the stopper from the decanter and empty the contents over his head."

Mr Ashwood laughed. "What, and waste an extremely good vintage?"

Eva laughed, too. She liked having him in her private space. It didn't feel strange or awkward. Few men cared to hear a woman's opinion. Noah Ashwood was different. He possessed the rare quality of being so remarkably masculine without the arrogance and the desperate need to take control.

She liked that.

She liked him—more than she should.

The memory of his fingers threading into her hair, the memory of his hot mouth moving so expertly, sent tingles to her toes. Oh, lust was a dangerous devil, indeed.

Thankfully, a knock on the door brought an end to her amorous musings, banished all notions of her raising her skirts and sitting astride Mr Ashwood's solid thighs.

"Come," she called, though her voice revealed something of her torment.

Henry entered. He had dressed in a hurry and appeared a little dishevelled. "You sent for me, ma'am."

"Come in and close the door."

From her sharp tone, the servant knew something was amiss. He did as she bade him and then waited, hands clasped behind his back, for instruction.

Eva glanced at Mr Ashwood, who settled back into the plush cushions as if about to watch an entertaining drama at the playhouse.

"This morning I asked you to take important documents to Mr Ashwood's office in Hart Street," she said, focusing her attention on the footman.

"Yes, ma'am." Henry's pale complexion was a sure sign of his guilt.

"When I questioned you later, you explained that you handed the documents to him personally. That is what you said?"

The footman nodded and glanced at the gentleman lounging on the sofa.

"And yet you lied. You did not see Mr Ashwood this morning. And so I must conclude one of two things. Either you thought the letters had value and so kept them, or—"

"No, ma'am. As God is my witness, I didn't steal the letters." A green vein in Henry's temple bulged as he pleaded his case. "I didn't take them, I swear. I can't lose this position, ma'am."

Eva's foolish heart softened. She knew Henry supported an

ailing mother, and three siblings who still lived at home. But perhaps her compassionate nature was the cause of her mounting problems.

"It's either that," she continued, forcing an air of authority into her tone, "or someone prevented you from taking the documents to Mr Ashwood."

Indeed, perhaps Henry knew the note would lead Mr Ashwood to the blackmailer. Perhaps Howard was to blame, and he controlled matters from the shadows. She would kill the coward herself if that proved the case.

"So, which is it, Henry?" Eva pressed. "Did you steal the documents? Did someone else force you to part with crucial evidence? My brother was desperate to have you serve as his valet. Perhaps that's where your loyalty lies."

"No, ma'am. Mr Dunn wanted me for his valet so I could run his errands. I took money to a place in Rosemary Lane. A terrible place full of cutthroats and vicious thugs."

"The Compass Inn," Mr Ashwood offered from his seat. "You gave money to the Turners? How much?"

"Three hundred pounds, sir, though Mr Turner said he'd cut off my b—" Henry swallowed and took a quick breath. "Mr Turner will do me an injury if I don't return with the full amount."

Shame burned Eva's cheeks. While living in her house, Howard had been secretly manipulating her staff. Just because he was the older brother, that did not give him the right to do as he pleased.

"As I'm the mistress of this house, you should have told me."

"The master said I'd lose my position if I didn't do as he said."

"The master!" Anger flared. "My brother is not the master here. And I can assure you, if he is alive, he can find somewhere else to rest his lousy limbs. I want his things packed, his room emptied."

"Perhaps you should take a moment and have a sip of port," Mr Ashwood said calmly.

"Oh, thank you, sir," Henry blurted. "This whole business has left my nerves in tatters."

"I was speaking to your mistress, Henry. We can discuss settling your nerves once you've explained what happened to the documents entrusted to your care."

Henry seemed reluctant to speak. He pressed his lips together so tightly she doubted the Spanish Inquisition could part them.

"If you fail to offer an explanation, Henry," Eva said, "I shall be forced to let you go."

An inner conflict saw the man scratch his head, rub his neck and tug at his ear. Eventually, he said, "Kathleen was going out to run errands and said she would take them."

"Kathleen? You gave the letters to Kathleen?"

"Yes, ma'am. I know I shouldn't have, but the locksmith is coming tomorrow, and Bardsley said I'm to watch him like a hawk. It meant having to do more chores this morning."

"You've arranged to have the locks changed?" Mr Ashwood interjected.

She cast him a sidelong glance. He was so relaxed, so composed.

"It's a dreadful expense, but I thought it best."

"I agree." Mr Ashwood turned his attention to her footman, his countenance darkening dramatically. "Do not give your mistress cause to doubt your loyalty again."

"N-no, sir," came Henry's shaky reply.

"Now, I am sure Miss Dunn would like to speak to Kathleen as a matter of urgency. Might you be trusted to fetch her?"

Henry nodded, but then hesitated. He looked to Eva and waited for confirmation, an act that brought a satisfied smile to Mr Ashwood's tempting lips.

"You may leave," she said. "Inform Kathleen that I wish to speak to her at once. You're not to leave her alone, not for a second, but must escort her here yourself."

Henry bowed and left the room.

"Your brother has a lot to answer for," Mr Ashwood said. "I'm inclined to give him a thorough beating though I bet his skin is as thick as his skull."

"I don't care what you do as long as I never have to set eyes on him again." She stared at the man who had broken his pledge, though she was far from annoyed. "You said you would remain silent while I questioned the staff."

He gave a half shrug. "I did. It was my heart that jumped to your defence. This case will soon be over, and I'll not have you suffer for their foolishness again."

She might have teased him, joked that he had no heart, but the feeling behind the comment held her enchanted. Mr Ashwood cared. He intervened, not because it was the logical thing to do, but because his emotions were engaged. He certainly kissed her like he wanted to twine souls.

Hmm.

She considered asking him to spend the night.

But of course she couldn't.

Lust had robbed her of all reason. Yet her desire for him went beyond a physical need. Deeper affections were engaged. She cared for him, too, far too much.

"I'm not as weak as you think," she said, though everyone seemed to ride roughshod over her. That's what came from being a woman with a kind heart. Men took advantage.

"I don't think you're weak. We live in a world where men have power. Hemming and Benham seek to assert their authority. They've learnt to get what they want through manipulation and fear."

"Then you must think me foolish for continually placing myself in harm's way." So many times, she had wanted to punch Mr Hemming on the nose and curse him to the devil. "But an unmarried lady has to provide for herself."

"I have no concept of what it's like to deal with lecherous men while trying to make a living."

"It's like a recurring nightmare."

"It's easy for me. I can defend my honour, fight with swords or pistols, wrestle naked in the park at dawn. You're forced to endure the torment or take undesirable work."

It was a serious point, and yet one particular piece of information left her intrigued. "You've stripped off your clothes and wrestled naked in the park?"

"Clothes can be restrictive. As I'm sure you discovered tonight."

Oh, did he have to allude to their kiss?

Her raging pulse had only just settled.

"Why do you seek to tease me?"

"I'm not teasing you, Eva. You deserve honesty from a man." He smoothed his hand down his muscular thigh. "All night, I've wanted to slip that silk gown off your shoulders, slide it down over every sweet curve until it's a claret pool on the floor."

Mother Mary!

Eva drew in a deep breath, but it barely filled her lungs. Her gown felt too tight, a dreadful inconvenience.

"You wish to wrestle with me, too?"

Mr Ashwood's emerald eyes glazed. "In a fashion. I want to make love to you, Eva." His voice was hypnotic. "I want mine to be the name on your lips when you reach the height of your pleasure."

Good heavens!

He made sin sound divine.

"Isn't the nomad afraid the reality will fall short of the dream?"

"I believe he might be about to have his awakening. To be blunt, madam, this nomad wants to plunge into the pool and wallow in the waters."

A knock on the door broke the spell, though Eva's blood burned with a ferocity she struggled to contain.

"Come," she called, almost choking on the word.

Kathleen shuffled into the room, her clumsy gait a means to incite pity. The maid's mouth and shoulders sagged, but Eva felt nothing but the potent thrum of desire. The need for physical pleasure proved overwhelming. The heat pooling in her sex made it hard to stand still. Indeed, she considered telling Kathleen they would discuss the matter in the morning.

"I expect you want to know why I didn't deliver the letters to Hart Street, ma'am," Kathleen said, spoiling Eva's erotic fantasy. "I expect you'll dismiss me without a reference."

"I expect I will," Eva said sharply. No longer would she put other people's feelings before her own.

Shocked upon hearing the admission, Kathleen burst into tears.

It was another ploy to gain sympathy.

Eva waited for the maid to stop blubbering. She did not offer a comforting arm or a consolatory handkerchief. No. Her patience had worn thin. All she truly cared about was continuing the arousing conversation with Noah Ashwood.

"I burnt the letters," Kathleen said between wet sniffs. "I did it for love, ma'am."

Mr Ashwood's mocking snort was audible.

"For love?" Eva stiffened. An arctic wind swept through her, banishing all amorous thoughts of the virile gentleman on the sofa. "Please tell me you're not talking about my brother."

The tight knot in her chest said this had everything to do with Howard.

"People misunderstand him, ma'am."

Oh, for the love of God!

"Then I suggest you start at the beginning." Eva snatched the port wine glass off the side table and swallowed a mouthful. The rich liquid warmed her throat. "I suggest you start at the point where my brother seduced you."

Kathleen smoothed her golden hair from her face—Howard enjoyed corrupting the angelic types—and her eyes turned dreamy. "No one has ever spoken to me the way Howard does, ma'am. He's so kind, so responsible."

Was it possible for someone to be so misguided?

Compared to Kathleen, Mr Hemming seemed rational.

"Oh, he's responsible," Eva mocked, "responsible for causing a mountain of misery."

"I know you were upset when he took the money, ma'am, but—"

"I don't give a damn about the money," she snapped. "I care that he stole my mother's jewels. I care that he preys on innocent women. I'll never forgive him for that."

No. Howard Dunn was no longer her brother.

In truth, she hoped they never found him.

"But don't you see?" Kathleen pleaded. "He was just trying to make things right. He was heartbroken when Mr Becker died. Grief does strange things to a man."

Mr Ashwood's weary sigh breezed through the room. "Grief

made him gamble away every penny he owned?" Cynicism dripped from every word. "Grief made him abuse women and steal from his own kin?"

"Yes, sir, but he wished to make amends. That's why I couldn't take the letters to Hart Street. If Howard sent the blackmail note, it was because he was desperate."

"So you do think he sent it," Mr Ashwood countered.

Kathleen shrugged.

"But I checked the note against a copy of my brother's hand-writing." Eva had spent hours examining every flourish. Instinct said Howard was guilty. But try as she might, she could not ignore the stark differences. Howard wrote with the same flamboyant air he did most things. "Howard did not write the note. Or if he did, he wrote it under duress."

"That's what I'm trying to say, ma'am. Howard is in trouble."

One did not need to be a wise seer to determine that.

"Why else would he have made such a silly demand?" Kathleen continued.

"What silly demand?"

Kathleen squirmed. "I—I have a confession, ma'am, one that will make Bardsley take his foot to my behind. It's ... It's about the theft of your boots."

In the brief second of calm, Eva realised that emotions were highly volatile. A few ill-timed words could turn burning desire into violent rage.

"I swear, I shall take my own foot to your behind." Eva's cheeks flamed as she tried to control her temper. "Mr Ashwood's time is precious. There are poor people without means who should be making use of his skills. Every problem he attempts to solve leads him back to you." She shot the gentleman an apologetic look. "Forgive me."

"It is not your fault," he said tenderly.

"I'm sorry, ma'am, but it was a matter of life or death."

"So Howard Dunn is alive," Mr Ashwood stated calmly. "Other than one unreliable sighting, no one has heard from him in two weeks. I find it odd his clothes are still in the armoire."

Kathleen shrugged and started sniffling again. "A boy brought this last week, ma'am." She reached into her apron pocket and moved to hand Eva a crumpled note.

"Give it to Mr Ashwood. I haven't got my spectacles, and I'm so angry, I cannot focus."

Mr Ashwood leant forward and took the note. He read it twice.

"It's from Howard. He instructed Kathleen to take your boots and shoes, put them in a coal sack and drop them into the garden of Number 12. Apparently, he did not sell your mother's jewels but hid them in the heels of your boots."

"Hid them? But that's impossible." Eva considered the pretty topaz and cannetille necklace. "The heels are too shallow. The soles on some are too flimsy. And why would he do that when I might send them to the cobbler?"

"I agree. It makes no sense."

Silence descended.

Mr Ashwood rubbed his sculpted jaw while lost in thought.

Kathleen's snivelling continued.

Then another thought struck her. "You don't think Howard hid the jewels in the pair I sent to the cobbler?" An icy shiver shot from her neck to her navel. "You don't think he got into a fight when he tried to reclaim—"

"Don't torment yourself with stories," Mr Ashwood said. "From what I've heard of your brother, murder is the only sin of which he is ignorant." Mr Ashwood pushed to his feet. "Excuse me a moment. I need to check something in your brother's room."

And with that, the gentleman left them.

The question that had been dancing on Eva's lips for the last two minutes demanded an audience. "Are you with child? Is that why you risked everything to help him?"

Kathleen broke into a whimper. "I thought so, ma'am, but no."

"And you've had relations here, under my roof?"

A solemn nod was the maid's only reply.

Contempt for her brother surfaced.

Had it not been for Mr Becker's promise to her mother, Eva would be working in service. Ensconced in his villa in Italy, her father hadn't paid her allowance in years. Everything she owned was thanks to Mr Becker's generosity. Writing had been the answer to her misfortune, a chance to earn an income, be independent. But in the end, she was no different from Kathleen. A man with a mind for seduction had sought to control her, to spoil her prospects, too.

Mr Ashwood returned, dragging Eva out of her melancholy. He carried an old pair of boots that were in fashion long before the turn of the century. Perhaps Howard liked to think of himself as a dashing Cavalier.

"Did you find those in Howard's room?" Eva couldn't imagine Howard owning something so terribly *passé*.

"They were hidden behind his polished Hessians." Mr Ashwood reached into his own boot and withdrew a blade.

Kathleen gasped in fright.

Eva couldn't admire the gentleman more if she tried.

"The heel is loose." Mr Ashwood used the blade to wedge the heel from the sole. "The nails have been removed before." Indeed, the boot came apart in his hands.

Something shiny and beautiful, something that sparkled beneath the soft glow of candlelight, fell to the floor.

Mr Ashwood discarded the boot and scooped up the rose-cut diamond earrings. He crossed the room, captured Eva's hand and placed them gently into her palm.

"These belong to you," he said in the slow hypnotic way that teased her senses. "With luck, we'll find the other stolen items, too."

For a moment she couldn't breathe.

Finding the earrings brought happiness beyond measure. And yet it was the way Mr Ashwood held her hand—as if she were as delicate and as precious as her mother's diamond jewels—that made her eyes widen in wonder.

"You may leave, Kathleen," Eva said, though it was Mr Ashwood who commanded her full attention. She couldn't tear her gaze away. Her desire for the man had been simmering since their passionate kiss. Since his daring declaration.

The maid sobbed. "Leave the house, ma'am?"

"Return to your room tonight. We will discuss your employment tomorrow."

"Oh, thank you, ma'am. I swear—"

"Good night, Kathleen."

The maid hurried from the room, her loud sniffs echoing through the hall.

"Based on the note, we must assume your brother is alive and hiding from those who seek to do him harm." Noah Ashwood ran his finger slowly over the sparkling earrings nestled in her palm. "I believe your brother blabbed to one of his creditors, told them the gems were hidden in your boots to bide time."

"That's a logical assumption."

"It's perhaps the only logical thought I've had all evening."

"Your mind is distracted?"

A smile played at the corners of his mouth. "My mind has been preoccupied ever since you mentioned a poison that can kill a man in seconds."

Eva arched a brow. "You fear I might kill you, Mr Ashwood?"

"I've spent sleepless nights imagining all the ways you might." He stroked her cheek, his vibrant green eyes possessing a sensual glint that made her shiver. "But it's late. I should leave you."

And yet she sensed his hesitation.

Amid all this mess, she knew one thing with absolute certainty. She wanted Noah Ashwood in every wicked way. She wanted to see his clothes flung about the floor, wanted to mould her body to his, feel his heat searing her skin. She wanted to know what it was like to feel pleasure from a man's touch. Life was precarious. What if she never felt this way again?

And so she inhaled deeply and said, "Stay."

CHAPTER 12

STAY!

The word wrapped around his heart with the same steely grip it did his cock. It was a tempting invitation. A host of erotic images bombarded his mind. He wanted Evangeline Dunn. He wanted to consume her, claim her, drive deep into her sumptuous body. He wanted to care for her, protect her, which was the most worrying part of this whole affair.

And it would be an affair.

A wild, passionate affair.

No longer could he deny his craving.

But Bower would know he'd spent the night, would reveal all to Lucius Daventry in the morning. Noah supposed he could devise a stratagem, leave the house, enter the alley leading to Castle Street, clamber over the wall into the garden of Number 12. But he refused to sneak about like a randy young buck.

Sod Daventry. Noah had proved himself to the Order a hundred times or more. Despite his need to help victims of crime, he could not temper his feelings for Miss Dunn.

But appeasing Daventry wasn't his only problem. The maid's confession led him to believe the Turners were responsible for attacking Eva in the street. The only way to prove the theory was to visit the stench-filled Rosemary Lane—home of The Compass Inn.

But he would deal with the issue tomorrow.

"You must think me extremely forward," she said when he failed to reply, her body stiffening as if fighting the first stab of humiliation.

"On the contrary. It just occurred to me that I have been negligent during this investigation."

Her shoulders relaxed. "Negligent? You? That's absurd."

"Yes, shocking, I know. But I failed to examine a vital piece of evidence." It was a mistake he was about to rectify. "I should have conducted a thorough inspection of your thigh. It's an important factor I've overlooked."

She swallowed. "An extremely important factor."

Desire flowed through him like a fast-flowing river. He stared at her parted lips, at the rapid rise and fall of her breasts as her breathing raced.

"Perhaps such an intimate exploration calls for more comfortable surroundings," he suggested, although the angel on his shoulder sought to remind him of his duty. The devil reminded him that loving any woman brought nothing but pain. For the first time in his life, he listened to neither.

"Then we should retire to my bedchamber while the mood for work still compels you." Beneath her innocent demeanour was a seductress in the making.

"Be assured, I'm compelled to work *hard* this evening."

"Then we should not delay."

She captured his hand and pulled him towards the door. An excitable energy vibrated between their palms. Anticipation had his heart pounding, his cock throbbing.

Once inside her bedchamber, she released his hand.

"Close the door, Noah." She kicked off her slippers and placed them carefully in a box on her dressing table, along with the dainty diamond earrings she clutched in her hand.

He closed the door. The click of the key in the lock was like sweet music to his raging lust—the introduction to this intriguing sonata.

"Is it bright enough for you to make your observations?" she said, unstoppering the bottle of rosewater on the side table and dabbing the scent on her wrists.

A single lamp cast the room in a soft golden glow. Her porcelain skin would look pearlescent beneath the seductive lighting.

"I intend to study the evidence closely." He could barely keep his breathing even. "One lamp is sufficient."

She touched her fingers to her neck, moistening her lips as she stroked absently back and forth. "I expect you'll need me out of this gown, though I have no wish to disturb Kathleen. I usually bathe before bed, though it's too late to lug buckets."

He crossed the room and closed the gap between them. "Then allow me to play lady's maid. Allow me to remove your clothes and draw damp linen over every inch of your skin."

She smiled, though he sensed her nerves. "Is that before or after you make a study of my bare thigh?"

It occurred to him that he should be mindful of her situation. "Eva, you understand what will happen if I do any of those things? You understand how events will naturally unfold?"

"Yes," she panted, lust clearly holding her body in its tight grip, too. "We will make love, Mr Ashwood, though I ask that you do not raise your expectations. Inexperience hinders one's pleasure, I'm told."

Was that another tale she'd heard from her godfather?

He smiled. "I am already satisfied beyond measure, and we're still fully clothed. But yes, we will make love, Eva. I imagine it will be wild and deeply passionate, though you may stop proceedings at any time. You need only say the word."

Her bright blue gaze dropped to his mouth. "Then while I still have command of my senses, let me say that I have never wanted a man the way I want you."

The knowledge sent a rush of blood to his heart, despite having little to spare. "And I have never wanted anything as much as I want you."

She seemed pleased. "Perhaps you should kiss me."

"We are equals in this bedchamber, madam," he teased. "Perhaps you should kiss me." When she hesitated, he added, "Embrace the woman who indulges her pleasures. Know that I am entirely at your disposal."

With sudden confidence, she touched her palms to his chest,

smoothed her hands over every taut muscle as she pushed his coat off his shoulders. "I would like to undress you, sir. Will you indulge me that?"

Damn right, he would!

"Noah," he reminded her, shrugging out of the garment and throwing it to the floor. "Kiss me first, and then you may tear these clothes off my back."

The first tentative brush of her lips fed the flames that had been simmering since he entered Newberry's ballroom and caught sight of her through the crowd. The sweet taste of her, the unique taste that had him in a delightful quandary, rippled through his body in penetrating notes and musical waves.

If this was a sonata, the teasing sweep of their tongues was the exposition. Desire laid bare. Raw. Exposed. Their need to explore this profound connection being the main theme of the composition.

It came as no surprise that the first movement progressed quickly. The soft, temperate caresses exploded into a frantic rhythm, a need to delve deep into each other's mouths, to taste, to drink, to feast. Breathless pants filled the air. Groans of pleasure rang through the room—the tempo stimulating and highly erotic.

Eva tried to unbutton his waistcoat while still devouring his mouth. His lips were anchored firmly to hers as he tugged her skirts up to her waist, stroked her bare thigh, grasped her bottom.

He should slow things down, but he tore his mouth from hers, swung her around and tugged at the row of tiny red buttons. Impatience made him clumsy. One button tumbled to the floor and went skittering across the rug.

"I shall pay for any repairs."

Eva pulled at the neckline. "Just get me out of this dress, Noah."

Had they made love many times before, he might have simply unbuttoned his breeches, bent her over and thrust hard from behind while she gripped the bedpost and sang his name. Such was his insatiable need for this woman. But they were kindred spirits. Their joining amounted to more than satisfying lustful urges.

Instead, he worked on the buttons, untied the bow, and pushed the sleeves from her shoulders. He slid the silk down over the gentle flare of her hips, leaving a claret pool on the floor.

When free of her petticoat, he set to work on her stays. Anticipation built again as he imagined reaching around and cupping her breasts, teasing her nipples to peak.

But the lady had something else in mind.

Her stays had barely hit the floor when she turned on her heel and flew into his arms. The clash of their mouths tore a groan from his throat. Eva grabbed the edges of his waistcoat and ripped the damn thing open.

Hellfire!

The need to bury himself inside her warm body overwhelmed him. And so, with his lips fixed hard to hers, he lifted her off the floor and carried her to the luxurious canopy bed. The need to hear her cries of pleasure, the need to feel her shudder beneath his touch, reached fever-pitch as he lowered her down onto the mattress.

"I must examine your thigh before we go any further." He removed his cravat as efficiently as the king's valet and dragged it from his neck.

Dreamy eyes—eyes glazed with the need to experience the dazzling heights of her climax—looked up at him. "Should I not remove my shift first?"

The answer was no. Seeing her naked form sprawled on the bed would be his undoing.

"Eva, the urge to taste you intimately has taken possession of my mind." He dragged his linen shirt over his head and threw it somewhere behind him.

She drew in a sharp breath, seemed fascinated by his bare chest. "Your body is magnificent."

"You're magnificent." She was the epitome of sublime.

The minx reached up and grasped the waistband of his breeches. "Hurry. Let's be magnificent together."

Perhaps *she* deserved the moniker *Dauntless*. It took every ounce of courage she possessed to grip Noah's breeches and trail her fingers down to the solid bulge demanding her attention. Of course, she wasn't in her right mind. A wild wantonness had taken command of her senses. A divine madness as potent as any drug.

"Hell." Noah closed his eyes, and his head fell back.

Through his breeches, his manhood swelled beneath her rhythmic touch. Watching him proved addictive. Knowing she had the power to arouse him sent her confidence soaring.

"You're not as innocent as you seem, minx." His voice was a husky whisper.

"Oh, I am. But I learnt a thing or two when spying on my godfather and his mistress."

He covered her hand to stall her. "At this rate, I'll embarrass myself and spill in my breeches." But that didn't stop him guiding her hand over his solid erection. "What else did you learn?"

Oh, she wished she hadn't mentioned it now. But the feel of him—swollen against her palm—encouraged her to be bold. "That a lady needs ... needs stimulation, too."

He moistened his lips. "To their detriment, some men fail to consider their partner's pleasure."

"But you're not one of those men."

"You sound so sure."

"I doubt there's a selfish bone in your body."

"I'm being selfish now." A wicked grin formed as he gripped the hem of her shift and slid it slowly up to her knees. "I'm of a mind to take everything I want."

Eva held her breath. Cool air danced over her skin, yet her body burned.

Noah pushed the garment past her thighs. "I shall start by attending to your injury." The rakish gleam in his eyes faded the instant he noticed the bruise. "Mother of all saints!"

"Hush. The servants will hear you."

"Love, they're going to hear a damn sight more than a curse." He stared at the ugly mark—a palette of purple and blue and black. "I know you said it was a nasty bruise but—"

"No doubt it will fade in a week."

"Then I must conduct a thorough examination every night, at least for the foreseeable future."

"Yes, you must."

The thought of having him in her bed, again and again, left her giddy. Her heart felt light in Noah Ashwood's company. Light, yet as full and as engorged as his manhood.

"You might change your mind when we progress beyond me gaping at your marred thigh."

Yes, the shock of seeing her injury had stolen the urgency from their lovemaking. But there was a way to solve that problem.

Eva sat up. She gathered her shift and drew it over her head, took his hand and pulled him down on top of her as she collapsed back onto the mattress.

The feel of his warm skin pressed against hers was her undoing. She claimed his mouth in a savage kiss. A kiss that cried of unrestrained longing. A passionate, erotic kiss full of pants and groans—an act of possession. Their tongues were so deep in each other's mouths she shuddered from the pleasure.

They writhed on the bed. Noah eased between her legs, grinding against her sex while still wearing his breeches.

Eva dragged her mouth from his. "Undress. Undress quickly."

He straightened, took a moment to catch his breath, but did not strip off his clothes as expected. His gaze drifted over her naked body like the kiss of the sun's rays—hot, inviting, scorching her skin. There was something carnal about the way he drew his bottom lip between his teeth as he admired her form.

"I'll undress in a moment." He touched his fingers lightly to her abdomen, seemed to marvel in the softness before trailing down to her intimate place. "I want to pleasure you first."

She knew what he intended to do. Once, she had walked into the dining room to find Mr Becker's hand beneath his mistress' skirts while the woman bounced happily on the chair.

A bolt of pleasure anchored her to the bed when Noah began massaging her sex. Her aching nipples hardened. Her gasps seemed to excite him, every soft caress robbing him of breath, too.

"Do you like me touching you like this, Eva?"

"Like it? It's divine."

But then, just as the sweet coil inside wound tighter, he stopped his magical ministrations. The longing, the unsated desire, was almost too much to bear. But Noah Ashwood was a man whose thorough approach to work applied equally in the bedchamber.

He came forward, braced on muscular arms, and kissed her passionately on the mouth. The kiss fed her growing need for him. But then he moved again, pressing his lips to her neck, to her breasts, feasting on her nipples until she no longer cared who heard her desperate pleas.

"Don't stop." She arched her back, threaded her hands into his hair.

"I don't intend to."

He kissed her abdomen, the brush of his mouth like the faint tickle of a feather, kissed her bruised thigh, teased her legs open. Her sex was exposed, laid bare while those greedy green eyes grew heavy at the sight. And then he was kissing her there, making love to her with his mouth and tongue.

"Good Lord." Eva clutched the coverlet in her fists.

Each sweeping stroke, each divine suck and lick, drove her to the brink of something wonderful. Inside, the pressure became intense. The strange force slowly engulfed her until her world shattered.

"Noah!" She came apart crying his name, shuddering against his mouth.

He cupped her sex as the tremors subsided. "You were beautiful in your release, Eva."

His husky voice reached her in some faraway place. She opened her eyes and their gazes locked over her naked body, spread on the bed like a feast. No one had ever called her beautiful. "Even when thrashing about like a madwoman?"

"Even then."

The warm feeling in her sex journeyed northward, settling around her heart. She could live like this forever. Days spent writing and helping the needy. Nights spent locked in his passionate embrace.

A sudden thought tore a gasp from her throat. "*He nestled down into the sweet valley and drank God's dew*. You weren't referring to the countryside when you wrote that line. After your expert attentions this evening, the words take on an entirely new meaning."

Noah stood. He ran his tongue over the seam of his lips and sighed. "Tasting you was beyond heavenly."

Her sex pulsed in response. This man knew how to say all the right things. "Then remove your clothes and let's skip to the end of the poem."

With a look that made her core muscles clench, he tugged off his boots. "I have no intention of rushing. I intend to thrust slow and deep into your welcoming body."

Eva's breath caught in her throat.

He held her in his emerald gaze as he unbuttoned his breeches. "I should warn you, I'm so hard it might come as a shock."

It came as a huge shock.

A highly aroused shock.

Noah Ashwood stood naked, bathed in a candlelit glow. Shadows danced over every chiselled contour. His muscular thighs looked as strong and as powerful as a gladiatorial champion. The lean planes of his abdomen drew the eye to the tantalising trail of hair leading down to his jutting manhood—smooth and as hard as marble.

"You're not afraid?" he said with a teasing glint in his eyes as he stroked the length of his impressive erection.

"Afraid and excited."

"We don't have to do this now." He glanced at the door. "We don't have to do this at all."

A fierce panic surged to her chest at the thought of him leaving. Her heart ached to join with him. Complicated emotions were at play. Too complicated to understand while her body thrummed with need. She doubted she would feel this way about any man again, and she was hardly a girl in her first bloom.

"You cannot tease me with mouth-watering confectionary and then close the box."

He laughed. "You have the look of a woman who wants to devour every last one."

"With such delights on offer, a lady is bound to be greedy."

He climbed onto the bed, crawling over her with panther-like grace, stopping to kiss her breasts, to take her nipples into his warm mouth, to suck, to tease, to drive her insane.

"Open your legs, love."

She opened for him and took him between her thighs.

"You're certain you want this, Eva?" He came down on top of her, his manhood pressing against her intimately.

"I've never wanted anything more." Every inch of her body burned.

He rocked his hips, breaching her entrance. "Do you think you can handle my intrusion, Miss Dunn?" he said, reminding her of the words spoken at their first meeting.

"I welcome your intrusion with bated breath, sir." She ached for it, yearned for it.

The mischievous twinkle in his eyes became something more profound as he eased himself into her body. "Then know that I shall treasure this gift always."

His endearing words caused an intense flurry of emotion. The sensation of being stretched, of their bodies joining, fed a need so deep it almost brought her to tears.

"You can touch me, Eva."

"Yes," she whispered, releasing the coverlet. She knew what would happen the moment she set her hands to his bare skin.

He was so hot, so hard. Her fingers throbbed as she stroked his back, grabbed hold of his hips.

"I'll try not to hurt you."

"I trust you," she breathed, relishing the weight of him pressing her into the mattress.

He kissed her as he rocked slowly in and out of her body, made love to her mouth in the same cautious way, bridling his lust, curbing his passion.

"Is this the first time you've made love to a virgin?" she said, tearing her mouth from his.

"I don't want to cause you pain."

Eva cupped his cheek. "I doubt you ever could. Do what you need to so we may move past the awkward part. Do it now. Do it quickly." She gripped his hips, urged him to take the final plunge. "I need you inside me, inside me fully."

Noah sucked in a sharp breath and thrust hard. "Hell and the devil!" he cursed as he buried himself to the hilt.

Merciful heaven!

She was suddenly full, full with him. Noah Ashwood. It took a second to remember how to breathe. Yes, it was a little uncomfortable, but nowhere near as painful as she'd feared. A rush of raw emotion mingled with a wave of divine pleasure. The need to hold him there and never let go proved as powerful as the need to feel those delicious tingles.

"God, Eva, you make me so hard." He withdrew slowly, then eased into her body in one long searing thrust, branding her, claiming a right she could never give to another man.

"Tell me what you want, Noah." She wanted to hear his deepest desires. "Trust me. Tell me what you want to do."

"I want you. I want to ride you hard, love, until we're sweating and panting."

"Do it then."

He needed no further inducement to kiss her in the wild, rampant way that had them writhing on the bed in an erotic dance. He was everywhere—consuming every part of her body. His potent essence swirled in her head. His masterful tongue plundered her mouth. He angled his hips, rubbing against her sex as his rigid shaft slipped into her, into her again and again with such skill.

The pleasurable waves gathered momentum with each undulation, taking her closer to that idyllic shore. Paradise was but a few thrusts away. The lapping sounds of their lovemaking, the slapping of their sweat-coated bodies only heightened her arousal.

She bit into his shoulder to muffle her cry, inhaling the earthy scent of his skin, and came apart with a violent shudder.

And while he found his release on the soft swell of her abdomen and his guttural groan punctuated the air, while he kept his promise and washed every inch of her skin with damp linen, only one thought came to mind.

She was in love with Noah Ashwood.

CHAPTER 13

NOAH LEAPT out of bed the second the loud crash reached his ears. Thankfully, he'd struggled to sleep, his mind occupied with the beautiful dilemma stretched naked beside him.

"Eva, wake up." He shoved into his breeches and threw on his shirt. "Eva!"

Hair mussed—and looking utterly irresistible—the lady raised her head from the pillow and peered through sleepy eyes. "Noah? What is it?"

"I'm not sure, but something is wrong."

Something was dreadfully wrong. He knew it the moment he dashed out into the hall and the acrid smell reached his nostrils. He knew it before opening the door to Howard Dunn's chamber only to be knocked back by a burst of orange flames.

Bloody hell!

"Fire!" Noah slammed the door shut. "Fire!" He raced back to Eva's bedchamber and yanked the bell repeatedly.

"Fire?" Eva came up on her knees, her lush breasts stealing his attention.

"Quick. Get dressed. Run downstairs and wake the servants. We need water."

The sudden hammering on the front door only added to the panic.

"That will be Bower." He snatched the pitcher of water from

138

the washstand and scooped up her discarded petticoat. "Let him in. Get him to help haul the buckets."

Knowing he hadn't time to waste, Noah removed his shirt, doused the linen and the petticoat with water, splashed what remained over his arms and chest. Then he charged back to Howard Dunn's chamber and attempted to tackle the flames.

Black smoke rose from the coverlet, clinging to the ceiling, crawling this way and that like an evil spirit doing the devil's work. The angry crackle of the beast on the bed would soon become a wild roar.

Holding the sodden garment aloft, he sidled closer and threw it onto the bed, smothering the flames. Before the fire sucked the water from the garment, he threw his shirt on top to bide time.

Bower appeared, empty-handed. "Stone the crows!"

"Quick! Fetch water!" Noah barked, but Bower was already bounding downstairs.

Eva arrived next, her silk wrapper hugging her body, her warm brown hair in disarray. The veins in her neck beat a visible pulse. "Good Lord!" With a shaky hand, she thrust a bucket of water at him.

"Stay back." Noah snatched the pail and threw the contents over the bed. "There's glass on the floor."

"Glass?" She coughed, then covered her mouth with her hand.

Noah coughed, too. "Don't breathe in the fumes."

He shooed her out onto the landing just as Bower returned with a bucket, water sloshing over the rim and down the man's leg. Glass crunched under the weight of his booted steps as he raced into the room.

"My guess is someone stuffed the neck of a spirit bottle with material and set it alight," he said. "The villain must have thrown it through the window, though that would have been one hell of a feat during the day let alone in the dark."

Fear rose like bile in his chest.

Had he not stayed the night, the house might have been an inferno.

Eva clutched the edges of her wrapper, the horror of what

might have been evident in every pained frown line. "Someone did this ... did this deliberately?"

"Without a doubt. Bower's swift reaction meant he must have witnessed the crime." In his wisdom, Bower had chosen to tackle the fire, not the blackguard.

The man in question joined them on the landing, his chest heaving from exertion. "The fire ... the fire's out, sir." Bower's gaze drifted to Noah's bare chest. "L-lucky you got to it when you did."

God's teeth!

Come first light, Lucius Daventry would have Noah off the case. He'd be filling ink pots and sharpening nibs until next Michaelmas.

"Did you see who did this?" Noah said, ready to throttle the coward who would threaten the life of an innocent woman.

Henry and Bardsley came rushing up the dimly lit stairs, carrying pots full of water. Both servants sidled past Noah without daring to glance at his chest.

"Douse the bed," Noah instructed before turning back to Bower. "Well?"

The man pushed his black hair from his brow. "The blighter had a good aim, I can tell you that." Bower's voice was as deep as the scar cutting through his left eyebrow. "Mr Daventry sent Jonah to keep me company. Being the fastest on his feet, he gave chase."

Relief rushed through Noah's veins. Jonah would catch the felon, of that there was no doubt.

Eva held her wrapper tight across her chest. "Who would do such a thing? Those poor women in the hospital must be scared out of their wits."

Those poor women?

That was one of the things he admired about her. She thought of others first despite being terrified, too.

"I imagine it's a warning from one of your brother's creditors." Noah might have rubbed her arm in comforting strokes had Bower not been standing there staring. "Equally, Lord Benham knows he cannot beat me in a fight and might have sought the coward's way to exact his revenge."

"Lord Benham has many faults," Eva said, "but this is the work of a coward, not a gentleman."

Noah had to agree. There was something desperate about the action. Upon reflection, neither Manning nor the Turners would raze a house to the ground. Not when it meant lessening the chance of them recouping their funds. They would want Eva alive to use as a bargaining tool.

Her eyes suddenly widened. "You don't think this has anything to do with Mr Hemming? He can be quite childish when he doesn't get his way."

A man in love attacked his rival, not the object of his affection. That said, feelings of jealousy and betrayal were the devil's poison.

"It wasn't your publisher who caused the fire, ma'am," Bower said, drawing his thick arms to his chest so the servants could squeeze past and return to the kitchen with their pans. "He came here earlier, not long after you left for the ball. He hid in the entrance to the alley. Waited there for a time."

Noah cursed between clenched teeth. "How do you know it was her publisher?"

"Jonah identified him. He kept watch in Tavistock Street this afternoon."

"How long did Mr Hemming remain in the alley?" Eva's strained tone conveyed her anxiety.

"Half an hour, ma'am. He walked to the door a few times, but couldn't raise the courage to knock."

Eva lifted her chin. "Well, I suppose that's some consolation. Hopefully, he won't bother me a—"

A loud bang on the front door made her jump.

Her nerves must be strung as tight as a bow.

"That might be Jonah, sir."

Eva glanced over the bannister. "Who is it, Bardsley?"

It wasn't Jonah, but a matron from the hospital come to offer assistance. Eva hurried downstairs to reassure the woman who explained she'd sent a porter to alert a constable.

"Have you noticed any other suspicious activity tonight?" Noah asked Bower while Eva was out of earshot. "Something besides the fact I'm standing here in nothing but my breeches."

A flicker of a smile touched Bower's lips. "A penny boy brought a note. I have it here in my pocket, sir." He tapped his chest. "Mr Daventry told me to intercept anyone who came knocking."

"Is the note addressed to Miss Dunn?"

"Yes, sir. I'll give it to the lady when she returns."

Noah nodded despite itching to know the contents and the identity of the sender.

"The fiend who threw the bottle, was he on horseback or foot?" Noah said.

"Foot, sir. I thought he was heading to the hospital, but then he crossed the road and disappeared into the alley. Jonah got ready to follow him, but the blackguard suddenly leapt from the shadows and hurled the bottle at the window."

"Then he's done this before." Noah scratched his head. The crime bore the mark of a heartless devil. Someone who didn't care if an innocent woman and her servants perished in a blaze. "Few men would hit the target the first time."

"There are capable thugs for hire if one's brave enough to enter the belly of St Giles, sir."

The Turners employed just such men to carry out their evil threats. Yet every instinct said the scoundrels were not to blame.

"That's all for now," he said. "Give Miss Dunn the note and then find Jonah. I want to question the reprobate before a constable arrives."

"Yes, sir."

Bower hastened downstairs. Noah went to inspect Howard Dunn's bedchamber, mindful not to tread on the shards of glass. He tore the sodden sheets and blankets off the bed, made sure the mattress and frame were not kindling and about to burst into flames. And then set about performing another important task.

"Noah!" Eva's panicked voice echoed along the landing. She came charging into her brother's bedchamber wearing her spectacles. "Noah, I have something to show—" She stopped abruptly when she found him sitting on the floor amid wet blankets and Howard Dunn's ruined boots. "What on earth are you doing?"

He raised his hand and dangled a pretty topaz necklace. "I believe this is yours."

She gasped, her eyes more dazzling than any precious gem. "My mother's necklace! Heavens. I never thought to see it again." She dropped to her knees beside him, snatching it from his grasp before kissing him quickly on the mouth.

He couldn't take his eyes off her as she stared at the delicate gold scrollwork. Happiness radiated, oozed from every fibre of her being. Knots formed in his chest as he held out his hand and offered her the ruby brooch.

The gesture earned him another kiss.

God, he wished he'd found a host of sentimental treasures.

She removed her spectacles and slipped them into the pocket of her wrapper before scanning the damaged boots. "The floor looks like a cobbler's workbench. Howard will be furious."

"Why? When I've finished with him, he'll not walk again."

Her exuberant smile returned. "What made you search for the jewels amid all the commotion?"

Ah, now to the difficult part.

"It's not safe here," he said, his tone conveying the full gravity of the situation. "I need you to pack a valise. I need you to get dressed and leave with me. Now. Tonight."

"Leave?" Confusion marred her brow. "I'll not have the fiend drive me from my home. And where would I go? I had barely enough money to buy boots without withdrawing my invest—"

"You don't need money. I need to keep you close until the threat passes."

"Close?" The uncertainty in her eyes faded.

"Somewhere I know you'll be safe."

"Where?"

"Wigmore Street."

"Wigmore Street?" Her breathing quickened. "But people will talk."

"You don't give a hoot what people think."

"No, not about me. But I care what they say about you."

He laughed. "It cannot be worse than what they say already." He didn't want her to think it was an excuse to take liberties.

"You would have your own chamber. I could retire to my room in Hart Street if necessary."

She remained silent.

Panic rose in his chest. "It would be a temporary arrangement."

"I—I'm not sure I would cope."

"Being in unfamiliar territory? Or are you worried I might become as obsessed with you as Hemming is?" There. The truth was better out than left to fester within.

Eva shook her head and drew her mouth into a serious line. "I'm not sure you would understand." She gazed at the pretty necklace clutched in her hand.

"Help me understand."

A brief silence ensued.

"Do you know what it's like to feel powerless? To have one's world pulled from under one's feet, to have—" She stopped abruptly. "Forgive me. Of course you do."

He wished he didn't know. "You feel empty yet heavy at the same time. You blame yourself for being weak. Strive to ensure you never feel that way again."

"Yes," she whispered. "So many people take freedom for granted."

"But one must question if we're ever truly free. There is always someone to please. Someone to hold you to account."

A sad sigh breezed from her lips. "Although stressful, this last week has been wonderful, too. I don't want Howard to live here. I'm tired of pandering to his whims. I want to wake in the morning knowing the house is quiet, knowing the day will be pleasantly uneventful."

"Eva, I'm just asking you to stay with me for a few days."

"I know." She shook her head again and laughed.

"You can have the run of the house. I'll stay out of your way."

"And yet I want to spend every waking minute with you." She exhaled deeply. "Oh, I'm a muddled mess of contradictions."

"A beautiful mess."

As their gazes locked, he saw his own confusion staring back. He understood her anxiety. Distrust was a hard thing to conquer.

More so, when one had been abandoned by the one person meant to provide support.

Then it occurred to him that he could give her a gift. Another gem to raise a smile. He would need to keep his wits. There would be no room for errors.

"What if you stayed in Wigmore Street so we might work together on the case? You would be there in a professional capacity, not because you need protection."

Her eyes widened as she absorbed his words. "Work with you?"

"Indeed."

"Won't Mr Daventry object?"

Damn right, he would. "I shall smooth things with Lucius Daventry." The row would be unpleasant.

"You'd take me with you to The Compass Inn?"

Inwardly, he groaned. "If we both deem it necessary, yes."

Hopefully, it wouldn't come to that.

"And to Mr Flannery's establishment?"

"Yes," he said, fearing he may live to regret his decision. "It may provide creative inspiration."

A rush of excitement had her jigging about on her knees. "Then I agree. I shall stay in Wigmore Street until my problems are resolved." Her gaze drifted to his bare chest, and he heard his own hunger reflected in her soft sigh.

"You have something to show me?" he said, assuming she wished to reveal the contents of the penny boy's note she clutched in her hand.

"Oh, yes!" She thrust the letter at him. "It's another threat."

Noah took the paper and scanned the missive.

This time the blackmailer included a brief sample of the article he intended to publish in the broadsheets. The wording was meant to incite public outrage. A woman living so close to the Lying-In Hospital—a place where the vulnerable were open to scandal and corruption—was obsessed with penning tales of murder. Was that not grounds to have her committed to an asylum?

Noah glanced at Eva. "The blackmailer has grown desperate."

"Yes, but you know there are men in society who will cause uproar. Seek to have me committed."

"And yet you seem unafraid."

"There's little point worrying about something that is unlikely to occur." She touched his arm. "Tell me we will find the devil before he rouses a storm."

"We will find him and hold him accountable for his actions. You have my word."

"It shouldn't be too difficult now he's told us where he will be." She motioned to the letter. "Although clearly he has no clue how resourceful you are."

Intrigued, Noah continued reading.

The villain asked for a thousand pounds to be packed into a valise and taken to Temple Gardens. They were to arrive at the stroke of midnight, two days hence, and leave the valise at Fountain Court, near the ancient oak tree in Middle Temple.

"He's chosen the court because there are at least five points of entry."

Eva smiled. "Because he believes it will be impossible for you to cover every exit. So we know the blackmailer is not Lord Benham."

Logic said she was right, but he wanted to hear her opinion. "And why is that?"

"Because the viscount knows you have at least four capable men at your disposal if one includes Mr Daventry. My brother knows nothing of your background. He knows the area well and often assisted Mr Becker in his frequent trips to the library."

She was right.

Howard Dunn was the most likely suspect.

"What about Hemming?"

She shivered at the mere mention of the man's name. "He would never publish such a damning article, not when people would hold him equally accountable."

"Unless jealousy drives him to cause a rift between us. Maybe he presumes a scandal would bring an end to our betrothal."

They might have examined Mr Hemming's motive further had it not been for a cacophony of shouts and curses erupting in the hall.

Eva shot to her feet and hurried to the landing. "Come quickly. Bower has returned with Jonah." She darted into her bedchamber, returned seconds later without her mother's jewels.

Noah yanked open the door to Howard Dunn's armoire. He took a neatly folded shirt from the shelf—though it looked a little too small—and dragged it over his head before racing downstairs.

Bower had taken Jonah to the kitchen. He was easing the badly beaten fellow into a chair and barking orders at the cook to fetch water and clean linen.

Jonah sat slumped forward, his long brown hair hanging loose from its queue. A trail of blood and spittle dribbled from his mouth. He clutched his ribs, struggled to catch his breath.

"What happened?" Noah took hold of Jonah's chin and examined his bloody nose. "Thankfully, it's not broken." He took a damp square of linen from Bower and dabbed the blood from the angry gash to Jonah's upper lip.

Jonah winced. "I—I had him ... caught him down near ... near Coal Yard." He sucked in a sharp breath as Noah continued his ministrations.

"He had you, too, judging by the state of your face."

Jonah shook his head. "He ... he didn't do this." He took shallow, measured breaths while hugging his chest. "A bunch of gin swiggers gathered near ... near the Kings Arms Yard ... came to his aid."

Bloody drunken fools. Were it not for their mounting problems, Noah would return with Bower and teach them all a hard lesson.

"Did you learn anything before the attack?" Noah took a pot of salve from the cook and smoothed it over Jonah's bulging plum of an eye. "Did he say who hired him?"

Jonah hissed as the salve stung. "When the fight started, the devil bolted. I heard him shout that some ugly nabob had a score to settle."

"Lord Benham," came Eva's frustrated whisper. "He's the only ugly nabob I know."

Undoubtedly. The lord might be a gentleman, but he was also a coward.

A sudden commotion in the hall heralded the arrival of the constable.

They spent thirty minutes giving their account of the terrifying event. Noah mentioned his connection to the magistrate, Sir Malcolm, which had the constable racing off to round up his colleagues to search for the rowdy gin swiggers.

Eva left Bardsley with a list of instructions, boarding the broken window being of primary concern. Twice, Kathleen pestered her mistress about keeping her position. Twice, Eva explained that she was not of a mind to think about that now.

"I'll need to report to Mr Daventry when I leave here," Bower said with some reluctance. "He'll want a full account of what's happened."

"Then you must give him a full account."

Bower nodded. He helped Jonah to his feet, and they made to leave.

The men had reached the hall when Noah called, "Bower."

The burly watchman glanced back over his shoulder. "Yes, sir."

"Thank you. Had I not woken when I did, your swift actions would have undoubtedly saved our lives."

Bower gave a curt nod.

It suddenly occurred to Noah that he had sent McGuffey home. "Might you wait and convey me to Wigmore Street? Miss Dunn will accompany me, too, as it's not safe for her here."

"I'll bring the carriage to Miss Dunn's door, sir."

"We'll be ready to leave in five minutes. And when you speak to Daventry, tell him I'll meet him in Hart Street in the morning."

After his showdown with Lucius Daventry, Noah would be in a perfect mood to tackle the devious Lord Benham.

CHAPTER 14

TEETH BARED, Lucius Daventry braced his hands on the opposite side of the desk in the Hart Street study. "You're off the case!"

Noah's temper flared as fast as a firework at Vauxhall. "Like hell I am!" He shot out of his seat, his need to defend his position firing him into action.

"Cole will take responsibility for finding Miss Dunn's brother."

"No!"

"No?" Daventry straightened. "Must I remind you that men risk their lives to oust the truth? Do you want to hear the story of how I dragged my friend from the Thames, a knife protruding from his chest?"

It was a tragic tale, one Noah had heard umpteen times. One used to explain the need for rules and order. "There's no need. I am in full command of my faculties."

"Ha! You've had intimate relations with a client. Miss Dunn is currently residing in Wigmore Street so you may continue this affair."

No, Miss Dunn was currently seated across the hall in the drawing room, Daventry's wife for company, listening to every word.

"My relationship with Miss Dunn has nothing to do with the case."

He thought of the intimate breakfast they'd shared. How beautiful she looked with strawberry jam coating her lips. How he'd enjoyed licking them clean.

Daventry snorted. "It has everything to do with the case. You attacked Lord Benham. I had to drag the truth from Cole this morning. Of course, he defended you, insisted you were provoked."

"Benham is a vile creature. He's lucky I didn't throttle him to death." And if he laid a hand on Eva again, Noah would do more than strangle the bastard.

"You rarely lose your temper," Daventry challenged. "Does that not speak volumes? I imagine your actions had Benham hiring a thug from the rookeries to exact revenge. You might have died had Bower not witnessed the attack."

That was the crux of Daventry's anxiety.

Panic manifesting as anger.

"I've risked my life many times. I might have died when Mr Fellows threatened me with a loaded pistol in the bank vault." Although he had known Fellows hadn't the courage to shoot. "I might have died when that French smuggler sent me hurling into the Thames."

"Precisely my point. The risk to life is greater when an agent is distracted."

"I'm not distracted. I'm in—" Noah stopped abruptly.

What was he? In awe of the woman who had spent the morning plotting ways to catch her blackmailer? Infatuated by the woman whose delectable mouth banished his nightmares? Inflamed by the depth of her passion? Intrigued?

"I'm interested in her opinion," Noah finished. Perhaps now was the time to reveal his plans, speak of his promise. "So much so, I've asked her to assist me in finding her brother."

Daventry stared, open-mouthed. Aghast.

"I thought it would distract her mind from the fact she might have died last night, might have lost her home," Noah added.

"Once again, you prove my point." Daventry's voice was tight with disapproval. "You've lost your mind. I'll not have her death on my conscience. No. Cole will investigate and inform Miss Dunn of the outcome."

Noah squared his shoulders. "I've never failed you before. I don't intend to fail you ever. Trust my judgement. Allow me to work with Miss Dunn and bring an end to her problems."

"No."

Surely Daventry could make allowances. "You worked with your wife to solve the case of Atticus Atwood's journals, so I'm sure you know what I must do."

Noah wasn't sure what he would do. He could not turn his back on his friends and colleagues, could not abandon Eva, either.

Daventry folded his arms across his broad chest. "Do you think I wanted to put Sybil in that position?" His raised voice was sure to gain the ladies' attention. "Fetch my wife. She will tell you I did everything in my power to protect her. Hell, she spent a year thinking I despised her just so I could keep her safe."

And yet everything had worked out perfectly.

Noah had never seen a couple more in love.

"And if you could change the course of history, if you had to do what was deemed right, would you? Would you let Bower deal with Sybil's problems while you watch from the comfort of your armchair?"

The questions caught Lucius Daventry by surprise. He took a moment to reflect before saying, "It's different. I loved her."

The blunt reply left Noah questioning his own feelings.

He thought about Eva constantly. There was something special about her, something he'd been aware of from the beginning. The magnetic pull proved too powerful to ignore. He was distracted, possessive, obsessed. Damn it, there was every chance he was in love, too.

"Would you change anything?" Noah reiterated.

Daventry looked Noah in the eye. "I wouldn't change a damn thing."

"Now can you see my dilemma?"

A light knock on the door had a frustrated Lucius Daventry charging across the room.

Sybil Daventry stood in the hall, her smile as vibrant as her curly copper hair. "We couldn't help but hear parts of your conversation. May we come in?"

"I don't think—"

"Please."

"Very well." Lucius Daventry stepped back, his rigid countenance softening as he stared at his wife.

"Miss Dunn has something she wants to say." Sybil touched her husband's arm affectionately, and he inclined his head in response. "I think it's important."

Daventry closed the door behind them. He carried another chair from the corner of the room and invited both ladies to sit. Then he moved to stand to the right of the desk, his powerful presence commanding everyone's attention.

"Well, Miss Dunn?" Daventry said. "Do you wish to defend Mr Ashwood?"

Noah glanced at Eva. She sat as confidently as she did the first day they met. If she was intimidated by the master of the Order, it wasn't apparent. After what she had endured, most women would take to their chambers complaining of a megrim.

"Sir, a catalogue of terrifying events first brought me to Hart Street," she said, her voice calm like the gentle flow of water on a breezeless day. "I wasn't sure what to expect, wasn't sure if anyone would help me, but my situation had grown desperate."

"We work to bring peace to the lives of the tormented," Daventry replied proudly. "It's a dangerous calling, Miss Dunn, as you discovered firsthand last night."

"More dangerous than I might ever have imagined." The hint of sadness in her eyes touched Noah's heart. "I could have picked any agent to hear my case, but I chose Mr Ashwood because it was evident he commanded everyone's respect. You must agree, respect is earned, and so I concluded that he must be a man worthy of such great esteem. Yes?"

Daventry glanced at his wife and with some reluctance said, "Yes, Miss Dunn. My colleague is exceptionally good at what he does."

"And it is clear the men look to him in your absence," she pressed. "They seek his guidance, value his opinion."

"Yes."

"Because he makes responsible decisions."

"Yes, Miss Dunn. Get to the point."

"State your issue with Mr Ashwood acting as my agent." Eva arched a challenging brow. "Be blunt, sir. I welcome your honesty. Nothing you say could cause me the least offence."

A rush of pride filled Noah's chest, mingling with a far more compelling emotion. Eva Dunn was the most remarkable woman he'd ever met. A woman he adored.

"Very well, Miss Dunn," Daventry said, keen to rise to the challenge. "My issue is you've been intimate. Ashwood kissed you in front of your publisher. He told the devil you were betrothed. As a gentleman, I shall not delve into the reason he was half-naked in your house at a ridiculous hour of the morning."

Eva raised her chin. "What happens privately between two consenting individuals has no bearing here, sir."

Sybil Daventry pursed her lips to hide a smile.

"I beg to differ," Daventry countered. "A man loses focus when his mind is absorbed with other things. I'll not condone such actions when it puts people's lives at risk."

Eva glanced at Noah, her gaze drifting slowly over his face and body as if he were as delicious as a meringue sculpture at Gunter's. "You do Mr Ashwood a disservice. You mistake him for a weak man. If I trust him with my life, then so should you."

A lump formed in Noah's throat. The only person to defend him with such passion had long since passed. He'd not thought anyone could replace his grandfather in his affections —until now.

"It's more complicated than that," Daventry said.

"Then let me make my position clear." Eva rose gracefully from the chair and straightened her skirts. "Despite knowing of the trauma I face if left to deal with my problems alone, I will walk out of this house and never bother Mr Ashwood again."

What the devil?

Noah's pulse soared. He had grown more than attached to the woman who admired his poetry.

"I will happily do that," she continued, "if it means he can keep his position with the Order, if he can continue to help people in the remarkable way he has helped me."

Good Lord!

No one had ever fought for him before.

A wave of euphoria surged through his body, chasing away the dark shadows plaguing his heart. The need to round the desk, take the woman in his arms and kiss her senseless left him jittery, restless.

"My husband's position demands he place the lives of his men over personal needs," Sybil said in support of Lucius Daventry. "But I shall ask him to recall a time when we sat in a carriage with the Wycliffs under similar circumstances. You claimed the right to protect me, Lucius, refused to listen to reason."

"It's different," he repeated.

"No, it isn't. And so I must ask you the same question Damian Wycliff asked his wife."

"There is no need. I recall it verbatim."

Still, Sybil said, "Can you not see what is happening here?"

Lucius Daventry remained silent.

His wife stood and closed the gap between them. She whispered something in his ear, something that made him close his eyes and sigh with contentment.

Noah wanted to touch Eva in the tender way Daventry touched his wife. He wanted the world to know her value, to see her the way he did.

"You put forward a persuasive argument, Miss Dunn." Daventry released his wife, and she returned to her seat. "As did Finlay Cole when he insisted on fighting your corner."

"Are you saying I can continue to assist Miss Dunn?" Noah asked, relief bursting through him. He would have done anything to prevent her from walking away. "So, she may accompany me on this investigation?"

Daventry cleared his throat. "Yes, but you will keep me informed of every decision, will allow me to assist you myself should it prove necessary."

"Agreed." A slight apprehension surfaced, brought about by the desire to have Eva Dunn all to himself. "I intend to visit Lord

Benham this afternoon. I shall tell him we apprehended the villain who started the fire and attempt to gain a confession."

"No. When in this mood, you're likely to punch the viscount."

"We could go," Sybil said, gesturing to Eva.

Daventry's jaw firmed. "No."

"You can arrange for Lord Newberry to accompany us," Sybil persisted. "Tell him that if his friend reveals all he knows about Miss Dunn's brother and the attack on her house, we shall never remind Newberry of his illegal dealings again."

"It's not safe," Noah countered. Having witnessed the way Benham abused Eva, he would never ask her to sit in a room with the devil.

"Lucius, you're on excellent terms with Sir Malcolm Langley," Sybil said. "Have the magistrate accompany us."

"Langley is plotting to arrest Manning today and is otherwise engaged."

Noah's chest felt a little lighter knowing Manning would be behind bars. But the villain was influential enough to order an attack from a prison cell.

"We should all go," Eva said, though the tightness around her eyes revealed her anxiety. "Lord Newberry can advise his friend, and you may all wait in the drawing room while I speak to Lord Benham alone."

"Alone? No!" Noah snapped. Fear hammered in his chest. "I'm likely to kill him the next time he hurts you."

"Noah, the sooner this matter is resolved, the sooner we can sleep easy at night," Eva said, not caring she had used his given name in front of the Daventrys. "I believe Lord Benham knows more about the situation with Howard than he professes." She paused. "Perhaps I could go with Mr Cole. He is sure to approach the matter objectively."

While Noah reined in his chaotic thoughts, Daventry said, "Miss Dunn has a point. After his bravery at Waterloo, there isn't a peer alive who would cross Finlay Cole. And you know Cole would protect her with his life."

Noah couldn't argue against sound logic. But he should be the one to protect her. What if something happened and he had to live with the guilt, forever blaming himself? And yet Daventry was right. A wise man did not deal with a situation from a place of heightened emotion. Noah had to draw strength from the man beneath the fears and doubts. The part that was a stable, ever calming presence.

"Agreed," he said. "On the condition I can remain outside in the carriage." He refused to spend the time pacing back and forth, fearing the worst.

Daventry nodded. "Agreed. I shall pay a visit to Newberry and have him caution his friend. Make the arrangements with Cole, and we'll reconvene later today."

When the Daventrys made no move to leave, Noah said, "May I have a moment alone with Miss Dunn?" The need to reward her for her impassioned speech still burned fiercely within.

The Daventrys removed to the drawing room without passing comment and seemed just as keen to spend time alone.

Noah closed the door gently. He took a few seconds to slow his racing pulse before turning around to face the woman who held him spellbound.

Eva stood a few feet away, concern etched on her brow. "What is it?" She seemed confused. "Are you angry with Mr Daventry? I thought he was remarkably fair considering."

"Perhaps because you put forward a convincing argument." A new and unclaimed emotion trickled through his body like brandy on a winter's night, warm and deeply satisfying. "You made me sound like a saint."

She gave a half shrug. "You are to me. I meant every word."

"But you were wrong when you called me responsible." He'd let his desires control him, behaved like a young buck in the first throes of manhood. "Even now, while the Daventrys sit just beyond this door, I want to gather you in my arms and indulge my cravings."

With a glint of passion in her eyes, she stepped closer. She reached out and placed her hand on his waistcoat, trailed her fingers over the muscles in his abdomen.

She did not need to speak. The sound of her laboured

breathing proved so erotic he was hard before she came up on her toes and kissed him.

A stolen kiss, a forbidden kiss, should be chaste and quiet and quick. But the moment their mouths met, an excitable energy exploded around them. They kissed with intemperate urgency, their bodies melding together, their hands moving rampantly, tugging clothing, touching, caressing.

But the kiss was far from chaste. Hardly quiet.

It was wild and reckless. Utter madness. Their greedy moans must have echoed through the house. They knocked over a chair in a scramble to reach the desk. He pushed papers onto the floor to clear a space, settled his hands on her waist and lifted her onto the wooden surface.

Her skirts were bunched past her knees and he was wedged between her thighs before he broke for breath.

They stopped for a second, panting, gasping, so damn hungry for each other.

Eva devoured him with her eyes, a sensual smile forming. "Things may progress beyond a kiss."

"I hope so, as I shall die if you don't touch me."

She reached out and cupped the bulge straining against his breeches, massaged his erection with a few teasing strokes. "If we're caught in a clinch, Mr Daventry will do more than remove you from the case."

"At this present moment, I don't give a damn." He kissed her, drew her bottom lip between his teeth but resisted the urge to bite.

"Perhaps we might continue our display of mutual appreciation later this afternoon," she said, mischief dancing in her eyes. "In a place where we might express ourselves fully. After all, it is Wednesday."

While all he wanted was to strip off his clothes and make love to her on the desk, he said, "There is a secluded spot at the bottom of my garden. I'll arrange a picnic and bring a delightful book of poems by a gentleman you know."

"And I shall straddle your hard body while you read them."

The comment wrenched a growl from his throat. "Just one last kiss before we go."

"One last kiss," she breathed, tugging his waistcoat and pulling him closer.

And so he spent the next five minutes showing her the depth of his gratitude, tasting her passionately in a bid to satisfy the crippling ache.

CHAPTER 15

"FOR MY DAMN SAKE, just tell them what they want to know and let that be an end to the matter." Lord Newberry's frustrated demand reached Eva's ears as she waited with Mr Cole in the hall of Lord Benham's house in Portman Square.

The snooty butler remained as stiff as a statue beside them and made no apology for the obvious row.

"I'll not have them question me like a criminal in my own house," the viscount countered. "If you don't bloody well throw them out, I will."

"Someone attempted to murder Miss Dunn last night," came Lord Newberry's reply. "When they apprehended the villain, he named you as the devil who hired him. Daventry has already mentioned the matter to Sir Malcolm Langley. Look, I want these bastards off my back."

Mr Cole glared at the study door before glancing at Eva. "Brace yourself. If he refuses to see us, I'm liable to kick down the door."

This time the butler released a faint gasp.

Eva smiled despite Mr Cole's gruff countenance. "These are new boots, though I'm more than happy to help, and have a reasonably good aim."

The faintest flicker of amusement passed over Mr Cole's features. "It may mean being arrested by a constable."

"A travesty of justice I shall write about in any newspaper willing to publish the article. Indeed, I shall print pamphlets, stand in the street and thrust them at every passer-by."

Mr Cole considered her through narrow eyes. "Daventry said you came to Ashwood's defence with the same fiery passion."

"I'll not have Mr Ashwood demeaned when he deserves the opposite. I might have died last night had he not been there to save me."

"The fact he was there at such an early hour of—"

A shout from the drawing room brought their conversation to a halt.

"Do they know who I am?" Lord Benham yelled.

"These bastards don't care who you are," Lord Newberry countered. "They find your weakness and keep stabbing with their damn blades. Just tell them what you told me."

The loud bang and vile curse proved the last straw for Mr Cole. He stepped forward, ignoring the butler's protests, and barged into the room.

Eva hurried along behind.

"You may have nothing better to do with your time," Mr Cole barked, folding his muscular arms across his chest, "but I'm a busy man. I'm due at Bow Street in an hour to meet with Sir Malcolm. I'm sure he'll be interested to hear why I kept him waiting."

"Don't forget your appointment with Peel, sir," Eva added, her temper roused by the arrogant glare of both pompous lords. "You promised to explain that Lord Benham hired the thug who sought to raze my house to the ground."

In truth, there wasn't a magistrate in the land willing to prosecute a member of the peerage. Still, her comment ruffled Lord Benham's feathers.

"Do you think I would take myself to the depths of the devil's underbelly and pay a miscreant to do my bidding?" Lord Benham stared down his hooked nose. "Now get the hell out of my house."

Panicked, Lord Newberry tried to reason with his friend. "Just tell them about the last time you saw Howard Dunn, and that will be the end of the matter."

"Listen to your friend, Benham." Mr Cole's tone was as menacing as the look in his eyes. "Prove your innocence else I fear Ashwood will call you out for insulting his mother, and for the shocking way you treated Miss Dunn. I'm sure I don't need to remind you of his skill with a pistol."

Lord Benham gritted his teeth, though uncertainty flashed in his eyes.

Eva hurried forward. "Be assured, my lord, my brother is no longer welcome in my house. It is only a matter of time before someone beats him to death and throws his body in the Thames. But do I deserve to suffer because of his foolish actions?"

The viscount sneered. "You're not the only person suffering, Miss Dunn. Why should you sleep peacefully when someone else must forever hide in the shadows?"

Hypocrite!

"Had you won the bet, my lord, you would be guilty of sentencing me to the same fate. But I suppose you do not consider my life as important."

The viscount remained silent.

"Did you pay someone to attack Miss Dunn's home?" Mr Cole snapped. "Was your mind clouded with the need for vengeance?"

"I know you hate me," Eva blurted, unable to suppress the sudden rush of emotion. There had been too many problems to deal with of late. "But do you really wish me dead?"

A muscle twitched beneath the viscount's beady left eye. "I do not hate you, Miss Dunn. I'm simply unused to rejection."

Eva took another tentative step closer. "Please, my lord. They say a kindness bestowed is repaid tenfold. Tell me what you know about my brother."

"Just tell her!" Lord Newberry interjected. It was plain to see he had his own interests at heart.

Lord Benham shot his friend an irate glare before turning to Eva. "I did see him in Cockburns, but not on the night I mentioned. It was two weeks ago now."

Eva's blood boiled. Her brother was an utter buffoon. "He was still gambling despite his mounting debts?"

"Gambling with what pittance he had left in his pocket. The proprietor refused to extend his credit."

"And did you speak to him?" Eva asked.

Lord Benham marched to the side table and unstoppered a crystal decanter. "I left before he did, waited in the alley." He filled a goblet with brandy, swallowed the contents and hissed a breath. "Dunn sauntered past as if he hadn't a care in the world, while my sister—"

The viscount refilled his glass and emptied it just as quickly.

"Did you speak to him, my lord?"

"Speak to him?" the viscount mocked. "No, Miss Dunn, I dragged him into the alley and gave him the beating of his life."

Eva sucked in a sharp breath.

"Did you kill him?" Mr Cole asked, though he sounded almost resigned to the fact the viscount would not admit liability.

"When he said he would marry Clara if I paid his debts and gave him a handsome monthly allowance, I considered squeezing the last breath from his lungs." Lord Benham gave a hard, cold-eyed smile. "But two knife-wielding thugs approached. They took Howard Dunn along with my signet ring and purse. I've not seen or heard from him since. I imagine they fed his carcass to a pack of wild dogs in the fighting pits."

The knowledge brought a surge of bile to Eva's throat. Yes, she wanted nothing more to do with her brother. But to know he met such a grisly end, made her sick to her stomach.

"When was this?" Mr Cole asked, unperturbed by the news.

"As I said, two weeks ago." The viscount refilled his glass and swallowed his resentment for the third time. "So you see, why would I hire someone to hurt Miss Dunn when I'm convinced her brother is dead?"

But if Howard was dead, who sent the blackmail note? Who demanded Kathleen gather Eva's shoes and dump them in a coal sack? Who started the fire in her brother's bedchamber?

"Besides," the viscount continued, "Clara would never forgive me if something happened to Miss Dunn."

For a moment, Eva just stared. So, it was all well and good to make her his mistress but not murder her in her bed. This vile creature was unaware of his own hypocrisy. That said, he certainly seemed to care for his sister. So much so, at some point, Eva might hope for a reunion with her friend.

"Thank you," Eva forced herself to say, knowing she would have to deal with this man if she wanted to see Clara and the child. She turned to Mr Cole. "Is there anything more you wish to ask?"

Mr Cole studied the viscount through suspicious eyes and said, "I'd like a brief description of the kidnappers. But otherwise, no. I'm satisfied we've heard the truth."

"Very well," the lord countered and proceeded to divulge characteristics that might apply to hundreds of men from the rookeries. "Now, if you've quite finished, get the hell out of my house."

Lord Benham's butler seemed just as relieved as Eva when she stepped over the threshold and out onto Portman Square. She took a moment to draw a deep breath, though terrible images of savage dogs bombarded her mind.

"Do those in the criminal underworld really throw their enemies into the fighting pits?" she asked Mr Cole. Try as she might, she could not banish the gory visions from her head. "Are men really so barbaric?"

"Some men rule by fear and have—" Mr Cole began, but Noah's coachman waved to capture his attention. Mr Cole marched towards the carriage and said, "What is it, McGuffey?"

"It's Mr Ashwood, sir. He saw someone watching the carriage." McGuffey was a young man with a kind, moon-shaped face. "He said he saw the same fellow outside his house this morning and took off after the blighter."

"Took off?" Mr Cole firmed his jaw and scanned the street. "Where?"

"They ran towards Seymour Street, sir." McGuffey pointed ahead. "He chased the cove into the mews."

"Wait here, Miss Dunn." Mr Cole darted away a mere second after issuing the command.

Surely he didn't expect her to sit in the carriage when she

might help calm Noah's temper? Besides, the thought of sitting alone outside Lord Benham's house filled her with dread.

"I shall follow them, McGuffey." Eva raised the hem of her skirts and was already hurrying away when she called over her shoulder, "Park the carriage on Seymour Street and wait there."

When Eva arrived at the mews, Noah and Mr Cole were already walking back through the cobbled alley. There was no sign of the cove mentioned. She took one look at Noah and knew something was seriously amiss. He strode towards her, hands fisted at his sides, a murderous look in his eyes, a silent rage building. She would not be surprised if he suddenly charged towards her, sword raised, screaming a battle cry.

Sick with worry, she looked to Mr Cole. "Wh-what happened?"

"We have another call to make," came Mr Cole's grave reply. "I would suggest you remain in the carriage when we visit Duke Street, but I expect we will need your calming influence."

Noah remained eerily quiet. The muscles in his shoulders were tight and tense, and she doubted he could grit his teeth any harder.

"Who lives in Duke Street?"

"A dead man," Noah muttered, looking straight through her.

"Hawkridge," Mr Cole informed.

"The man you chased worked for your uncle?" Fearing the worst, she peered beyond Noah's broad shoulders. Deep down, she knew he would never take his grievance out on the man paid to spy. "Where is the fellow now?"

"He escaped through the alley into Berkeley Street." Mr Cole's strained voice brimmed with apprehension.

They returned to the carriage and Noah assisted Eva's ascent. His gentle hand on her back was so opposed to the anger radiating.

They barely spoke during the forty minutes it took McGuffey to navigate the mile and a half across town. Despite the many stops and starts as they journeyed through the bustling streets, nothing calmed Noah's temper.

"Assist Miss Dunn from the carriage, Cole," came Noah's

barked instruction as he vaulted to the pavement and marched towards the impressive facade of Number 5 Duke Street.

"Ashwood can appear rather brusque when in a temper," Mr Cole said, sounding almost friendly. "You must understand that his uncle has caused no end of trouble since inheriting the title."

Eva placed a comforting hand on Mr Cole's arm, and the man recoiled. "Sir, I know what it's like to suffer because of a bothersome family member. Nothing Mr Ashwood could say or do would change my good opinion of him."

Mr Cole gave a curt nod, and they moved to stand behind the gentleman hammering the brass knocker as if he wished to wake the dead.

A footman dressed in blue livery opened the door. His concerned frown became a welcoming smile, and he gazed at Mr Ashwood as if he were the prodigal son returned.

"I trust Hawkridge is at home."

"Yes, sir." The eager footman stepped back from the door and bid them entrance. "Knowles will announce you at once."

Noah patted the servant on the upper arm, and for the briefest moment his anger dissipated. "It's good to see you, William."

"Likewise, sir." The footman lowered his voice. "Things aren't the same here since his lordship's passing."

"No. My grandfather was such a lively fellow. I imagine the house feels empty without him."

"Terribly so, sir."

The grey-haired butler appeared, his proud bearing softening the moment he laid eyes on Noah. "Mr Ashwood." The older man's smile was blinding. "Good afternoon, sir."

"Good afternoon, Knowles. I'm here to see my uncle, though I should warn you the visit will be unpleasant."

Both servants seemed rather pleased at the prospect.

"You won't want tea then, sir," Knowles teased.

"Not unless you wish to see the best china smashed into a hundred pieces." Noah clasped the older man's shoulder and lowered his voice, "Now, I wish to save you both from bearing the brunt of your master's wrath, so we'll play the usual game."

Both men nodded.

A few seconds of silence ensued before Noah suddenly shouted, "Move out of my way! You'll let me in, else I shall take the damn door off its hinges."

"But, sir!" Knowles cried while William thumped the door and rattled the knocker. "Wait here! Let me see if the master is at home!"

"I know he's here. I want to see Hawkridge. Now!"

Knowles smiled and pointed to the study door. "Sir! You can't go in there. Not without an appointment."

A painfully thin lady with a solemn face appeared at the top of the stairs, though she made no attempt to control the situation.

Noah charged towards the door and marched into the room.

Mr Cole gestured for Eva to follow.

"What the devil do you mean barging in here like you own the house?" Lord Hawkridge slammed his hand on the desk and jumped from the chair in protest. "Knowles! Knowles! Call the constable!"

"Yes, call the damn constable." Fists clenched, Noah rounded the desk. "I have evidence my uncle has committed a crime."

The lord's eyes widened in shock as Noah grabbed the pompous oaf by his lapels and dragged him to the plush bergere chair near the hearth.

"Get your damn hands off me," Lord Hawkridge warned, though his outrage was but a flicker of a spark compared to Noah's roaring flame.

Noah threw his uncle into the seat. "I've just questioned your hired lackey, Eric Blighty. He admitted following me to Miss Dunn's house, spoke of a visit to Southwark last night."

Lord Hawkridge sneered, though his beady brown eyes shifted rapidly. "Blighty? I've never heard of the devil."

"I suppose you know nothing about him meeting a gang who work near the Wheatsheaf Brewery." Noah braced his hands on the arms of the chair and pressed closer to the quivering lord. "Nothing about him paying a thug to hurl a bottle through Miss Dunn's window."

Eva gasped upon hearing the news.

Lord Hawkridge hired the thug?

Why would the peer wish to harm her?

"I h-haven't the faintest clue what you're t-talking about," came the lord's stammering reply. "Like your father, you're a trouble starter who seeks to cause mischief."

Noah ground his teeth. "Every twitch and pained expression says you're lying."

"It won't be difficult to find the villain," Mr Cole said. "Peel's vow to tackle organised gangs is crucial to reform. And men like that are quick to blab if it means escaping the noose."

"You've overstepped the mark," Noah continued, poking his uncle in the chest. "Everyone knows you're bitter because I inherited the lion's share while you got nothing but the entailed property. That's the reason you've wasted years trying to prove I'm illegitimate, trying to persuade my grandfather to amend his will. But you could have killed an innocent woman. And for what? Out of spite? Because you would do anything to prevent me from marrying? Because you hope I die so you can claim everything I own?"

Lord Hawkridge found an ounce of courage from somewhere and said, "I'd rather die than have my brother's offspring take the title."

"Then you're in luck." Noah straightened. "I'll take that as an admission of guilt and so you'd best dust off your pistols. Only one of us will walk away the victor."

Eva gasped. "No! You'll not risk your life on my account."

"Daventry will cast you out of the Order," Mr Cole cautioned. "There is no honour in killing a man. You'll be forced to live abroad. Your name will carry eternal shame. That's not what your grandfather wanted. That's never been what you wanted."

Panic gripped Eva around the throat. "Please, don't do this. There must be another solution."

Noah turned on his uncle. "Why could you not simply sire an heir and be done with it? Why could you not look to fill the house with a brood of boys ready to take your place?"

"Do you not think I've tried?" The lord's words dripped with contempt. "I had the pick of the crop and chose the only damn woman in the *ton* who is barren. No wonder she came with a sizeable dowry."

Lord Hawkridge spoke as if his wife were a broodmare. No doubt, he wished to put the muzzle of a pistol to her head and pull the trigger, go hunting for a filly. Perhaps the woman with the saddest eyes Eva had ever seen, might wish for a quick end to her torment, too.

"That useless vessel will be the ruin of my family." Lord Hawkridge's features twisted in disdain. "That pathetic woman will be my damn downfall."

Eva couldn't bear to hear another derogatory word from this fool's lips. Thankfully, she didn't have to suffer another disparaging remark. Without warning, Noah drew his fist back and threw a punch that snapped his uncle's head sideways.

There was a stunned moment of silence before Lord Hawkridge cried out and clutched his jaw.

"That is for the insult shown to your wife, for speaking ill of her when in company." Noah drew his fist back again, and his uncle flinched. "I would wager you're the one who cannot sire an heir. Everything about you is rotten to the core. My father knew it to be true. My grandfather knew it, too."

Eva stepped forward. She curled her fingers around Noah's bulging bicep and eased his raised arm to his side. "All the more reason you should not waste your life exacting revenge. This ingrate isn't worth the time or trouble, and I pity the woman who has to suffer his vile condemnation."

The woman who deserved Eva's pity appeared like an apparition in the doorway. Her gaunt face and pale complexion spoke of months of sustained torment.

"Your father had the utmost respect for Mr Ashwood," the wraith-like figure said so quietly the words were barely audible. "Can we not welcome him as family and put this dreaded business behind us?"

Lord Hawkridge stared at the frail creature as if he wished to banish her back to the nether realm. "Remove yourself, madam. You have not been summoned."

The lady managed to rouse strength from somewhere. "Does

it matter which Ashwood bears the title? Does it matter if your nephew is the heir?"

Lord Hawkridge ground his teeth. "I'll not have the son of a wastrel take the seat." He jabbed his finger towards the door. "Now, why don't you go for a walk in the garden, my dear. With luck, you'll catch a chill and bring a speedy end to all my problems."

Eva held her temper, but it took a tremendous effort not to punch the lord. "Come, Mr Ashwood," she said, staring down her nose at the pathetic toad in the chair. "There is no point wasting your breath, and I refuse to let you risk your life for this worthless creature."

"Go to hell!" the lord retaliated. "And take that useless bint with you."

"Miss Dunn is right, Uncle," Noah countered. "A lead ball to the chest is too good for you. When you take your last breath, I pray the Lord delivers a fitting punishment. A humiliating end for the deplorable way you treat your wife." Noah tugged the cuffs of his coat. "In the meantime, I intend to ensure Peel is aware of your complicity. I intend to spend my waking hours ensuring every peer in the land knows of your cowardly misdeeds."

Noah did not give him a chance to reply. He captured Eva's elbow and led her out into the hall, ignoring the muttered curses emanating from the study.

Lady Hawkridge was already climbing the stairs, no doubt keen to remove herself from the whip of another vile tirade.

"Gertrude," Noah called.

The lady gripped the rail with bony fingers and glanced back over her shoulder. "I shall be fine, Mr Ashwood. Do not concern yourself with my predicament."

"You should not have to suffer like this. As you know, I own an estate in Gloucestershire. Say the word, and you may retire there at your earliest convenience."

Eva's heart swelled at his generosity. She might have fallen in love with him all over again were she not already besotted.

"That's extremely kind, sir, but I refuse to run from my

responsibilities." She turned and continued her solemn walk as if ascending the crude wooden steps to the gallows.

Knowles and William were waiting at the front door.

The butler thrust a wicker basket into Noah's arms and whispered, "Mrs Drysdale assembled a few items for you, sir. She knows how you love her almond cake and plum jam."

Noah's eyes shone with genuine affection. He asked Knowles to pass on his thanks, clutched the butler's shoulder and added, "Should Lady Hawkridge ever need assistance, send word to me in Wigmore Street."

Knowles nodded.

Noah cast a wistful glance along the hallway as they all departed.

They climbed into the carriage, travelled for a few minutes in silence until Eva said, "One cannot help but fear for Lady Hawkridge's mental state. Perhaps I could write to her, encourage her to accept your offer."

Noah sighed and brushed his hand through his hair. "Hawkridge won't let her leave. He needs someone to blame for his misgivings. I made the offer because I want her to know she has somewhere to go should the situation become unbearable."

"It's hard to believe you're from the same family," she replied.

"Why do you think my grandfather left me everything that wasn't entailed?"

No one spoke for a while, not until Mr Cole said, "When we return to Hart Street we need to update Daventry on our findings." He repeated what Lord Benham had told them about the last time he'd seen Howard.

"Very well," Noah replied. "We need to tell Daventry about the second blackmail note. And I need to visit the Turners." He gave Eva his full attention. "I pray they're responsible for kidnapping your brother, and not Manning."

"I don't think it matters either way." It was strange, but she had already resigned herself to the fact Howard was dead. A man could only dance with the devil so many times before getting burned.

"But the Turners can wait," Noah suddenly said. "Once I've updated Daventry, I have an appointment I cannot postpone."

"An appointment?" Eva feared he would return to Duke Street alone and seek to end the bitter feud with his uncle.

But the corners of Noah's lips curled in the sensual way that made her heart thunder and her muscles weak.

"It's Wednesday," he said. "I have something important to do." His sinful gaze swept over her body. "Something that cannot wait."

CHAPTER 16

THE ANGER SIMMERING in Noah's veins dissipated the moment he glimpsed Eva approaching on the garden path. It was six in the evening, and the sun shone while making its slow descent. The warm breeze ruffled his hair, blew away the bitter emotions that had plagued him since beating a confession from his uncle's lackey.

Despite the constant trickle of water from the fountain, he heard the crunch of Eva's footsteps on the gravel path as she passed through the willow tunnel. She appeared from between the fragrant pink rose bushes, her eyes bright, her smile dazzling.

"Well," she began, taking in the picnic laid out on the blanket. Her gaze drifted to the enclosed garden and the borders teeming with vibrant summer flowers. "This is certainly more private than the park."

"It's my sanctuary." A place where he came to relax and forget about the traumas of the day. "No one will disturb us out here. The topiary hedge prevents anyone from spying on us from the upper windows next door."

"I trust we have Mrs Drysdale to thank for the picnic."

"She liked to spoil me when I lived with my grandfather and has filled the basket with my favourite delicacies." Although nothing could surpass the sweet taste of Eva Dunn's lips. "And

I've brought a book of lewd poems should you wish to hear the words of a genius."

Eva arched a coy brow. "Are you attempting to seduce me, Mr Ashwood?"

He glanced at her plain grey dress, noted that her breasts were not as high or firm. "It seems you're in the mind for more than a picnic, Miss Dunn. Either that, or I need to dismiss the maid."

The temptress smoothed her hands from her breasts to her hips. "Stays are most inconvenient when frolicking in the garden."

Minx!

He gestured to the beautiful blooms that gave off the sweetest scent. A scent nowhere near as intoxicating as the smell of her skin. "Do you know the name of those roses?"

"No, but I can see you're dying to tell me."

"*Cuisse de Nymph* or Thigh of Nymph when translated." Indeed, the heads were soft and pink and pleasing to the eye.

"What a remarkable coincidence."

"So remarkable it's as if fate lured you here. What better place to continue my detailed examination?"

She glanced at the selection of food on the blanket—cured ham, chicken pie, almond cake and plum jam. "Are you hungry? Are we to eat before you make a thorough study of my thigh?"

"Hungry? I've been ravenous all day." He was more than ready to slip his tongue into her sex and feast. "But there's no rush. I like watching you eat. Observing you wrap your mouth around a juicy slice of pie might prove arousing."

"Then let us indulge our appetites." She glanced up at the cloudless sky. "There's no reason why we cannot remain out here for hours."

"No reason at all." He took her hand and guided her to the blue plaid blanket. "Don't be polite. Once you've tasted the pie, you'll be begging Mrs Drysdale to bake another."

She sat down, removed her boots and tucked her legs under her skirts. Noah offered her a choice of wine or lemonade.

"After the day we've had, wine will better settle my nerves."

Noah examined the bottle and laughed. "Knowles saw fit to slip a bottle of my grandfather's best burgundy into the basket."

"Will your uncle not dismiss him for theft when he notices?"

"Hawkridge doesn't waste time monitoring the wine cellar. And Gertrude is treated more like a scullery maid than the mistress of the house."

Hawkridge feared that if he left Gertrude to manage the household affairs, she would rob him blind and disappear into the night. Noah wished his uncle would banish his wife to the country where she might find some semblance of peace.

Noah removed the cork from the bottle and set the wine aside. He shrugged out of his coat, hung it on the low branch of the apple tree and sat on the blanket.

"Your uncle controls those around him with an iron fist." Eva took the china plate and held it in her lap. "You can feel the oppressive atmosphere the moment you enter the house."

Noah cut a slice of pie and placed it on her plate. "Things were so different when my grandfather was alive. The staff were happy. When he died, I offered them all positions in Wigmore Street, but Knowles' family have served every Lord Hawkridge for two hundred years."

"And he didn't want to be the one in a long, proud line to neglect his duty."

"No. The rest of the staff are loyal to Knowles. They're like a family."

Eva accepted a fork. She cut the pie and slipped a small piece into her mouth. "Mmm. Delicious." Her expression turned pensive as she swallowed the morsel. "I still don't know what to do about Kathleen. I cannot trust her, but Howard is so sly, so manipulative, I feel somewhat to blame."

Most people would cast the maid out without a thought, but Eva cared for those less blessed. Her inner beauty was the reason he found her so damn irresistible.

"No doubt your brother tempted Kathleen with dreams of a bright future." To a maid, the prospect of becoming a gentleman's mistress had some appeal. "I can give her a position at my estate in Gloucestershire if it eases your conscience."

Eva put her hand to her chest. "You would do that? For me?"

"Without hesitation."

For a heartbeat, maybe two, they stared into each other's eyes.

"I don't know what to say."

He smiled. "Say yes and let that be the end of the matter."

Again, she stared. "You have a way of solving all my problems. When I'm with you, I feel as if I could tackle the world."

He put down his plate and captured her hand. "When I'm with you, I feel an inner peace I never thought possible."

"It proves the point that beyond dark storm clouds the sun is still shining. Had Howard not behaved so abominably, I would not have come to Hart Street. I wouldn't have met you."

The thought left an empty void in his chest. "I'd like to think we would have met somewhere. At my publisher's office, perhaps. Oh, on the subject of Mr Lydford, he sent word he will meet with you on Friday."

"Friday?" Her look of delight faded almost instantly. "Maybe I should wait before meeting him. I fear I've lost the ability to commit words to paper."

When one's mind was diverted, it was impossible to be creative. And Eva had been plagued by a host of distractions of late. "You need inspiration, that is all."

"That's easy to say."

Yes, he knew what it was like to sit at a desk, fingers stained with ink, surrounded by a mound of crumpled paper.

"You could write about a maid who is manipulated by her employer's brother, and so she sets out to ruin him by clever means. Write a terrifying tale of consequences."

"A tale of consequences," she mused. The sudden flash in her eyes said he had piqued her interest. "Yes. It could be a lesson to all gentlemen that one should never underestimate a female opponent."

"Indeed." There were many ways to help unfortunate members of society. A poet or novelist had the perfect opportunity to enlighten the upper echelons. "If the message saves one poor maid from suffering Kathleen's experience, it will be worth the effort."

"You're right," she said, her countenance brightening. "What would I do without you?"

What would he do without her was more to the point.

The thought roused a deep-rooted insecurity. To have happiness snatched from one's grasp caused unbearable pain, tremendous heartache. Every instinct advised he learn from history. But if working with Cole had taught him anything, it was that a life spent living in the past was a life filled with bitterness. The need to help his friend break the tragic cycle was the reason he had insisted on Lady Adair playing chaperone.

"Hopefully, you'll never have to face that dilemma," he said in the lighthearted way that failed to reveal his innermost fears.

Indeed, he was suddenly captured by the beauty of the moment. The sweet smell of roses permeated the air. The verdant canopy offered an idyllic haven where a man might indulge his passions. The incredible woman seated next to him on the blanket roused a yearning he needed to satisfy. Satisfy now if she was willing.

"Shall I read a poem?" He took the green leather-bound book from beside the basket. "Is there one you prefer?"

She looked to his mouth and then into his eyes. "It's hard to choose. I find *The Path to Nirvana* quite intriguing."

Minx!

Did she have a full grasp of its meaning? he wondered.

"*The Path to Nirvana*," he repeated, thrilled by her choice. "What do you suppose it reveals about my innermost desires, Miss Dunn?"

She moistened her lips, bit down on the plump, pink flesh he was eager to suck. "My godfather said that the maiden riding the stallion to Nirvana is a metaphor for an intimate act."

Thomas Becker had gone down another notch in Noah's estimation, not because he was wrong. "And Mr Becker thought that an appropriate conversation to have with his charge?"

"Not at all." The breeze whipped loose strands of hair across her face, and she laughed as she brushed them back. "He read it to his mistress. I heard him say it was a poem about a path to heightened pleasure. A poem about ecstasy."

Fool!

"It is a poem about freedom. Freedom from constraints, yes. Strong men are happy to relinquish control. But Nirvana is a place free from worry and external pain." A place he'd longed to visit. Indeed, he had entered the gates of paradise when nestled between Eva Dunn's soft thighs.

She considered his words for a moment. "So, left without guidance, the stallion would simply stand in the meadow and eat the sweet grass. He would wander idly."

"Precisely." Oh, she understood him so well. "Instead, he is taken to paradise by the only maiden who knows the way."

Eva swallowed visibly. "The maiden rides without a saddle. She rides bareback."

"Because he trusts her, and longs for the intimate connection."

"She feels every hard muscle moving between her sweat-soaked thighs."

Hell! Eva knew exactly what to say to raise a reaction. "It takes a special maiden to command such power." He drew his gaze down her body, noted her erect nipples pushing against the simple sprig muslin. "It takes a woman like you, Eva."

She stroked the elegant column of her throat as if hot, parched. "This is an interesting conversation, though I have never been more aroused than I am at this moment."

Noah was aroused, too. His cock was so hard it was about to burst from his breeches. "Then ride me, love. Take me to Nirvana."

His provocative invitation brought a sensual glint to her eyes. "You believe I know the way?"

"I know you do."

She laughed. "Then hurry, make space." Her urgency was evident in every shallow breath.

She did not need to tell him twice.

In a mad flurry of activity, he wrapped the pie in the muslin cloth and placed it in the basket. An excitable energy charged the air as she handed him the slab of cake, quickly gathered the plates and made room on the blanket. He snatched the wine bottle, was about to force the cork into the neck when she grabbed the bottle from his hand and took a swig.

"Don't be shy," he teased, though he loved that she felt free enough to express herself. "May I have some?" She offered him the bottle, but he shook his head. "I want to drink from your mouth, Eva."

Her eyes widened. She shuffled closer, took another sip, came up on her knees and kissed him. The rich burgundy trickled into his mouth, but he was more intoxicated by her than he was the wine.

She pulled back, the seam of her lips stained red. "Would you care for more, Mr Ashwood?"

"You know damn well I would."

A growl rumbled in his throat. He slid his arm around her waist and pulled her to his body. There was no time for slow coaxing, for being gentle. With a surge of carnal lust, he penetrated her lips and mated with her mouth.

Hunger clawed at his insides.

Urgent. Restless.

Every sweep of her tongue hardened his cock. The need to lay her down and spread her wide consumed him. The urge to pleasure her, love her, threatened to destroy all rationale, too.

He tore his mouth from hers, snatched the wine bottle from her hand and took a large swig. And then he threw it to the ground and kissed her again. The rich wine mingled in their mouths, dripped down her chin. He licked every drop. He rained kisses along her jaw and throat until the fire inside became a raging inferno.

"Ride me, love," he panted. "I need to be inside you."

Breathless, and with eyes glazed with desire, she glanced at the blanket. "Tell me what to do. Show me how to please you."

Damn. Did she not know that simply being with her brought him untold pleasure? Did she not know that everything about her—her smile, her witty comments, her caring nature—drew him like a magnet?

Love filled his heart.

The feeling burst through his body with such force it left him desperate for their union.

"I shall lean against the apple tree, and you can sit astride me."

"Then hurry, Noah. What about our clothes?"

"We cannot undress here during the daylight." They could visit the secret garden on a night when the moon was a waning crescent, strip naked and indulge their fantasies.

Noah moved to sit on the grass, the trunk of the small tree providing support. Eva watched, open-mouthed, as he unbuttoned his breeches and drew his cock free.

A pleasurable sigh breezed from her lips as she bunched her skirts to her thighs and came to sit astride him.

"Take me into your body, love." Anticipation burned. "Claim me, Eva, as no one else can."

Her nerves only heightened the experience. While he took himself in hand and acted as guide, she lowered herself down slowly, so damn slowly they must have heard his groan in the house.

"Oh," she gasped as she sheathed him to the root.

God, she was divine.

While she sat looking enraptured by the feel of him, he reached up and pulled the pins from her hair. "Now you just need to find a rhythm."

She shook the silk tendrils loose so they cascaded over her shoulders. "Hmm. There's something thrilling about being in the garden." She seemed happy, carefree.

He cupped her nape and drew her mouth to his. The need to convey the emotion brimming in his heart resulted in a passionate kiss, the tantalising strokes of their tongues like sustenance for the soul. But then the minx began moving, rising like a siren of the sea, sliding down on his cock to claim him as her captive.

He reached under her skirts, gripped her bare buttocks with both hands, helped her to ride him hard.

"Touch me, Noah," she panted. "Ease this infernal ache."

With a firm hold of her buttocks, he found the right angle, the pressure needed to stimulate her sex. Merciful Lord! She was so damn wet, so damn hot and greedy. The sudden thought that he couldn't live without her bombarded his mind.

"When I visit The Compass Inn tonight, tell me you'll wait

179

here," he said before he lost the last logical thread of thought. "Tell me you'll wait. I need to know you're safe."

"I'll wait," she breathed, the canter becoming a frantic gallop.

"Can you feel every hard muscle between your sweat-soaked thighs, Eva?" His heart raced with thundering beats as she rode him closer to an idyllic paradise.

"Yes."

He released her buttocks, wrapped his arms around her waist and closed his mouth over her erect nipple, sucking it through the muslin. She came almost instantly, convulsing around him, milking him so hard he feared he wouldn't withdraw in time. It was utter madness, but he'd never felt more alive, never happier, never so free.

Indeed, he withdrew with seconds to spare, pumping his seed over her inner thigh. And while they caught their breath, and he fumbled in his coat pocket for a handkerchief, he knew, beyond a shadow of doubt, he was going to marry Eva Dunn. He was going to love this woman until the end of his days.

CHAPTER 17

THE COMPASS INN on Rosemary Lane was home to those who made a living from dishonest pursuits. Light-fingered boys who received their education on the prison hulk in Woolwich were adopted into nurseries of crime. They grew up to be equally immoral creatures who preyed on the weak, and so the perpetual cycle continued.

Few gentlemen ventured to this part of town at night. One could not walk a few feet without being accosted by vagrants begging for alms, or impoverished children scavenging for scraps. The filthy streets teemed with drunks and fraudsters and half-naked whores canny enough to steal a man's purse while pumping his cock.

It was one of the reasons Noah worked for Lucius Daventry. Giving a boy a penny today would not help fill his belly tomorrow. But the master of the Order had opened numerous schools to educate orphaned children, to at least give them hope of a brighter future.

Noah had instructed McGuffey to park the carriage near Tower Hill, a five-minute walk from the tavern, less if a man had to take to his heels and run.

"So, you plan to bribe the Turners?" Cole said, gripping the black walking cane that sheathed a swordstick.

"I plan to offer an inducement that might lead to information, yes," Noah said as they navigated the crowded street that resembled a vestibule of hell.

"You're going to pay Howard Dunn's debt," Cole stated with some disapproval.

What else was Noah supposed to do?

If by some miracle Howard Dunn was alive, his debts were so great he'd spend time in the Marshalsea. And despite Eva's protestations, he feared the fool would take advantage of her compassionate nature.

"I've information that might negate some of the debt," Noah said before pausing to tell a scantily clad bawd he had no interest in her wares. "But the need to bring an end to Eva's troubles is my only motivation."

Cole shook his head at the large-breasted woman, too. "Did I not warn you she would work her way under your skin?"

Noah's thoughts turned to the eager maiden who'd made love to him in the garden. "You make the feeling sound like an annoying itch. Yet it's more akin to a warm brandy flowing through one's veins."

"You're in love with her, then." Cole seemed so confident in the statement, he did not wait for a reply. "That complicates matters."

"I don't see how, but we will continue this conversation later."

They had reached the shabby doors of The Compass Inn. The chipped frame, cracked panes and the pungent smell of stale piss told a man what to expect beyond the dingy entrance. But despite the air of unruliness on the street, the mournful sound of a sailor's ballad echoed from within.

They were about to step inside when the doors of the rundown tavern burst open, forcing them to jump back.

"What the devil?" Noah complained.

"Clear out of the way, gov'nor," cried a scrawny chap pushing a lifeless body in a wheelbarrow. "Though I've room for another cadaver."

With more strength than he looked to have in his spindly arms, the miscreant pushed the barrow into the alley and returned seconds later with an empty cart.

Noah turned to Cole. "You know they'll take your sword-stick." The Turners employed a man to frisk every patron for weapons.

"Yes, but carrying a weapon sends a clear message."

"What, that we're not cowards?" Noah said.

"Precisely."

"Come. The sooner we get this business over with, the better."

Inside The Compass Inn, the atmosphere was subdued. The Turners ran their criminal operation with an iron fist. The small group of sailors and lightskirts seated around the crude wooden tables sat quietly sipping ale, listening to a one-armed man sing a maudlin ballad about a ship sunken in a storm.

Through the dim candlelight, Noah peered at the round table in the far corner of the room. The Turners were seated amid the swirling mist of smoke rising from their cheroots.

Another spindle-thin fellow blocked their path. The scar running from his forehead to his cheek said the man was more formidable than he looked.

"State your name and your business," the lout said as if he stood guard at St James' Palace.

"Noah Ashwood. I have an appointment."

A gentleman did not arrive at The Compass Inn without seeking permission. Thankfully, one of Daventry's men—an ex-sailor whose brother had served the Turners for years—had arranged the meeting.

The man glanced at Cole's cane. "Leave all weapons at the door," he said, lifting the lid of a wicker basket on the floor beside him.

Cole deposited his cane. Then he raised his arms and allowed the fellow to rummage in his pockets and slip his fingers into the tops of his boots. After giving Noah a good frisk, and once satis-fied they were not about to slit the brothers' throats, the man gestured for them to pass.

The journey to the table was like the walk to the defendant's dock. People glared at them like riled members of a jury, assuming their guilt. The Turners were waiting at the bench, ready to don their black caps and deliver the grim verdict.

"Ashwood, is it?" said the ugly brother with beady eyes and a high forehead, the one who looked like the snarling bull terrier sitting in the basket. "You've come to pay a debt, you say."

"I've come to enquire after the health of Mr Howard Dunn and to settle his account."

"We're not nursemaids," replied the brother with golden hair and angelic good looks—the one said to be doubly dangerous. He puffed on his cheroot. "What makes you think we know anything about the man's ailments?"

Cole cleared his throat. "Because the two men seated at the table closest to the hearth are the ones who stole Lord Benham's purse and signet ring. The same men who snatched Howard Dunn off the lord two weeks ago."

"No one has seen Howard Dunn since," Noah added. "I need to know what happened to him before I settle his debt."

The brothers' expressions darkened. So much so, the dog's ears pricked, and the animal bared his teeth. The ugly Turner silenced the beast, then whispered something to his brother. Muttered curses followed. The air turned volatile, as if the men were getting ready to whip up a storm.

Noah waited, his heart thundering in his chest. But these men had no respect for cowards. "I think it a fair request."

The angelic brother turned to Cole. "The lord who told you about his purse and signet ring, do you take him for a liar?"

"He had no reason to lie."

"So, it's as we thought," one Turner said cryptically.

The angel snapped his fingers at a burly man standing guard nearby. Then, quietly and calmly, three men rounded on the table near the hearth. Both suspected kidnappers were dragged to their feet and escorted through a door near the bar. At no time during the event did the crowd stop sipping their ale or the one-armed man stop singing.

"Let no one say the Turners suffer traitors." The ugly brother's sinister chuckle revealed a mouth filled with rotten teeth.

"Your men failed to mention they stole the purse and signet ring," Noah said, jumping to the obvious conclusion.

"It must 'ave slipped their minds the way that scheming toff slipped their grasp."

Noah gasped, though wasn't shocked. "Howard Dunn escaped?"

From the beginning, he'd suspected Eva's brother had sent the blackmail note. The devious devil must have secret lodgings somewhere. Indeed, why else would he have left all his clothes in Brownlow Street?

"Escaped, or the crafty beggar paid them buggers to let him go."

The dog's growl conveyed the Turners' annoyance.

"So, am I to understand you had nothing to do with stealing a sack of lady's shoes and boots?" Noah made sure not to mention the hidden gems lest the Turners send a man to Brownlow Street to have a good rummage.

"Shoes and boots?" The angel brushed a golden lock from his brow and laughed. "Do we look like common minstrels out to make a shilling?"

So, why would Howard Dunn write to Kathleen and tell her to steal the wrong boots? The visit to The Compass Inn was meant to bring clarity, yet Noah was as confused as ever.

"Rest assured," Noah said, trying to keep control of his temper, "when I find Howard Dunn I shall kill him myself."

"Then you might claim the reward."

"Reward?"

"We've put a price on his head."

Bloody hell!

Noah needed to bring an end to the Turners' involvement, not act as their lackey. "I'll pay Howard Dunn's debt now, on the condition you revoke the order and regard the matter settled."

The brothers glanced at each other, clearly suspicious.

"And why would you pay the debt of a man you want to kill?" came the expected challenge.

Noah wasn't ashamed to admit the truth. "Because I'm in love with his sister and want the rogue out of her life." It was the first time he had voiced his feelings aloud. The rush of panic didn't come. Everything about his declaration felt right.

"I've never met a woman worth a shilling," the golden-haired Turner mused. "Three thousand is a mighty debt to pay for a bit of skirt."

Noah might have mentioned the three hundred pounds Henry was supposed to have paid, but he knew not to chance his luck. "I'll give you two thousand, plus information that might save you a small fortune and protect your pride."

The brutish looking Turner snorted. "Do all fancy folk talk in riddles? Give us a clue to this information before we strike a deal."

As soon as Noah discovered Dunn owed the Turners a debt, he remembered his encounter at the docks. To the criminal fraternity, information was more precious than gold, and it helped to build trust.

"Your man is fighting le Diable next week," Noah said. "I know a secret about the Frenchman that will save you from suffering a crushing defeat."

This time the angel bared his teeth. "Then you'd better spill your guts. And you'd better not take us for fools."

Noah explained how he had captured a French smuggler whose passenger proved as interesting as the chests of tea and casks of brandy.

"Diable has an identical twin, one considerably less skilled. No doubt you will have witnessed the Frenchman's recent loss and weighed your fighter's odds against him."

Both brothers cursed.

Both brothers gritted their teeth.

"You need to prepare your man to fight the real Diable," Noah continued, "not the weak imitation. That, or you can attempt to locate the twins and take vengeance for their duplicity."

"Oh, we'll have vengeance all right," the brute said. "Make no mistake."

Noah reached into his coat pocket and withdrew the banknotes. "I have your word Howard Dunn fled, and you've not seen him since?" When the men nodded, Noah slapped the notes on the table and added, "To your knowledge, Dunn is still alive?"

Both men shrugged.

The ugly brother covered the notes with his gnarled hand. "I hear we're not the only ones out for blood, but this settles the debt."

"I have your word that's the end of the matter?"

"You have our word," they said in unison.

The pretty brother suddenly came to his feet, the loud scraping of the chair on the boards failing to capture the crowd's attention. "Let me see you to the door, Mr Ashwood."

Noah braced himself. A nervous tension thrummed in the air. The Turners were fair men, but vicious and unpredictable when in a temper.

They walked towards the door amid the mournful ballad that had the one-armed man weeping. The scrawny fellow keeping guard at the entrance raised the lid on the wicker basket and invited Cole to take his swordstick.

"The information about Diable," the pretty brother began, "it's worth more than a thousand pounds. Never let it be said the Turners don't show their gratitude. And so we're in your debt, Mr Ashwood." He gestured to the lean fellow with the terrible scar. "Send word to Wynn when you want to call it in."

"You trust my word regarding Diable?"

The brother gave a sinister grin. "You're not a fool. A lie to a Turner is like a death wish." And with that, he turned on his heel and sauntered back to his corner table.

Noah and Cole left the subdued crowd in the tavern and rejoined the recalcitrant mob on the streets. They spent the brief walk back to Tower Hill discussing what they knew about Howard Dunn.

"He has to be the one who sent the blackmail note," Noah said. Howard Dunn would wish he'd been captured by the Turners when Noah was finished with him. "And you're certain he has no friends who might have provided lodgings?"

"Quite certain. Most people gave him the cut when they learned he owed money to unscrupulous lenders."

"Then he is living somewhere in town. Somewhere close to Temple Gardens by my reckoning."

Thankfully, they reached the carriage without incident. Noah instructed McGuffey to take Cole to Golden Square before returning to Wigmore Street.

They sat in companionable silence as the carriage rumbled through the dim thoroughfares. Noah's thoughts turned to the enchanting woman waiting for him at home. The profound yearning made him think of Cole's plight.

"I know I insisted Lady Adair play chaperone," Noah began in a bid to gauge his friend's reaction, "but I'm surprised she made herself available at such short notice."

Cole was no fool. He could spot a poacher's trap hidden in the undergrowth from a hundred yards. "I presume she attends every major function. It would have been no hardship."

"I didn't mean to make things awkward, but knew she would assist you without question." One only had to spend a few minutes in a room with Sophia and Cole to feel the tension, the desperation, the suppressed passion in the air.

Cole turned and stared out of the window. "I've no desire to discuss my relationship with Sophia Adair." His voice held a steely edge. "The matter is closed. Done. One cannot alter the past."

And yet the past tormented him, ate away at his soul. As Cole's friend, Noah felt compelled to help him find peace.

Noah stared through the gloom. "You did nothing wrong. You were not to blame."

Cole released a sigh. "Sophia thought I was dead. She explained her reasons for marrying, and I respect them."

No. Deep down, he was still hurt, still bitter. "I'm not talking about Sophia." He was talking about the woman Cole married while still nursing a broken heart. "I'm talking about your wife. I'm talking about Hannah."

The atmosphere in the carriage changed instantly. Noah could feel the panic, could sense the crippling torment before Cole shot forward in the seat and rapped hard on the roof.

"I cannot do this now," Cole said as the carriage came crashing to a halt. "I shall meet you in Hart Street tomorrow as planned." And with that, Cole vaulted to the pavement, slammed the door and stalked off into the night.

Noah spent the rest of the journey struggling to know how to help his friend. Cole's grief had as much to do with his failings as it did the loss of his wife.

It was almost midnight by the time the carriage rolled up outside Noah's home on Wigmore Street. No doubt Eva was asleep, and yet his need to ease the insistent ache saw him approach her bedchamber.

The soft glow of candlelight crept through the gap beneath the door, sending his heart lurching. The splash of water reached his ears along with the melodic voice that drew him like a siren's song.

He knocked on the door. "Eva. May I come in?" The question had a sexual connotation, and he imagined driving deep into her welcoming body, banishing all his woes.

"Noah?"

"Yes."

"Yes, come in."

Excitement thrummed in his veins as he turned the door-knob and entered the room. The lady was lounging in a bathtub near the fire, her bare skin glistening in the light of the dancing flames. Her hair was tied loosely, teasing tendrils caressing the elegant column of her throat. Firm, round breasts bobbed in the water, dusky pink nipples peeking above the surface. Never had he seen a more alluring sight.

"I feel like a nomad stumbling upon a glistening oasis," he said. Indeed, his mouth was so damn dry. "Is it not a little late to bathe?"

"I wished to occupy myself while waiting for you. Would you care to slip into my water? It's still warm, and you look like you need something to relax those tight muscles."

There was a lightness in the air, a playful energy that soothed the soul and brought instant solace. He could get used to having her in his home. He could get used to this feeling of contentment.

"I don't want to disturb you."

She narrowed her gaze. "What happened at The Compass Inn?"

"By all accounts, your brother is alive." He hoped the information brought relief, though he couldn't help but experience some trepidation. "He escaped his kidnappers, though one wonders why he did not return home."

"Because Howard is the blackmailer," she said, rising out of the water like a goddess of the sea.

Water trickled over every inch of her skin, dripping from the delightful pink nipples he was eager to suck. He tried to ignore the purple bruise marring her thigh. Howard Dunn would pay for that, too, once Noah caught the blighter.

Eva slipped into her wrapper but did not tie the silk belt. She padded over to him, kissed him in the slow, open-mouthed way that conveyed abiding affection.

"Come. The water will ease the tension," she said, smoothing her hands over his tight shoulders. "We will worry about Howard tomorrow. When we catch him at Temple Gardens, I think we should take him to Sir Malcolm. A stint in the Marshalsea might teach my brother a lesson."

Noah might have challenged her opinion had she not begun to unbutton his waistcoat in the brazen way that sent his thoughts scattering. He might have questioned why a man drowning in debt would demand a measly thousand pounds.

But then Eva tugged his shirt from his breeches and ran her hand over his erection. And for the next two hours, he forgot anyone else in the world existed.

CHAPTER 18

IT WAS three in the afternoon when Henry arrived in Wigmore Street in a state of blind panic. Eva's footman could barely catch his breath as he stood in Noah's drawing room, shaking and clutching a note.

"Just take a moment," Eva said. The poor man's face glowed beetroot-red. Beads of sweat clung to his brow. "Did you run the whole way?" It must be nigh on two miles to Brownlow Street.

"Yes, ma'am," he panted, struggling to maintain the decorum expected from one's footman.

Noah strode to the row of decanters on the side table and splashed brandy into a crystal goblet. "Here, swallow this." He offered Henry the goblet and waited for him to down the contents before returning the glass to the tray.

The spirit calmed the footman. "Mr Hemming c-called, ma'am."

Hearing the devil's name chilled Eva's blood. "Yes, and what did he want?"

"He heard about the fire and came to offer his assistance."

Had suspicion for the arson attack not fallen on Lord Hawkridge, Eva might easily blame a coward like Mr Hemming for the dreadful deed.

"I told him you weren't at home, ma'am, but he barged into the house and insisted on waiting for your return."

The man was a damn menace. A veritable pest. "And where did he wait?"

Suspicion sparked. She would lay odds the publisher used the opportunity to search her study. He was obsessed with her stories, kept demanding to read her current work in progress.

"In the study, ma'am."

Conniving devil!

"Bardsley caught him rummaging through your desk and told him to leave," Henry continued, "but Mr Hemming got angry. He said he wasn't leaving until he'd spoken to you."

A hard lump formed in her throat. "Please tell me you didn't give him this address."

"Hemming won't dare approach my door," Noah said, confident in his assertion.

Henry shook his head. "Bardsley said you were staying with friends."

Eva sighed. "Mr Hemming knows I have no friends."

"Yes, ma'am. He started ranting and raving that an evil schemer had taken advantage of your good nature." Henry glanced at Noah. "No offence meant, sir. I'm just stating what the man said."

"None taken. Though I wonder if it occurred to you that Hemming might have followed you here."

"That's why I ran, sir. Mr Hemming wrote this note and asked me to deliver it to Miss Dunn." Henry stepped forward and handed Eva the note. "After seeing Mr Hemming's wild temper, Bardsley said to wait half an hour before leaving."

Eva shivered. It was as if Mr Hemming stood behind her, his icy fingers trailing down her spine. "You're certain he didn't follow you?"

"He did follow me, ma'am, that's why I ran. But I lost him in Queen Street by cutting through the warrens around Seven Dials."

Eva looked to Noah, who seemed unperturbed by the news. She donned her spectacles, broke the seal and took a moment to read the missive. A hollow pit opened in her stomach as she absorbed the words on the page. Good grief! The man had lost his mind. Madness had consumed his spirit and turned him into a blithering idiot.

"Thank you, Henry," she said, drowning in disbelief.

Noah knew something was amiss and so said to her footman, "Visit the kitchen and Cook will feed you. And have my butler, Kenning, give you the fare for a hackney ride home."

Henry bowed. "Thank you, sir. And may I ask what I should tell Mr Hemming if he returns?"

"Tell him you will call the constable the next time he forces his way into the house," Noah replied. "I shall have a man come to stay for a few days until we resolve the matter. You may go."

Henry bowed and left.

"Well?" Noah said. "What devilment is Hemming spouting now?"

Eva took a moment to compose herself before saying, "Unless I break our betrothal and marry Mr Hemming, he will file papers stating he writes under the pseudonym Cain Dunnavan. He intends to take ownership of my work."

"But that's absurd," Noah said, though he seemed remarkably calm. "It's just a ploy to get your attention. Once we've dealt with your brother tonight, we shall visit Mr Hemming. And when we meet Mr Lydford tomorrow, he will advise you on the best course of action to take."

Eva wished she had his confidence and composure. But she had experienced Mr Hemming's manipulative tactics firsthand. The man was obsessed with his own self-importance, felt he had a right of entitlement. He exploited others without conscience or shame.

"You have nothing to fear from Mr Hemming," Noah said, for he must have sensed her anxiety. He stood and offered his hand. "Come. We're due in Hart Street in an hour. When it comes to our rendezvous in Temple Gardens, Daventry will want to ensure the plan is flawless."

Eva slipped her hand into his, but his warm grip did not banish the sense of dread. No matter how much they planned, they could not predict every eventuality.

"Howard is an imbecile," she said, "but is desperate for

funds." Why else would her brother continue to hide in the shadows? "Bear in mind he is capable of anything."

Noah brought her hand to his lips and kissed her palm. "Don't worry about Howard. He won't hurt you. Besides, I have no intention of letting you out of my sight."

●

They arrived at Fountain Court from different directions long before the stroke of midnight. Eva, Noah and Mr Cole came by carriage and alighted on Bouverie Street, cutting through King's Bench Walk amid the formidable shadows of buildings occupying the hallowed ground. Mr Sloane and Mr D'Angelo arrived by wherry and had been instructed to pay the waterman to wait. Mr Daventry and Bower arrived via the narrow alley leading from The Strand.

Amid the shady walks and gloomy buildings surrounding Middle Temple, the small fountain burst from the flagged courtyard like an oasis deep in the desert. And yet the constant trickle of water brought no comfort, no lasting relief. Indeed, the eerie atmosphere only added to Eva's fear of impending danger.

They spent ten minutes waiting for everyone to arrive before depositing the valise near the ancient oak tree and taking their positions. Time ticked by slowly. The agonising wait was akin to teetering on a precipice, wondering when one might fall.

"What time is it?" she whispered as they hid near the steps between Fountain Court and the gardens.

The light breeze brought the fragrant smell of summer flowers—mignonette and chrysanthemums—though the sweet scent did nothing to alleviate her unease.

"There's no point pulling out my watch," Noah said, his gaze fixed on the leather valise.

Mr Cole had climbed the nearby post, blown out the lamp and plunged them into darkness.

"We're sure to hear a chime from somewhere," Noah added.

Soon, various bells across town chimed the midnight hour, the sounds echoing in the distance like a death knell. But they lacked synchronicity, and Eva struggled to keep count. Was it an omen? A warning that nothing flowed smoothly? Even the best-laid plans went awry.

"Hush," Noah whispered, though they had done nothing more than breathe.

They waited.

Seconds felt like minutes.

Minutes felt like hours.

The air thrummed with a choking tension.

What if Howard did something reckless?

What if he pulled a pistol and shot blindly in the dark?

But there was no time to feed her anxiety. The clip of booted steps on the flagstones cut through the stillness.

Merciful Mary!

"He's here," Noah mouthed, and then made a hand signal to Mr Daventry who hid near the opposite set of steps.

A figure appeared from the right, slinking through the shadows, avoiding the faint glow of the lamp in the courtyard. The man moved stealthily. His shifty nature marked him as the blackmailer come to collect his prize. Indeed, he stopped near the tree and gaped at the brown leather bag.

"Wait until he picks it up and walks away," Mr Cole whispered.

Eva's heartbeat thumped loudly in her ears. Every muscle in her body was ready to charge at the wastrel and knock sense into his thick skull. Yet this lean figure lacked her brother's confident bearing. His gait lacked the arrogance of one who believed himself above mere mortals.

The fellow glanced left and right in the gloom before crouching down beside the bag and unbuckling the straps. After a quick ferret inside, he scooped the bag into his arms, took to his heels and bolted.

The small courtyard erupted into a hive of activity. Shouts and barked orders flew like arrows through the darkness, hitting their targets. Mr Sloane appeared and gave chase as the mystery blackmailer darted through an alley to the left.

Everyone followed suit, except for Mr Daventry who cried that he would trap the villain in the next courtyard.

"I don't think it's Howard," Eva panted, gripping Noah's

hand. She had to yank her skirts past her calves to keep his fast pace. "Howard has a certain way of walking, lofty and dandified."

"A man doesn't care about such things when darting about like a frightened rabbit."

"It's not Howard," she repeated. The fleeing silhouette did not look like Mr Hemming, either.

"Whoever he is, he's fast on his feet," Mr Cole panted as their quarry headed along Middle Temple Lane.

Eva had thought the blackmailer was remarkably clever for choosing the Temple as the meeting ground, though she realised her error when the fool ran into a dead end. Still, that didn't stop him from attempting to climb the brick wall. In his desperation to escape, he was forced to drop the valise.

Noah released her hand and sprinted forward. He grabbed the fiend by the back of his coat and pulled him to the ground.

"Argh! Get off m-me," the fiend cried as a mad scuffle ensued. "Let me go!"

Noah pulled the fool to his feet and drew his arm back, ready to launch his fist.

"W-wait!" the man cried, covering his face with his hands. "I —I can explain."

The moment Eva heard the stutter, she knew the blackmail-er's identity. "Mr Smith?"

Noah released the clerk and took a moment to study the man's face. "Smith? What the devil?"

"I'm s-sorry," he said, squinting as he scanned the ground for his lost spectacles.

Eva picked up the clerk's eyeglasses and straightened the wires before handing them to him.

"Th-thank you, Miss Dunn." The clerk put on his spectacles and then stumbled in terror upon witnessing six capable men glaring back at him.

"We demand an explanation!" Noah snapped, his temper barely contained.

Cornered, the clerk had no option but to comply. "And you sh-shall have one if you give me a minute to catch my breath."

Noah folded his arms across his chest. "Well?"

Eva stepped forward. The young man was sure to find her

less intimidating. "Does Mr Hemming know you're blackmailing me?" Perhaps the publisher had sent his clerk to do his dirty deeds. "Does he know you arranged this meeting tonight?"

The clerk hung his head. "No, Miss Dunn."

Noah turned on his heel and muttered a curse.

"You're entirely to blame?" she asked incredulously. "You don't strike me as the sort of man who would threaten a lady so cruelly. Have you no conscience?"

Mr Smith let out a whimper. "I—I was desperate, Miss Dunn. Y-you don't know what it's like working with Mr Hemming. It's only a matter of time before I lose my position."

"Oh, spare me your pitiful tale," Noah mocked. "You're a liar and a thief and deserve the worst kind of punishment."

"Wait a moment," Eva said before Noah dragged the fellow to the nearest police office. "Why would you lose your position? Does it have to do with me parting ways with Mr Hemming?" Surely not. The man published other notable works and made more than a reasonable living.

Mr Smith shook his head. "No, Miss Dunn. He's lost his mind. If he's not for Bedlam, he'll be for the hangman's noose."

The hangman's noose?

Mr Hemming was a little unstable, but not to that extent. "Mr Smith, if this is a ploy to incite pity, it won't work. Either explain yourself properly, or I shall walk away, and you may deal with Mr Ashwood."

Noah bared his teeth and growled.

"You sent the first blackmail note before I terminated my contract with Mr Hemming," she continued. "You sent it before that dreadful night, the night you witnessed the violent scene in his office."

Eva felt the heat of Noah's penetrating stare. She had failed to convey the force Mr Hemming had used to pin her against the bookcase.

The clerk dragged his hand down his face. "Mr Hemming will kill me if I tell you."

"And I will kill you if you don't," Noah countered.

Silence ensued, but eventually Mr Smith said, "Mr H-Hemming made me write the first blackmail note."

"I see." Eva wasn't surprised. "Was it a ploy to lure me to his office?" It's what she had first suspected.

The clerk took to wringing his hands. "It's more complicated. There's more—"

"Stop dithering and come to the bloody point!" Noah barked. He inhaled deeply before turning to Eva. "Forgive me. If he doesn't spill his guts soon, I'm likely to throttle him."

The comment whipped Mr Smith into a panic. "It all started the night your brother came to the office, miss," he gabbled.

"My brother went to see Mr Hemming?"

"We were working late, until the early hours. Mr Dunn arrived in a terrible state. Blood oozed from a cut above his eye, and it looked like his nose was broken."

"No doubt from the beating he'd had off Benham," Noah said.

"Or from the Turners' men," Mr Cole added.

"He'd come to see if he could borrow money. That's when he told Mr Hemming about his troubles. That's when they came up with their cruel plan."

Cruel plan?

For a moment, Eva's world stopped spinning.

A sudden bout of nausea made her want to heave.

What had she done to deserve such vile treatment?

"What sort of pl—" Her voice broke on the last word.

Noah placed his hand at the small of her back. The comforting gesture gave her the confidence to continue.

"What sort of plan?" she repeated.

The clerk glanced warily at the group of men surrounding him. "Mr H-Hemming would keep your brother safe from the vicious thugs who were after him and get you to withdraw money from the bank to help pay his debts."

Oh, the sly scoundrels!

"And what would Mr Hemming get in return?" she said, though it seemed fairly obvious now.

"Mr Dunn gave his permission for you to wed Mr H-Hemming and agreed to put an announcement in *The Times*."

Eva snorted. "My brother does not decide who I marry."

"Once you were wed, and Mr Hemming had control, he

promised to settle your brother's debts in full. In the meantime, they arranged to frighten you into submission. The plan was you'd come running to Mr H-Hemming, desperate for his help."

What had once seemed like the worst of storms, terrifying and impossible to navigate, now appeared as nothing more than a light shower. Two pathetic individuals, two weak men who hadn't an ounce of common sense between them, had sought to use her for their own gain.

"When you say frighten me, I assume they arranged for Kathleen to steal my shoes and boots." Lord, that meant they had hired the monster to attack her in the street.

"They read about the murder of your cobbler and had the idea. Mr Dunn said he could get the maid to do his bidding."

Eva fell silent, consumed by the depth of their deception.

So, the night she had turned to Mr Hemming for help—the night he touched her inappropriately—he was already plotting and scheming with her brother.

Noah cleared his throat. "That doesn't explain why you've come to claim the bounty. Nor does it explain why Mr Hemming has no notion you're here."

"Because Smith wrote the second note without their knowledge," Mr Daventry surmised. "He was going to take the money and run."

"I had no choice." The clerk was overcome with panic again. "Mr Hemming has lost his mind, Miss Dunn. It all started the day you came to the office with Mr Ashwood. And he's not been right since."

She should have known Mr Hemming would seek revenge. "Mr Hemming lost control of his faculties long ago," she said.

"Not like this, miss. Mr Hemming was in a devil of a temper. He wanted your brother to help kidnap you and force you into marriage, but Mr Dunn refused when he heard you were betrothed to Mr Ashwood."

Was it too much to hope that Howard cared, that he sought her happiness? Of course it was! She was not that naive. "Probably because he thought Mr Ashwood the better option when it comes to borrowing funds."

"Then he's a fool if he believes I'd give him a damn penny,"

Noah said. "I'd put him on a ship bound for the Americas before I'd fund his gambling habit."

If only that were possible. She would certainly sleep easier at night knowing her brother was thousands of miles away.

"So, where is my brother now? You must have some inkling as to where he is staying." And why hadn't he come home?

The clerk started shaking, shaking uncontrollably. "I—I had nothing to do with it, Miss Dunn."

Impatience saw Noah grab the man by his lapels. "Just tell us what the hell happened!"

"They argued, and then—" The clerk struggled to catch his breath. "Then Mr Hemming hit Mr Dunn on the head with a paperweight."

The information tore a gasp from Eva's throat. She started shaking, too. "Good heavens! Is he dead?"

Part of her wanted the clerk to say yes. Did she not deserve some peace? Part of her hoped the answer was no. Would she not always blame herself for not dealing with Mr Hemming sooner?

"No, he's not dead. Mr Hemming is keeping him prisoner." Mr Smith began whimpering like a hungry child. "He said I was guilty of aiding him and would swing from the neck, too, if caught."

"Hence the reason you wrote the second blackmail note," Mr Cole added.

Noah released the clerk and allowed him a moment to gather his composure before asking, "Where is Hemming holding him?"

"In the a-attic," the clerk stammered. "Above the office in Tavistock Street."

CHAPTER 19

Despite the late hour, Tavistock Street was a hive of activity. Patrons burst from the theatres and cluttered the pavements like an army of ants. The bawds who sold their wares from alleyways and doorways snatched punters as they passed and disappeared for a five-minute fumble. Beggars loitered, waiting to accost the drunken fools stumbling from coffeehouses, brothels and gaming hells. Covent Garden was a playground for the wealthy. A hunting ground for those who made their living on the streets.

Daventry had taken the clerk to Bow Street to make a statement, securing a case against Hemming being a priority. Sloane and D'Angelo had taken the wherry back from Temple Gardens and would arrive in Tavistock Street in due course.

"Every instinct tells me you should wait in the carriage," Noah said as his conveyance rolled to a stop fifty yards from the publisher's office.

While Eva had every right to help free her brother from his prison, he feared she might be too lenient, feared Hemming might hurt her in a bid to escape.

"I'll be perfectly safe," she said, glancing at Cole and Bower seated opposite. "Besides, I presume Mr Hemming will be at home in bed at this hour."

Cole's hum rang with doubt. "In my experience, a felon rarely leaves a hostage unattended. I expect Hemming will be close."

Beside him, Eva trembled at the mention of the publisher's name. She cast Noah a sidelong glance and smiled. "What can Mr Hemming do when I have three strong men as my protectors?"

It was Noah's turn to shiver. Hemming could fire a pistol in the dark and hit the wrong target. He could throw a punch. She might fall, hit her head on the grate. The rooms inside were small and cramped. How could he protect her during the mad scramble, the chaos?

Both Bower and Cole stared at him, waiting for his reply.

The weight of responsibility bore down on his shoulders. No man deserved to live with the pain of regret, but Eva was in just as much danger in the carriage as she was inside Hemming's office.

Noah met the men's gazes. "Keep her between us at all times. I shall lead the way. Cole will take the rear. Bower, you will wait at the bottom of the stairs should Hemming or Dunn attempt to escape."

Both men nodded.

They alighted the carriage, veered around the pedestrians who seemed happy to amble and were in no rush to get home. They entered the alley through the wrought-iron gate next to the apothecary. As expected, the door leading to Hemming's premises was locked.

"Allow me, sir," Bower said, rummaging in the deep pocket of his greatcoat. He removed a ring of odd-shaped keys and began sifting through them.

"We could give the door a hard kick," Cole said.

"What, and alert Hemming of our intentions?" Noah wanted to take Hemming by surprise. It was the best way of ensuring no harm came to the lady standing nervously beside him.

Bower tried various keys before finally muttering that he'd found the right one. With the key firmly in the lock, he produced a length of wire and slipped it into the hole. It took a few seconds of fiddling before he opened the door leading to the narrow hall.

"You're wasted as a butler," Noah whispered.

Bower smiled. "I seem to spend more time on the streets, sir, than dressed in finery."

They mounted the flight of stairs cautiously, the odd board creaking beneath their feet, hoping to hell they didn't alert Hemming. Cole and Eva waited on the landing while Noah checked the clerk's office. Once confident there was no one hiding in the shadows, Noah eased the door closed, locked it and slipped the key into his coat pocket.

"Do you not have a weapon?" Eva whispered, the cold grip of fear wrapped around every word.

Noah shook his head and tapped his finger to his lips. Now was not the time to explain that a coward with a pistol would likely fire when his opponent flashed a blade.

They crept along the landing. The door to Hemming's office was ajar, the room beyond dark, eerily silent.

Noah gestured to Cole, indicating he intended to examine the room before mounting the next flight of stairs. Indeed, he slipped inside and was gone less than a minute before returning and pointing to the ceiling.

The stairs leading to the third and fourth floors were narrower. Every step creaked as they made their ascent. If Howard Dunn was being held captive in the attic, he would be expecting their arrival.

They paused on the landing leading to two small wooden doors. Noah shrugged and motioned to the left. He tiptoed closer to the door. The absence of candlelight spilling out from the gap between the jamb and the ill-fitting frame suggested the room might be empty.

Noah breathed to settle his racing heart and then wrapped his fingers around the handle. A faint gasp from behind made him pause and glance over his shoulder.

Eva had covered her mouth with her hand, her eyes wide with panic. It was as if she were about to witness her worst nightmare—a terrifying scene concocted from a wild imagination. No doubt she pictured Hemming waiting to lunge at them in the dark, bludgeon them to death. Like Noah, did she wonder if Smith had lied to lure them into a trap and both devils were hiding behind the door, eager to exact their revenge?

But then another emotion mingled with the frantic look in her eyes. A tender emotion that squeezed his heart. She placed her hand on his arm. "Please be careful," she mouthed. "I cannot lose you. I love you."

His world stopped.

Every nerve in his body thrummed.

The power of those last three words proved to be invigorating and crippling. They roused hope and fear. Excitement and dread. It would be so easy to run, to protect his heart. But he couldn't live without her.

A muffled groan echoing from beyond the paint-chipped door put paid to his need to tell her he loved her, too. A loud thud followed, like someone stomping on the boards or the weight of a body falling from a bed.

Forced to concentrate on their present dilemma, Noah tried the door and found it locked.

"Step back," he said as the ghostly mumbles in the darkness grew louder. He barged the door with his shoulder, the frame splintering and snagging his coat.

The attic room was a dingy, cluttered space, the air musty and damp. Hazy slivers of moonlight pierced through the dirty skylight, landing on the mounds of paper and books stacked high in the gloom. Broken chairs and old trunks littered the floor. Cobwebs clung to the rafters. The mumbles emanated from the truckle bed near the old shipping crates that still carried a whiff of tea.

Guard raised, and filled with clawing apprehension, Noah approached.

A man lay curled on the floor, his arms and legs bound with rope, a filthy rag tied around his mouth. His clothes were dusty and splattered with blood. The stench of stale sweat wafted into the air along with the sickly sweet smell of opium. Anger and frustration had the man squirming and banging his feet on the floor, though he had no hope of breaking free of his restraints.

The light pad of footsteps behind brought Cole and Eva. Cole made a quick scan of the area before disappearing to inspect the second attic room. Eva stepped closer and stared while Noah hauled the fellow to his feet.

"Howard," she whispered, studying the man's swollen face, but she did not sigh with relief. She did not race forward, desperate to untie the ropes.

Howard Dunn was a handsome man with a weak chin and sloping shoulders, though he looked tired, pale and thin. Bruises —some small, some green, some blue—marred his cheeks and forehead. A trail of dried blood ran from a crusty clump of brown hair, down his neck, staining his shirt.

Noah might have pitied the reprobate had he not moaned and groaned and thrust his bound hands at him, demanding he remove the constraints at once. Even with his mouth gagged and his feet secured with rope, even with the injuries that made him appear vulnerable, arrogance oozed from every fibre of his being.

Noah was about to untie the gag when Eva said, "Wait. There's something I want to say before he spouts his vile diatribe." She closed the gap between them and stopped but two feet away. "You've been causing mischief, Howard," she said, her tone unsurprisingly cold. "Perhaps I should just leave you to rot in the attic."

Dunn's eyes grew wide, the fading bruises beneath a sure sign he'd broken his nose. He mumbled incessantly while thrusting his tied hands at Eva. He nodded and jerked his head as if pleading with his tormenter.

"The strange thing is I don't care about the dreadful things you've done to me," she said, bitterness imbuing her tone. "I don't care that you plotted to extort money, that you colluded with a man whose only motive is to control me."

As she broke for breath, the ingrate thrust his hands in her direction and mumbled like a madman.

But then Eva slapped his face, the shock of it taking the wind from his sails. "That is for taking Mother's jewels," she said, her voice breaking. "Mother suffered for years before her death. I remember the day she pressed the earrings into my hand and said she hoped I might wear them on my wedding day."

A tear trickled down Eva's cheek. Pain twisted around her beautiful features as grief surfaced. Noah knew the feeling well— the dreaded emptiness, the choking ache.

Every instinct said to leave the rogue in his bug-ridden bed.

He should let Bower and Cole deal with the devils and take Eva home. But then she drew her fist back and punched her brother in the stomach.

The man might have crumpled to the floor had Noah not been holding him upright.

"That's for Clara, not for me. I shall never forgive you for corrupting her, for luring her into one of your pathetic traps to gain funds. Lord Benham would rather his sister were ruined than have her married to a scoundrel like you."

Noah thought of his own mother's plight. Perhaps he should warn Benham that some women were not strong enough to deal with shame. One had to hope that the bond with her child gave Clara Swales a reason to live.

"As for the child you sired," Eva continued, the tears flowing freely now. "Had I a pistol to hand, I would shoot you between the legs. No child deserves to live with the pain of having a heartless prig for a father."

"I second that," Noah said, pride and love for this woman ready to burst from his chest. "Now we just need to find a pistol."

Eva managed a weak smile as she drew her hand across her cheeks to dry her tears. "Shall we see what he has to say for himself?" She shuffled back, keen to put a little distance between her and the unpredictable devil.

Noah reached behind the rogue, ready to untie the filthy neckcloth used as a gag. But Howard Dunn suddenly raised his bound arms, jabbing them at Eva like a man possessed. Frightened, she shuffled back further and almost stumbled over the old trunks.

Noah was of a mind to punch Dunn, too. "Stop whining." He yanked the neckcloth from the fool's mouth. "And be careful what you say else I shall shove my fist down your throat."

Howard Dunn gasped for breath and only managed to form a single word. A word of warning. "Hemming!"

As if conjured from the depths of hell, Hemming suddenly sprang up from inside the trunk. Before Noah could pull his blade from his boot, Hemming grabbed Eva around the neck and pressed the muzzle of a pocket pistol to her temple.

Cole heard Eva's scream and came to a crashing halt in the doorway.

"Stay back!" Hemming gathered Eva tight to his body, using her as a human shield. "Stay back else I shall shoot, and neither of us will have her."

The wild terror in Eva's eyes rendered Noah frozen to the spot.

"Harm a hair on her head and I'll kill you with my bare hands," Noah countered. "Lower the pistol. We know about the blackmail note and your devious plans. Smith told us everything."

He didn't mention Smith was at Bow Street making a statement to implicate Hemming in exchange for his freedom. Hemming needed to believe he had a chance of escaping, else heaven knows what he might do in desperation.

Hemming ground his teeth. "It's your damn fault. Seducing her with your picnics and poetry."

"I'm in love with her," Noah said, raising his hands in mock surrender. He needed Hemming to fire a shot at him. Amid the frenzy, Cole would take the blackguard down. "You'll have to shoot me as I'm determined to have her for my wife."

Recognition replaced the panic in Eva's eyes. "He's lying. I have changed my mind. You were right. I fear Mr Ashwood wants to control me once we're wed."

"And yet you didn't heed my warning," Hemming snarled.

"I'm going to marry her," Noah reiterated.

He was not acting or playing a role. He would marry Eva Dunn and love her for the rest of his life. She would bear him strong sons and spirited daughters. They would never disrespect each other as their parents had done, never abandon their children.

"Let us leave," Eva pleaded with Hemming. "Let's go somewhere quiet, away from here, and discuss what we should do now."

"No!" Noah challenged.

But then the bane of Eva's existence flexed his vocal cords. "Don't leave with him, Evangeline. The man is as mad as a March hare."

Hemming couldn't take the chance that Eva might listen to her brother, and so he shuffled back towards the door while keeping a firm grip on his prize.

Cole met Noah's gaze and stepped aside.

"You can't let him take her!" came Dunn's outraged reply. "I need her to help me out of a fix."

Noah turned and punched the fool hard in the chest, knocking him back onto the truckle bed. "You've lost the right to act like the concerned brother." Dunn was likely to say something to make Hemming shoot. "This is your damn fault."

And it was Noah's fault, too. He should have forced Eva to remain in the carriage. He should have conducted a thorough search of the trunks and crates. Daventry was right. But he'd been so blind with rage upon seeing the snake slithering in his bindings he'd lost focus.

Hemming edged out of the door, dragging Eva with him.

Noah followed slowly, mindful not to make any sudden movements.

"Don't take another step," Hemming said, guiding Eva sideways down the first few steps. "Move, and I'll shoot her."

Their descent was awkward and clumsy. It proved almost impossible to navigate the dark stairway while holding a woman hostage and pointing a pistol at her head. Eva stumbled, but the devil caught her.

The choking lump in Noah's throat pressed against his windpipe. History often repeated itself. Families tended to suffer the same crippling blows. A man might be destined to lose every woman he loved. Perhaps it was foolish to hope, to dream.

But there was a stark difference in this scenario. Noah's mother had smiled and professed all would be well. Eva's ghostly complexion and trembling lips spoke of terror. She wanted to live. The truth of it was plain to see.

Amid the gloom of the stairwell, their gazes met.

No doubt she could sense his torment as clearly as he sensed her fear. Perhaps that was why she made the sudden move, took advantage of an opportunity. When she drew a deep breath, he knew she was about to do something reckless.

"Don't," Noah mouthed, shaking his head.

But he was too late.

The moment Hemming moved to step down, Eva elbowed him so hard in the stomach the man lost his footing.

In the sudden panic, the pistol flew out of Hemming's hand and bounced down the stairs. The succession of loud thuds echoed and would surely alert Bower.

Arms flailing and nostrils flaring, Hemming tried to grab onto something stable.

Aware of the imminent danger, Noah raced forward just as Hemming grabbed the back of Eva's pelisse to prevent himself from falling.

Time slowed.

Bile lodged in Noah's throat as he watched Eva stumble back. The look of horror on her face cut through his heart, sharper than any blade. No. It could not end like this. No. He could not watch another woman he loved perish. It would be the end of him. The end of everything.

Eva managed to grip the handrail with her left hand. She reached out to Noah with her free hand, a desperate plea for him to save her. He was able to grab hold of her wrist seconds before Hemming lost his grip of her pelisse and tumbled down the stairs.

Relief stole the strength from Noah's legs. He flopped down onto the step and dragged Eva into his arms. Their breathless pants mingled as they embraced. He stroked her hair, muttered thankful prayers. He felt so blessed to have a second chance he almost forgot about Hemming.

"Watch out!" Cole cried, throwing himself on top of them as the shot rang through the stairwell.

In those few seconds when no one moved, a man couldn't help but fear the worst. Cole was deathly still as he smothered them with his muscular body. Noah was aware of the rise and fall of Eva's chest, aware that he had escaped being hit by the lead ball. And the hurried thud of footsteps retreating on the stairs spoke of Hemming's escape.

"Eva, are you all right?"

"Yes, though I fear Mr Cole is hurt."

"Cole?"

Silence.

"Cole!"

A groan rumbled deep in his friend's chest.

"Good God! Have you been hit?"

"No." Cole released a painful moan as he attempted to stand. Dust clung to the shoulders of his black coat. The lead ball must have hit the plaster somewhere above their heads. "It's just my damn leg."

The old war wound plagued him during the winter months and those times when he exerted himself.

"You risked your life to save ours, Mr Cole," Eva said, somewhat in awe of the man. She came to her feet, though her limbs still trembled. "You might have died."

One would expect to see a flash of relief in Cole's eyes, but it was the opposite. He looked disappointed, disappointed the Lord had not claimed his soul and saved him from his torment. For a while now, Noah had feared that Cole's acts of bravery stemmed from a desire to die.

Shouts from the ground floor reached their ears.

"That must be Bower. He must have caught the devil."

They descended the stairs with care. Eva gripped the handrail as if she feared she might fall again. Cole hobbled slowly behind them, though he had taken to suppressing his groans.

Bower was alone in the alley leading to Tavistock Street.

"Where the hell is he?" Noah glared at Bower. "Tell me how in blazes he escaped!" Was there to be no end to the fiend's tricks?

Bower caught his breath. "He's on the street, sir. He came a cropper—"

Noah didn't wait to hear the rest. He captured Eva's hand and led her out onto Tavistock Street.

A thick trail of burgundy blood led from the wrought-iron gates, past the goldsmith shop and stopping at Hemming's lifeless body sprawled on the pavement. People congregated a few feet away, pointing, staring, whispering amongst themselves, while two constables tried to edge them back.

Amid the chaos, Daventry hurried across the road with Sir Malcolm. The portly, grey-haired magistrate looked at Noah, his expression oddly grave. Noah could have sworn he noticed a hint of pity swimming in both men's eyes. Strange.

"What happened to Hemming?" Noah said as three more constables came running from the direction of York Street. "He threatened to kill Miss Dunn before shooting at us on the stairs."

Perhaps the fool had fallen awkwardly, though that still didn't account for the excessive loss of blood.

"A man stepped up to Hemming at the gates just as we arrived," Daventry said. His voice was calmer than expected, yet something was troubling him. "He slit Hemming's throat before bolting. The publisher staggered some way before collapsing on the pavement."

"So he's dead?" Eva said as if afraid the man had nine lives.

"Undoubtedly."

"I recognised the felon as one of Manning's men," Sir Malcolm said, pausing to shout instructions to the constables who seemed incapable of controlling the crowd. "After learning of your troubles, Miss Dunn, I suspect he mistook Mr Hemming for your brother. There's only one way the man might have learnt of your brother's location, but that's an internal matter."

He meant the only way the felon could have arrived so promptly was if someone at Bow Street had turned traitor.

"I see," Eva said.

An awkward silence ensued.

"I thought you were busy dealing with Manning, Sir Malcolm?" Noah said when he could no longer stay his curiosity. Every bone in his body said something was wrong. Both men were acting strangely. "How did Daventry persuade you to come here and assist with our case?"

"I'm here on other business," Sir Malcolm said, albeit reluctantly. "Is there somewhere we might speak privately?"

Privately?

What the devil did Sir Malcolm want with him?

"We can speak here." Impatience burned. "I have nothing to hide from Cole or Miss Dunn."

Sir Malcolm's pained expression drew attention to his heavily wrinkled brow. "It's about your uncle."

"Hawkridge? What of him?"

Sir Malcolm swallowed deeply. "I'm afraid Lord Hawkridge is dead."

Dead?

It took a few seconds to absorb the information.

"Dead? How? Tell me he didn't trip down the stairs and break his neck." Noah snorted, despite the rising panic in his chest.

"His valet found him dead in his bedchamber this evening," Sir Malcolm replied. "By all accounts, he retired earlier this afternoon with his wife. The staff presumed ... well, I'm sure you understand your uncle's need for an heir."

A host of scenarios formed, the most prevalent being his uncle died from the strain of trying to sire his successor. "Then I must attend Lady Hawkridge."

Sir Malcolm winced. "Lady Hawkridge has disappeared. There's some suspicion she killed your uncle and escaped via the adjoining door. Both were locked when the servants tried to enter."

Noah struggled to absorb the information. Poor Gertrude. The woman must have been pushed to her limits.

"I can vouch that the lady wasn't in her right mind yesterday," Noah said, knowing she would likely hang if found. "Though I wonder how a woman so slight had the strength to overpower my uncle."

Sir Malcolm's cheeks flamed. "I believe she hit him over the head with a chamber pot. Numerous times. The contents of which were found smeared on his chest." The magistrate glanced at the body of Hemming sprawled on the pavement. "But I need you to come with me."

Noah gripped Eva's hand. "I cannot leave now."

"Mr Daventry will liaise with Sergeant Reeves and deal with things here," Sir Malcolm said.

Eva squeezed Noah's hand. "You should go. The servants must be beside themselves with worry. Mr Sloane and Mr D'Angelo will be here soon. I shall stay with Mr Daventry and Mr Cole, see what is to be done about my brother."

Noah forgot the fool was still tied up in the attic.

An internal war raged.

He didn't want to leave her.

Cole gripped Noah's shoulder. "I shall not leave Miss Dunn's side until she is safely back in Wigmore Street. You have other responsibilities to deal with at present. Trust me to act in your stead."

Eva continued to offer words of reassurance until he agreed to accompany the magistrate.

With some reluctance, Noah left Eva and his colleagues and climbed into Sir Malcolm's coach. He stared out of the window at the gruesome scene, watched Cole hobbling on his left leg as he walked with Eva and Daventry back through the wrought-iron gate. Eva stopped. She glanced back at the coach and offered a weak smile.

For the first time in his life, Noah knew what he wanted.

He wanted to work for the Order, wanted to marry Eva Dunn, lead a full and enriched life. He did not want to be the next Lord Hawkridge. Indeed, he feared nothing would ever be the same again.

CHAPTER 20

"You can't leave," Mr Cole said tersely. He gripped the arm of the sofa in Noah's drawing room and stood. "You'll not desert him. I'll not let you go, not until Ashwood returns."

"You must sit down, Mr Cole. You need to rest your leg." Eva crossed the room and forced him back into the seat. "And I'm not deserting him. I must return home to Brownlow Street at some point." She swallowed in an attempt to hold back the tears. "Now the threat has been dealt with, I'm sure Mr Ashwood will be glad to get back to normality."

Except he wouldn't be Mr Ashwood anymore. He would be Lord Hawkridge, a man of title and responsibility. Such a respectable gentleman would need to marry a lady of excellent breeding. A gentle creature who said the right things and behaved with dignity. Not a woman whose heart ruled her head. Not a woman who wrote novels and made love in the garden. Not a woman who longed to kneel at his feet and take his manhood into her mouth.

"Besides, it is almost six o'clock in the morning." She captured Mr Cole's booted foot and lifted it gently onto the low stool. "After the night we've had, we all need sleep."

"I'm not a fool, Miss Dunn."

"No, but I imagine you know all about sacrifice."

"He's in love with you."

Her heart almost burst from her chest. "And I'm in love with him."

She was so in love with Noah Ashwood she would not make him choose between her and his position. She would not let him torment himself or be forever plagued by guilt.

"Then why must you run away?" Mr Cole challenged.

"You're his friend. You know his worth. Noah was made for great things." More important things than passion and pleasure. "With my tainted history, I shall be a stain on his character."

"If you think he will let you go, you're mistaken."

Oh, why must Mr Cole make things more difficult? Could he not see that her heart was breaking? Could he not see that she would crumple to the floor at any moment, a blubbering wreck?

Eva lifted her chin. "He'll have to marry and sire an heir. And he's not the sort of man to keep a mistress." Not that she could make love to a man who had a wife.

The slam of the front door and the clip of booted footsteps prompted Mr Cole to say, "Ah, let us see what Ashwood has to say about the matter. I'm rather glad I have a seat for this."

Eva arched a brow. "If I didn't know better, I might believe you're amused."

After having a brief conversation with Kenning, Noah strode into the drawing room.

Eva's heart lurched.

Tears threatened to fall.

"Forgive me. I didn't realise I would be so long. We've been out searching for Gertrude." He looked exhausted, world-weary. Those magnificent green eyes had lost their confident sparkle. "Lord knows where the woman has gone. If she has any sense, she will be halfway to France by now." He walked towards the decanters on the side table, stopped abruptly when he noticed her valise on the floor next to the chair. "What the devil's going on?"

Before she could form a word, Mr Cole said, "Miss Dunn is of a mind to save you. She is returning home so you may concentrate your efforts on playing the dutiful peer."

Eva gritted her teeth and resisted the urge to kick Mr Cole's injured leg.

Shock, and something infinitely more disturbing, flashed in Noah's eyes as he absorbed the information. "You're leaving? You're returning to Brownlow Street?"

"I don't want to be a distraction, not now you have more pressing matters to deal with." This was not a conversation she wanted to have in the presence of Mr Cole. She was bound to cry. "And Howard is no longer a concern. As soon as Mr Daventry explained that the blade that killed Mr Hemming was meant for my brother, he accepted five thousand pounds and passage on the next ship sailing to Italy."

"As Dunn hasn't committed a crime and is guilty of nothing more than tormenting his sister," Mr Cole explained, "Daventry and Bower bungled him into the carriage and left for the docks."

But Noah didn't seem remotely interested in her brother's fate. "You don't think I would make time for you, Eva?" he said in a low voice. "After my experiences, you don't think I know what is important?"

Every bone and muscle in her body throbbed with the need to kiss him, to strip off his clothes, take him into her aching body and never let go.

"Noah, I'm simply returning home now the threat has passed, as we agreed."

"No, you're leaving because you think I'm to inherit. You think that changes things."

"Of course it changes things."

Noah shook his head. "Gertrude might be carrying an heir."

"I think that is highly unlikely."

"Well, yes, particularly after Sir Malcolm spoke to her lady's maid, but nothing is set in stone."

Eva glanced at Mr Cole, who didn't seem remotely embarrassed that he was party to this conversation.

"We all need sleep," she reiterated. "McGuffey will take me back to Brownlow Street, and we can discuss this later."

Noah remained silent for a moment, then he crossed the room and came to stand a mere foot away. "You forget, I once looked into a woman's eyes when she lied and professed all was well. Sometimes, later never comes. And so we will have this out now, madam." His determined gaze remained fixed on her when he said, "I shall call on you later today, Cole. Won't you excuse us?"

Without warning, Noah scooped Eva into his arms and headed for the door.

She might have protested, attempted to wriggle free, but the feel of being held so close to his hard body proved divine. Love, and an insatiable longing, saw her thread her arms around his neck as he carried her to his bedchamber.

The heavy blue curtains were drawn, blocking out the early morning rays. The smell of Noah's teasing cologne clung to the air, and she inhaled the potent scent.

"Now, let us deal with the real problem," he said, lowering her down onto his plush mattress. He crossed the room and locked the door. "Just in case you attempt to escape."

That wasn't the reason he held her captive.

He was going to make love to her.

He was going to make it impossible for her to walk away.

Noah returned to stand at the foot of the bed. "I almost lost you tonight. My world collapsed around me as I anticipated you falling down the stairs." He shrugged out of his coat, and it fell to the floor. "I watched that devil press a pistol to your head. The sheer terror in your eyes will haunt me for the rest of my days."

"I know," she whispered, tears welling as she imagined every tragic outcome. "You wanted him to shoot you, but I would give my life to save yours."

Noah finished unbuttoning his waistcoat, and that hit the floor, too. "Then what makes you think I would let you walk out of my life without protest?"

"You're a man who takes responsibility seriously," she countered, though she couldn't concentrate knowing he was about to discard his cravat, that his shirt would soon follow. "That's the reason I chose you to take my case."

A sinful smile played on his lips. "You still maintain that's the reason you picked me?"

When he drew his shirt over his head, she inhaled a sharp breath. Merciful heaven. The need to press her lips to his bronzed skin danced like a devil inside.

"Your strength of character was evident the first moment we met," she said, the burning heat between her thighs distracting her, too.

"No, there was more to our first meeting than that." He unbuttoned the band on his breeches. "Think."

For a woman who had suffered at the hands of Lord Benham and her publisher, stepping into a room occupied by four powerful men had been unnerving. But the second she locked gazes with Noah Ashwood, she had instinctively known all would be well.

"There was a familiarity, an awareness, a deep sense of comfort in my chest the moment we met. I found you interesting." Her heart raced the second he tugged off his boots. "I thought you were the most handsome man I had ever seen. I fell in love with you so quickly I'm still struggling to catch my breath."

His smile widened. "You fascinated me from the beginning, too. It became impossible to deny my need for you, and I knew then this was more than a fleeting infatuation. I knew I'd fall madly in love with you."

"Noah," she breathed as he pushed his breeches past his lean hips to reveal his erection.

Oh, her body was aflame.

He palmed the solid length, hummed with pleasure while his emerald eyes held her captive on the bed.

Why did he not touch her?

"You're trying to seduce me into believing a title doesn't matter," she said, desperate to have him spread her wide and push deep into her body.

"No, love, I'm about to show you how good we are together." He came forward, placed his hands on her knees and pushed her skirts up to her waist. "Marry me. Love me. Bear my children. Become the next Lady Hawkridge if that is our destiny. But whatever fate has in store, I need you."

Were she not already intoxicated with desire, his words would have left her giddy.

"But I work for a living and cannot deny my creative passions."

He crawled onto the bed and settled between her thighs. "I work, too, and intend to continue serving the Order." He pushed into her body. "You're so wet, Eva."

The moist sound of their joining heightened her pleasure. "But there'll be no time—"

"We will manage somehow. We will manage together."

"Oh, Noah." She wrapped her thighs around his hips and vowed never to let go.

"Marry me," he repeated, withdrawing to the point she felt empty without him. "Let me love you."

"Yes." She gripped the muscles in his back as he thrust into her body.

"Yes, you'll marry me? Or yes, you welcome my attentions?"

"Yes, to both. I love you."

"I love you." He kissed her then, kissed her and made love to her like a thirsty nomad dying to drink the water.

Four weeks later

The wedding took place in the chapel on the grounds of Drummond's Folly, Noah's rambling estate in Gloucestershire. It was a private affair attended by close friends. In the absence of family, Eva had asked Cole to stand in her father's stead, an honour he had not refused, but one he had not necessarily welcomed.

Eva looked so stunning in pale blue, Noah could do nothing but stare like a besotted fool. Her bright smile stole the breath from his lungs. Every time she touched her fingers to her mother's diamond earrings, she dazzled him with her radiant glow. She had been so tormented on the day they met he could not have envisioned her looking so happy. He almost burst with happiness, too, when they were pronounced "*Man and Wife together*".

They removed to the house for an informal breakfast. Later, they mingled in the drawing room with their friends. For a while, Noah stood by the hearth, sipping his brandy, watching Eva laugh and thread arms with Sybil Daventry.

"Our wives have become good friends," Daventry said, moving to stand beside Noah.

"I must thank Sybil for all her help. Eva was most grateful for her advice and company."

"And I should express my gratitude. My wife made a few choice purchases while selecting garments for your wife's wedding night." Daventry brought his brandy goblet to his lips and continued to stare at the ladies. "When it comes to grabbing my attention and making a point, together they can be quite the tour de force."

"Friendship is important when one has no family," Noah said.

"When I played escort on their many shopping trips, they brought a concerning issue to light." Daventry glanced around the room. "Where's Cole?"

Noah looked through the large sash window and scanned the rose garden. "He went for a walk. I don't expect to see him for the rest of the day."

Cole struggled with excessive displays of affection, and Noah couldn't keep his hands off his wife.

Daventry released a weary sigh. "Sybil fears he is slipping deeper into the darkness. Eva believes he will soon be so consumed in misery no one will reach him."

Noah could not dispute either opinion. "I've tried broaching the subject of his wife, but he won't listen. Guilt eats away at him."

"Were they in love?"

There were different sorts of love. Noah believed Cole loved Sophia Adair. But Cole had loved Hannah in his own way, too. "They cared for each other."

Daventry remained silent for a few seconds. "I have something to tell you, and would value your opinion."

Noah was all ears. "Something about Cole?"

Daventry nodded. "Lady Adair approached me a few days ago, asking to hire Cole as her agent."

"Her agent?" Hellfire! Cole would go berserk if he knew. "And what is the nature of her dilemma?"

"You must not repeat this to a living soul, but Lady Adair has a secret." Daventry paused. "Her sister resides at Blackborne. Everyone thinks she lives abroad, for reasons I cannot divulge. But Lady Adair is convinced someone has attempted to abduct her sister and has begged for Cole's help. I'm told Blackborne is a rather eerie place located in the heart of a haunted wood."

Noah rubbed his jaw. "I'm not sure a house full of ghosts is the right place for Cole."

"Sometimes, a man must face his demons."

While Noah considered pleading with Daventry to dismiss the idea as folly, instinct said it was a chance for Cole to find redemption. Still, Lady Adair was hardly a poor soul without connections.

"Must I remind you that we do not come to the aid of wealthy members of the *ton*?" he said.

"No, but Lady Adair has agreed to make a substantial contribution to a women's refuge. Were it anyone else I would have refused. But I would not be sending Cole to save Sophia Adair. I rather hope the lady might save him."

Noah feared Cole was beyond saving, that he would always blame himself for his wife's death. But one had to believe that love could break down walls, cross barriers. "Then you have my support, but be prepared. Cole is certain to refuse."

"I'll wait until we return to London tomorrow before informing him of my decision. I don't want you breaking up a fight between your friends on your wedding day."

Daventry gripped Noah's shoulder and agreed to inform him of Cole's decision before crossing the room to join Sloane and D'Angelo.

The conversation with Daventry occupied Noah's thoughts until Eva approached. She came up on her tiptoes and kissed his cheek.

"You seem distracted," she said. "Are you annoyed I've left you alone for so long?"

He gathered her hand and pressed his lips to her knuckles. "I could never be annoyed with you. But perhaps now is the right time for me to give you a wedding gift."

Eva's eyes widened. "A gift? But I have nothing for you."

"Love, I can think of many ways you might make amends."

She batted him playfully on the arm. "All pertaining to us stripping out of these clothes I assume."

"Undoubtedly." Noah withdrew the note from his pocket and handed it to her. "Once you've read this, I hope you'll want to ravish me senseless."

"We could sneak away for half an hour," she said, quickly peeling back the folds. After squinting to study the missive, she handed it back to him. "You read it. I haven't my spectacles to hand."

Noah read the note from Lord Benham granting Eva permission to visit Clara.

Eva slapped her hand to her chest in surprise. "I cannot believe it. How did you—" Excitement danced in her eyes. "Did you bribe him? Threaten him?"

"I gave him my assurance your brother will never set foot on English soil again. And I suggested, as Lady Hawkridge, you would be a good ally. Clara will be welcome in our home, but should you wish to visit Northumberland, I would insist on accompanying you."

"I don't know what to say." Regardless of the fact they were in company, she flung her arms around his neck. "Let's go for a walk in the garden, somewhere quiet and secluded, so I may show you the depth of my gratitude."

"Cole is wandering about aimlessly, and we're sure to stumble upon him. Catching us in a clinch will probably drive him deeper into despair."

"Then let us retire to our bedchamber."

"I have a better idea. The study is closer, and you know I'm rather partial to polished surfaces."

Eva laughed. "Do you intend to perch on the desk and display your muscular thighs to advantage? Like you did on that first day when you were eager to gain my attention?"

He couldn't help but laugh. "You were so busy scribbling you failed to notice my manly attributes. And though Mr Lydford is willing to publish anything you write, you never did tell me your idea for a plot."

She arched a brow and lowered her voice. "I thought I could

write about a woman who falls madly in love with her enquiry agent while embroiled in a tale of mystery and mayhem."

Noah moistened his lips. "Intriguing. On their wedding day, does she lead him into the study and have her wicked way? Does she push him back onto the desk and take his manhood into her mouth? Does she straddle his thighs and ride him to Nirvana?"

Eva smiled and captured his hand. "No, I was going to suggest she join him in his business, become the first lady of the Order, but I much prefer your ending."

THANK YOU!

Thank you for reading **Dauntless.**

What is Sophia Adair's secret?
Amid all her troubles, will she drag Cole from the darkness?
Will Cole banish his demons and seek his heart's desire?
Find out in ...

Raven
Gentlemen of the Order - Book 2

More titles by Adele Clee

To Save a Sinner
A Curse of the Heart
What Every Lord Wants
The Secret To Your Surrender
A Simple Case of Seduction

Lost Ladies of London

The Mysterious Miss Flint
The Deceptive Lady Darby
The Scandalous Lady Sandford
The Daring Miss Darcy

Avenging Lords

At Last the Rogue Returns
A Wicked Wager
Valentine's Vow
A Gentleman's Curse

Scandalous Sons

And the Widow Wore Scarlet
The Mark of a Rogue
When Scandal Came to Town
The Mystery of Mr Daventry

Gentlemen of the Order

Dauntless
Raven
Valiant
Dark Angel

Made in United States
Orlando, FL
12 January 2023

28572990R00139